"Readers who love a grumpy-to-smitten hero will swoon."

—*Kirkus Reviews*

"A dashing Regency romance featuring a wounded earl and an unyielding heroine with strong convictions."

—*Library Journal*

The Duke Is But a Dream

"Plenty of chemistry and passion . . . A deeply satisfying tale of love persevering despite social constraints."

—*Publishers Weekly*

"In this story of finding yourself, it's the family the central characters create together that's the most satisfying discovery of all." —*BookPage*

"Again she creates relatable heroines similar in force and tone to those created by her sister historical romance authors Tessa Dare and Sophie Jordan." —*Booklist*

First Earl I See Tonight

"A kind, funny heroine is the perfect match for a stoic, brooding hero in Bennett's delightful first Debutante Diaries Regency romance. Sexy, clever . . . will bring smiles to its readers." —*Publishers Weekly*
(starred review)

"We love a heroine who doesn't wait to be rescued, so thank you, Anna Bennett! . . . A crumbling estate, mysterious letters, and a villain hiding among friends add a dash of intrigue to this tantalizing Regency adventure."

—*Apple Books Review*
(Apple Books Best of the Month)

By Anna Bennett

IT TAKES A RAKE
ONE DUKE DOWN
GIRLS BEFORE EARLS
WHEN YOU WISH UPON A ROGUE
THE DUKE IS BUT A DREAM
FIRST EARL I SEE TONIGHT
THE ROGUE IS BACK IN TOWN
I DARED THE DUKE
MY BROWN-EYED EARL

It Takes a Rake

ANNA BENNETT

St. Martin's Paperbacks

First published in the United States by St. Martin's Paperbacks, an imprint of St. Martin's Publishing Group.

IT TAKES A RAKE

Copyright © 2023 by Anna Bennett.

For information, address St. Martin's Publishing Group, 120 Broadway, New York, NY 10271.

www.stmartins.com

ISBN: 978-1-250-79395-9

Our books may be purchased in bulk for promotional, educational, or business use. Please contact your local bookseller or the Macmillan Corporate and Premium Sales Department at 1-800-221-7945, ext. 5442, or by email at MacmillanSpecialMarkets@macmillan.com.

Printed in the United States of America

St. Martin's Paperbacks edition / February 2024

10 9 8 7 6 5 4 3 2 1

To Lisa—
There's no one I'd rather share a bottle of prosecco with.

Chapter 1

Forty-eight months and seventeen days away from Belle-haven Bay should have cured Leo of his infatuation with Miss Kitty Beckett—the beautiful, talented heiress who considered him her nemesis. Leo's head for numbers meant he grasped the staggering improbability of a match between Kitty and him with brutal clarity, so he'd done what any logical man in his position would do. He'd set about ridding himself of his inconvenient feelings, using the normally prescribed methods.

Working grueling hours at his new architectural practice.

Flirting with other pretty young women.

Drinking copious amounts of brandy.

Unfortunately, none of those remedies had made him forget the devilish dimple in Kitty's cheek or the irrepressible gleam in her eyes. Hell, Leo could scarcely go an hour without being haunted by memories of them sparring in his grandfather's office and reluctantly declaring a truce as they shared a sandwich on the beach.

It didn't matter that he was a far different man than he'd been back then. More confident, more worldly, more jaded. The truth was that he was still, one hundred percent, smitten with Miss Kitty Beckett.

And she was quite oblivious to the fact.

Now he was getting his first glimpse of her in four years, and he drank in the sight like parched earth soaking up a drought-ending rain. She stood in Lady Rufflebum's opulent ballroom chatting with her close friend, the Duchess of Hawking, seemingly unaware of the moonstruck expressions of the young bucks orbiting her. Kitty was the sun, and they were mere mortals content to bask in her warmth. To admire her from afar.

It wasn't difficult to see why. Her gold-spun hair glistened in the candlelight; her incandescent smile banished the shadows. Her beauty had, no doubt, brought many a man to his knees, and Leo supposed he was no exception. But what had captivated him, making it impossible for him to move on, was the way she challenged everything he thought he knew. About architecture, competition, and the fairer sex.

Years ago, when they'd both worked as apprentices in his grandfather's shop, Leo would squint at his straight-edge and pretend to take measurements while stealing glances at Kitty as she drew at the desk across from him. He could still picture the sure, graceful sweeps of her hand. The nimble, steady movements of her fingers. The fire that sparked in her eyes as she transformed a blank page in her sketchbook into a design so lifelike, so inspired, so ingenious that it took his breath away.

Naturally, when she'd held up her creation and asked for his opinion, his cocky seventeen-year-old self had shrugged and said, "Congratulations. You've created the perfect dwelling for a gargoyle and his fairy bride."

Despite being two years his junior, Kitty wasn't cowed in the slightest. "If anyone is familiar with the preferences of gargoyles, I daresay it's you. Never fear, I shall include plenty of bedchambers for you and your gargoyle-fairy children. Let us hope they will resemble their mother, poor unfortunate soul."

He brushed off the barb as if he hadn't felt its sting. "There's nothing objectively wrong with your drawing. It's actually quite good," he admitted, making him the reigning king of understatement. "But in case you hadn't noticed, golden spires and stained-glass windows aren't exactly commonplace here in Bellehaven. A building like yours wouldn't fit in at all."

She'd tossed a curl over her shoulder. It was a habit of hers that he absolutely adored—mostly because it was a telltale sign that he'd touched a nerve. But, true to form, Kitty quickly regained her composure. "That's the difference between you and me," she said icily. "*I* am not content to blend in."

He'd scoffed, pretending that barb hadn't also met its mark. "No?" he countered. "You wouldn't walk through the doors of the Salty Mermaid wearing a ball gown."

"Wouldn't I?" She narrowed her eyes and held his gaze in a silent challenge. He didn't look away. Not when his cheeks grew hot. Not when desire punched him in the gut and traveled south.

After an interminable amount of time, she clucked her tongue and smiled serenely. "It's as though you don't know me at all, Leo Lockland."

The way she'd said his name—as if it were part curse, part incantation—delighted him. Of all her quirks, it was a favorite, second only to the hair flip.

The next day she'd glided into the shop wearing a ball gown and stood directly beside his desk, waiting for him to acknowledge her.

He took his time finishing his calculation, which, incidentally, hadn't a chance in hell of being correct, then glanced up at her. If there was one bone in his body that wasn't already head over heels for her, safe to say it now was. "Nice gown. But this isn't the Salty Mermaid," he said with a smug smile.

She silently reached into the delicate reticule dangling from her wrist, withdrew a shot glass, and clunked it on his desk. The scent of brandy tickled his nose.

"Nathan Gutridge sends his regards," she said smoothly, referring to the pub's burly barkeep. "He hopes he can count on you for the annual cricket match." With that, she took her seat across from him, withdrew her sketchbook from the desk drawer, and began working.

Damn distracting, that. How was he supposed to concentrate on measurements and scale while she was draped in silk and lace? "You're not going to wear that all day, are you?"

She blinked slowly, as if his question were more absurd than her gown. Then she laughed. Not a dainty titter or delicate giggle, but a genuine, full-bellied laugh that made him feel like he could fly. Her laugh edged the hair flip out of first place.

"Of course I'm wearing this gown all day," she said blithely. "In fact, I might wear it all bloody week."

His and Kitty's relationship had always been based on an odd combination of fierce competition and grudging respect. But beneath the barbs and the banter—on his side, at least—was a constant longing. It had burned for so many years and was such a part of him that he could almost forget it was there.

Until he'd come face-to-face with her again.

In the years he'd been away she'd grown even more beautiful—something he didn't think possible. One look at her obliterated every defense he'd carefully erected around his heart.

He'd left behind a burgeoning architectural practice in London so that he could be close to his recently widowed mother in Bellehaven. On his first night home, his mother mentioned that despite Kitty Beckett's many suitors, she was still single. Leo had snorted at that out of pure habit. He couldn't let his mother know that he had a decade-old crush on Kitty. But hope sprouted in his chest.

He prided himself in being a practical sort. He dealt in measurements and calculations, nails and mortar, timber and stone. He believed in physical labor and standing by his word. But despite his protestations, Kitty had always had a knack for bringing out the dreamer in him.

Surely, by now they'd outgrown their silly rivalry. Maybe, finally, she could see him in a different light. Not as a competitor, but as a warm-blooded man. Improbable as it seemed, tonight she had him wondering if a beautiful, ridiculously talented heiress could fall for a decent, hard-working bloke like him.

There was only one way to find out.

He strode across the ballroom toward her, sliding a palm over his chest in hopes of quieting the thumping of his heart. When he was a mere ten yards away, a gentleman approached her, lifted her gloved hand, and pressed a kiss to the back.

It was all quite within the bounds of proper behavior, but the man's lazy grin and possessive grasp rubbed Leo the wrong way. He bristled as the bloody rogue whisked Kitty in the opposite direction, toward the dance floor.

"Leo Lockland. Is that really you?" He recognized the feminine voice behind him. It belonged to Kitty's friend.

He dragged his gaze away from Kitty, mustered a smile for the young duchess, and closed the distance between them. "Good evening, Your Grace."

"Come now," she protested with a graceful wave of her hand. "You must call me Poppy. After all, it wasn't so long ago that we were building sandcastles together."

"You're looking very well," he said, relieved to see that despite recently becoming a duchess, she was the same freckle-faced, down-to-earth girl he'd grown up with. He'd been closer in age to her older brother, but Dane had spent more time eating sand than trying to build with it. Poppy had been Leo's ally and a fierce defender of sandcastles. "I owe you belated congratulations on both your marriage and the birth of your daughter. I'm happy for you, Poppy."

"Thank you." She gave his hand an affectionate squeeze. "It's nice to have you back in Bellehaven. It's been ages, hasn't it? I thought I might see you when—"

She stopped before completing the thought, but Leo knew what she'd been about to say. She'd expected him to come home last year. For his father's funeral. But Leo hadn't.

Poppy pasted on a smile. "In any event, I'm glad you're here now. Will you be staying long?"

Leo nodded. "I sold my apartment in London. I'm moving back permanently," he explained. "To be closer to my mother and to take over my grandfather's practice."

"That's wonderful," Poppy said brightly. "I wish I could introduce you to my husband, but he's in London at the moment. Our daughter, Alexa, and I will be joining him tomorrow and will stay for several weeks while we attend to some business matters."

"My mother mentioned that you've been helping the local fishermen expand their operations," Leo said. "She says that, thanks to you, Bellehaven will soon be the fishing capital of England."

"Initially, I simply wanted our fisheries to be able to compete with the new ships off the coast," Poppy said with a smile. "But I confess I like the sound of your mother's idea."

The duchess's gaze flicked to the dance floor where Kitty waltzed with a tall, dark-haired toff, and her smile faded a notch—as if she didn't much care for the man. But that might have been wishful thinking on Leo's part.

He lifted his chin in Kitty's direction. "I see some things haven't changed. She still has legions of admirers."

"Indeed." Faint lines marred the duchess's forehead, confirming his earlier impression. "The problem isn't so much with quantity as it is quality," she added vaguely.

Leo arched a brow. "You don't approve of her dance partner?"

Poppy's color rose. "I didn't mean to disparage the marquess. I'm sure the matchmaking mamas consider him a good match."

"But you don't?"

Poppy leaned closer and whispered, "Lord Hadenwood is handsome, charming, and wealthy," she began, as if these were strikes against him. "Accustomed to having beautiful young ladies falling at his feet. He flits between balls and soirees, leaving a trail of romantic conquests in his wake."

Leo grunted, indicating she needn't elaborate further. "He's a rake."

She shrugged helplessly. "Many young women are drawn to his type."

"Including Kitty?" he asked, fully aware that he was dancing close to a line.

The duchess hesitated. "I know your relationship with her has always been a bit . . ."

"Adversarial?" he offered.

She shot him a grateful smile. "Right. But you know her better than most. She is not easily manipulated, and yet, she's never been able to resist a challenge. I fear she'll be so engaged in idle flirtations, so knee-deep in battles of wits that she won't notice when a genuinely good and kind man tries to capture her affections."

Leo mustered a sympathetic chuckle. "So you're saying nice blokes don't stand a chance against rakes?"

"I would not go that far," Poppy said. "But I must admit that when it comes to winning a woman's heart, a man with a silver tongue, a wicked grin, and a dangerous air has something of an unfair advantage."

The duchess's words were still echoing in his head as Kitty twirled past him in a blur of golden curls and sea-green silk, tugging a piece of his heart along behind her.

Maybe it was a good thing that he hadn't been able to pull her aside and tell her that he'd thought of her every day and dreamt of her every night.

Because if being nice was a curse, he was doomed.

He didn't stand a chance in hell with Kitty Beckett.

Kitty prided herself on being able to spot a rake at one hundred paces, and her current dance partner, Lord Hadenwood, was a prime example from his tousled hair to his polished Hessian boots. The question was whether he was the right sort of rake for her.

Namely the sort who was practical enough to marry, kind enough to be a good father, and enlightened enough to support her career goals. She needed a man who was decent but who wouldn't demand all of her heart. Because she couldn't give it.

Some evenings Kitty felt as though she was on the hunt for a unicorn—and destined to find nothing but donkeys.

"Tonight's ball rivals any that I have attended in London," the marquess said loftily. "I confess I am surprised."

"Bellehaven isn't so very far from civilization," Kitty teased. "I like to think that what we lack in culture we make up for with charm."

"Any deficits this town may have are more than made up for by your charms," he said with a predictably wicked grin. But he was mistaken if he thought she'd be swept off her feet with a pretty compliment. After all, courtship was a perilous game for an heiress with ambition, and she refused to engage feelings or allow herself to be backed into a corner. Her plans and dreams were too precious to risk.

"Perhaps one day I shall design a maritime museum for Bellehaven," she said as they glided across the dance floor. "A building to celebrate our rich history and vibrant culture."

The marquess missed a step, but quickly recovered. "You? Design a building?" he asked, clearly perplexed.

She pasted on a smile. "I worked as an apprentice for several years and plan to start my own architectural practice soon."

He shook his head as if he must have heard her incorrectly. "I was under the impression that you . . . that is, I thought you were . . ."

"Wealthy?" she provided, issuing a challenge with her direct gaze.

He shot her an apologetic smile. "Fortune aside, why would a woman with your beauty choose to dabble in trade?"

Dabble? She opened her mouth to issue a scathing retort but decided to save her breath.

Lord Hadenwood was not her sort of rake, but no matter. There were plenty more rogues in England. Surely one of them would meet her criteria.

They danced the rest of the set in icy silence, and when

the music finally ended, Kitty lifted her chin. "You needn't worry about returning me to the duchess's side. I shall find my own way."

"Very good," he said, mumbling apologies as he slunk away.

Free at last, Kitty turned and located Poppy on the perimeter of the dance floor. The fiery-haired duchess was a dear friend. She, Kitty, and Hazel, who had been her teacher and friend even before she'd married Kitty's uncle, had formed a close-knit trio called the Belles. Initially they'd bonded over their grief, as all three young women had lost their mothers far too soon. But they'd found strength in each other and now shared everything from gowns, to books, to secrets. Kitty was the youngest of the three and the only one who was unmarried. She was also, unfortunately, the most likely to find trouble, despite her recent attempts to get her life in order.

Eager to tell Poppy about her disappointing dance partner, Kitty glided toward the duchess, only to find her deep in conversation with a strange man.

He was a buttoned-up sort, with hair so closely cropped that it revealed an inch of tanned skin at the back of his neck. He wore a nondescript blue jacket, buckskin trousers, and plain polished boots. She couldn't see his face, and yet, there was something familiar about the way he stood, arms crossed, feet shoulder-distance apart, weight on his heels. Almost as if he were scouting a potential property or overseeing a construction site. In fact, he looked rather like—

Bloody hell.

But no. Leo Lockland didn't possess shoulders that broad. He certainly didn't have those muscular thighs or that chiseled jaw. His hair was lighter—the bright yellow of pineapple pulp, not the dusky-brown of driftwood. It couldn't be him, and yet, it seemed fitting that Leo would barge his way into her thoughts, unbidden.

She found herself thinking of him at the oddest times. Last week, when she'd finished designing a new addition for the cottage where Poppy's father lived, she wondered if Leo would have teased her about the mermaid carved into the peak of the roof, which lent it the look of a great ship's prow. And whenever she smelled freshly baked strawberry tarts, she couldn't help but recall his annoying habit of shoving a whole tart into his mouth at once. If she didn't know better, she'd think he'd been raised by heathens.

In truth, Leo was not so different from the blasted blister on her heel. Irritating. Maddening. Distracting.

To make matters infinitely worse, he was a brilliant architect. He had a gift for numbers, measurements, and calculations. Give him a drawing, a pencil, and a quarter of an hour, and he could compute the precise length of the beams needed for a ceiling, the number of planks needed for the walls, and the number of stones needed for the chimney. Then he'd go a step further and figure the price of the building materials down to the halfpenny.

Numbers had never been her strong suit, blast it all.

Determined to put him out of her mind, she crossed the room to join Poppy and ask for an introduction to the stranger.

"Kitty," her friend said brightly, "look who's returned to Bellehaven!"

The man turned, met her gaze, and held it. Though she'd never participated in a duel, she imagined this was how it must feel the moment after taking one's paces and facing one's opponent. On guard. Ready to do battle. Oddly exhilarated.

"Leo Lockland," she said, with the sort of enthusiasm

normally reserved for tooth extractions and undertakers. "You've returned."

"It's good to see you, Kitty." His voice was deeper, richer than she remembered.

"It's Kat now," she said coolly.

Leo's brows rose a fraction of an inch. "I was standing here, one second ago, when the duchess called you Kitty."

She counted to three in her head. "Poppy is like a sister to me. The same rules don't apply," she replied slowly, as if she were speaking to a child.

"I've known you since you wore braids."

"That's why I did not insist that you address me as Miss Beckett," she retorted. "A decision which I am now regretting."

Leo cocked his head, conceding the point. "Then I guess I'll count myself lucky."

"It's been an age since we've seen you here," Kitty said, keeping her tone neutral lest he think she'd missed him. "I am sorry about your father."

His jaw twitched. "Thank you."

An awkward silence ensued, and Poppy cleared her throat. "How long have you been away, Leo?"

"Four years," he said, his voice laced with something akin to regret.

Poppy clucked her tongue as if she couldn't imagine being away from her beloved sea for so great a time. "You must have missed the salty spray of the ocean, the soothing rumble of the waves."

"Indeed." Leo's gaze flicked to Kitty and back to the duchess. "I have missed much about Bellehaven."

Kitty barely refrained from rolling her eyes. After working with her in his grandfather's office for three years and being a constant thorn in her side for the entire duration, he'd left without a word.

She supposed she shouldn't have been surprised, for that was the way of the world. People came into her life, stayed for a bit, then vanished, like bottles drifting out to sea. But each person who left took a piece of her with them, leaving her a bit more hollow, a bit more brittle on the inside.

Sometimes death stole people away, as it had her parents when she was just a girl. Other times happier circumstances—perhaps marriage or a new family— pulled her closest friends in different directions. No one was to blame, really. But the least a person could do was say goodbye, and Leo had not. She'd been more wounded by his sudden departure than she cared to admit, even to herself. Perhaps *especially* to herself.

Now he was back, acting as though he expected to pick up where they'd left off. But time had not stood still for Kitty. She'd continued her apprenticeship under Leo's kindly grandfather, Mr. Sandford. She'd honed her skills and begun to make a name for herself. Now she was count- ing the days until she officially came into her inheritance and could strike out on her own.

"Kitty, er, Kat," Leo said. "I wondered if I might have a word."

She inclined her head. "Go on."

"In private," he amended.

"I shall leave you alone," Poppy said, her shrewd eyes narrowing slightly. To Leo, she added, "I hope you will pay a visit when my husband and I return to Bellehaven in the fall. In the meantime, please look after Kitty."

"I don't require looking after," Kitty huffed, indignant, as her friend glided away. "And, in case you hadn't noticed, he's hardly a suitable governess!"

"She knows how to ruffle your feathers," Leo said with a wink.

In all the hours they'd spent working directly across from each other, he'd never winked at her like that. As if he knew all her secrets. Suddenly warm, she withdrew her fan from her reticule.

She shot him a too-sweet smile, hoping to get back on familiar footing. "What did you wish to discuss?"

He hesitated a beat, so she continued. "Allow me to guess. You're upset because your favorite drafting pencil has gone missing, and you think I've hidden it." She'd certainly been guilty of that a time or two.

His eyes crinkled at the corners. The lines there were deeper than she recalled, but in a way that suited him, dash it all. "No," he said. "Try again."

"You've discovered that your accounts ledger is off by three pennies, and you're so distraught you need me to prevent you from hurling yourself off Brigand's Bluff." He'd always been a bit of a perfectionist.

"That's not it, either," he said, gazing at her as if she should be able to read his mind.

To be fair, she'd once been quite good at ascertaining the direction of his thoughts. But a great deal of time had passed since he'd left, and she hadn't received so much as a single letter. Perhaps she'd been foolish to expect to receive correspondence from a boy with whom she'd quarreled almost daily. Indeed, they'd once traded insults with the same ease that civil people exchanged pleasantries.

But then he'd trotted off to London, and the loss of their rivalry left a gaping void. Her life had felt much like a parlor where the sofa had been suddenly removed. Even a threadbare, wobbly, tea-stained sofa was preferable to no sofa at all. A parlor without any sofa was simply awkward and empty and . . . sad.

So Kitty had done what she needed to do. What she'd

done before when people left. She'd rearranged the other parts of her life in an attempt to fill the space.

But now Leo was back, and she wasn't at all certain she knew him anymore.

At last he said, "Could we go someplace quieter to sit and talk? Perhaps the terrace?"

The unexpected seriousness in his expression rattled her, and she suddenly regretted teasing him. What if his grandfather or mother was unwell? Or if he was in some sort of trouble? "Of course," she said, despite the full dance card dangling from her wrist. "Let's go."

They were halfway to the French doors when Mayor Martin hopped onto the dais where the orchestra sat, bows resting on their laps. "Ladies and gentlemen," the mayor boomed across the ballroom, "may I have your attention, please?"

Kitty and Leo paused near the potted ferns. "What's this about?" he asked, as the crowd around them gradually hushed.

"For weeks, the mayor's been hinting he has big news to share at tonight's ball," Kitty whispered. "The town's all a-twitter, but he's been quite tight-lipped. Can our talk wait until after the announcement?"

"Of course," he said with a self-deprecating shrug. "I'm nothing if not patient."

A retort was on the tip of Kitty's tongue, but she swallowed it when the mayor launched into his speech.

"Many thanks to Lady Rufflebum, our lovely hostess, for inviting us all to her annual summer ball. I can think of no better way to begin the busy tourist season. I am honored to inform you that plans are underway for all of Bellehaven's usual events, including the locals versus out-of-towners cricket match on the beach, our famous regatta at the docks, and the Regatta Ball in our beautiful assembly rooms."

As cheers and applause erupted around the ballroom, Kitty glanced at Leo and said, "Some things don't change."

He nodded, thoughtful. "Maybe not. I'm hoping some things do."

His words settled in her belly like a butterfly landing on a bloom. That uncharacteristically dreamy, faraway look in his eyes could mean only one thing: Leo Lockland fancied a woman in Bellehaven. Probably someone sweet and agreeable. Someone who wouldn't dare look at him crosswise, much less contradict him. Maybe he'd even written to her while he was in London.

Kitty smiled to herself and mentally tucked that bit of speculation securely into her reticule, for it would surely be useful at some point. Of course she was curious as to the identity of the poor girl, but she would find out soon enough. And then she'd have a bit of ammunition to toss Leo's way the next time he made the mistake of needling her.

The mayor cleared his throat, snapping Kitty's attention back to long-awaited announcement.

"Thanks to the generosity of our benefactor, the countess, I am able to reveal a new, exciting opportunity for our town. As you are all aware, Bellehaven has been growing by leaps and bounds. We anticipate the construction of several new buildings in the next decade, and, to that end, we are sponsoring a design contest."

A shiver of excitement skittered down Kitty's spine, and she perked up her ears in order to hear over the excited murmurs of the guests around her and Leo.

"The rules of the contest are simple," the mayor continued. "Each entry will consist of a building design for a structure of the participant's choosing. The designs will be judged in three distinct areas: visual appeal, technical merit, and the potential benefit to our fair town."

"Unbelievable," Leo whispered in awe.

Kitty's fingertips went numb. This was precisely the opportunity she needed to prove her skills before she moved to London. She had to win the contest, and she *would*— no matter what it took.

"Submissions are due the day before the regatta," Mayor Martin continued, "and the winner will be announced at the Regatta Ball. The winning architect shall receive a monetary prize of one hundred pounds. More importantly, their building shall grace a prime location on Main Street, adjacent to the beach. Construction on the new project will begin in September."

The words buzzed in Kitty's ears like fireflies in a jar. This contest was her chance to be recognized as an architect. To show that she was capable of designing a structure that Bellehaven could be proud of. She swayed slightly, and a firm hand pressed against the small of her back.

"Are you all right?" Leo murmured. "You look a little flushed."

"I'm fine," she said, both irritated that he noticed and grateful for his concern. "But I could do with some fresh air."

"Follow me." He led the way around clusters of guests and the refreshment table to the French doors leading to the terrace. They crossed the flagstone patio and sat on a stone half-wall bathed in the moonlight. A chorus of insects serenaded them from the lush garden, but all Kitty could think of was the design contest. It was a chance to make a name for herself, to leave her mark, and create something beautiful for Bellehaven.

She was confident in her ability to bring a vision to life

on paper—drawing was her forte and passion. Numbers, on the other hand, were a headache and necessary evil. She'd been honing her technical skills in recent years, but the project she had in mind was going to push the limits of her knowledge, and she couldn't risk losing the contest over a silly computation error.

Which led her to two stark, rather humbling conclusions.

First, Leo Lockland, her longtime nemesis, was likely to be her greatest rival in the contest.

Second, she was going to swallow her pride and ask him for a favor.

Chapter 2

If Leo's calculations were correct—and they usually were—Kitty's shoulder was only three and seven-eighths inches away from his. Her hand rested on the stone wall where they sat, a mere two and five-sixteenths inches away from his thigh. And for the first time in years, they were completely alone. His heartbeat thundered in his chest as if he'd sprinted a mile to get to the countess's terrace.

If he didn't know Kitty so well, he might have misread the flush of her cheeks, the rapid rise and fall of her chest, and the frenetic tapping of her slipper on the flagstone terrace. But he was neither so hopeful nor so foolish as to imagine that those signs had anything to do with him or their closeness.

Kitty was entirely fixated on the mayor's announcement about Bellehaven's building design contest. She had the same feverish look about her that she'd always had when she was in the throes of envisioning a new project. He'd forgotten how beautiful she looked when she was inspired. How arousing it was when her lips moved—as if she were silently enumerating the elements she'd incorporate into her creation.

She blinked at him and shook her head as though she'd almost forgotten he was there. "I know you wished to talk about something," she said. "But may I ask you something first?"

Leo nodded. Clearly, this was not the moment to confess his feelings for her. "I presume this is about the contest?"

She looked into his eyes and blew out a long breath. "Are you going to enter?"

"I don't know," he said truthfully.

She scoffed, incredulous. "How could you not know?"

"I haven't had time to sufficiently weigh the pros and cons, much less consider what sort of building I'd design."

With a frustrated sigh, she stood and paced the terrace in front of him. "Is it necessary to nail down every little detail? Must you be so deliberate about everything?"

He smiled, grateful that he hadn't lost his knack for getting under her skin. "How about if I turn the question around. Do *you* want me to enter the contest?"

"No and yes."

He scratched his head, at a loss. "Care to elaborate?"

"No, I don't want you to enter because, though I'm loathe to admit it, you are likely my strongest competition," she admitted, and Leo could only imagine what it had cost her.

"And yes because . . . ?"

"Yes, because I don't want to win by default. I want to win knowing that my design was the best. That it outshone every other entry and won on its merits." She exhaled slowly. "You should enter."

"I'm finishing designs for a couple of clients over the next two weeks," he said. "But I'll think about it."

She walked back to the stone wall, sat beside him, and swallowed. "In the meantime, I have a favor to ask of you." She closed her eyes for a moment, then looked deep into his. He'd never seen Kitty Beckett so vulnerable, so exposed.

And in that moment, he would have given her anything. If she'd asked him to rob the next coach that came to town, he'd have donned a mask, hopped on his horse, and hidden in a shrub by the road. He was powerless to refuse her when she looked so genuine. So soft.

"What sort of favor?" he asked, his voice a little raspy to his own ears.

"I wondered if you'd help me with my entry for the contest." The words spilled out as if she'd been holding them in for a while. "My technical skills have improved vastly since we last worked together, so I wouldn't be asking you to do everything. I just need someone to consult with as questions arise, and to occasionally review my work to make sure my calculations are sound."

"I suppose I could help," he said, trying not to appear too eager.

A warm smile lit her face. "Thank you. I wouldn't have asked, but I've never undertaken a project of this scope before, and this contest is a unique chance for me."

"I understand," he said truthfully. He didn't know any other female architects. Couldn't imagine they'd have the same opportunities he had. "What are you going to design?"

She gazed out at the moonlit garden, and her face took on a dreamy look. "I'm not ready to share quite yet. It's still coming into focus. But it's going to be something the likes of which Bellehaven has never seen."

"I don't doubt it."

"In any event, you mustn't let your involvement with my project prevent you from entering the contest," she said, earnestly. "May the best design win."

He arched a brow in his best villain impersonation.

"There could be a conflict of interest. Aren't you afraid I'll try to sabotage your project?"

"Sabotage," she repeated with a chuckle. "That's rich."

"One misplaced decimal could be disastrous," he said, suppressing a shudder at the thought. "Are you certain you trust me?"

"With numbers?" she qualified. "Yes, I do. Besides, you're not capable of carrying out an evil plan. You couldn't be ruthless if you tried."

He sat back, mildly offended. "You don't think I could?"

She patted his knee like she was consoling a schoolboy who'd had his lunch pail stolen. "Not in a million years. You're far too . . . nice." She winced, as if she'd just delivered news that he had a ghastly illness.

He was still digesting this as she smoothed the skirt of her gown and folded her hands on her lap.

"I'm glad that's settled," she said brightly. "You shall act as a consultant on my contest entry. And now you must tell me what I may do for you in return."

Leo blinked. "You don't need to do anything for me."

"I absolutely must," she said firmly. "I wouldn't rest easy otherwise."

"Why? Are you worried I'll hold the favor over your head? Blackmail you?"

She chuckled again and dabbed the corner of one eye with a fingertip as if some of her mirth had leaked out. "I believe we've already established that you're too honorable to sabotage anything. I'm afraid we must add blackmail to the list of things you're incapable of."

It was true, damn it all. And though he supposed it was a compliment, it sounded more like a fatal flaw. "Very well, Miss Beckett," he drawled. "If you insist on making this an even exchange, tell me: What can you offer me in return for my services?"

She lifted her chin, squared her shoulders, and frowned, thoughtful. "I could sketch a design for you—for one of your current projects perhaps?"

He would have loved to have one of her sketches—but not for a job. He'd rather have something she drew just for him. But he couldn't ask her that without revealing his feelings for her, and he wasn't ready to do that. Yet.

He shook his head. "No, thank you. My current clients are accustomed to my dry, functional drawings. If I gave them a glimpse of your talent, I'd only be setting them up for disappointment in the future."

Her mouth quirked adorably. "I take it you still regard the use of watercolors and pastels as frivolous?"

"Not so much frivolous as beyond me," he confessed. "I've come to terms with it."

"Each of us has their cross to bear," she said philosophically. "Let me see. There must be something else you need. Some sort of service I could provide." She tapped the tip of her index finger against her plump lower lip, then her eyes went wide with inspiration. "I could reintroduce you to some of the young ladies in town."

He narrowed his eyes, suspicious. "Why would you do that?"

She shrugged innocently. "I assumed you'd be interested in finding a nice, agreeable woman to settle down with."

Holy hell. "I don't need you to play matchmaker, Kitty."

"It's Kat," she reminded him coolly. "And you needn't sound so offended. I simply thought you could use some assistance in that area. You've been away for a while, after all, and there are some recent newcomers to Bellehaven—eligible young ladies who would suit you."

Leo raked a hand through his hair and took a turn at pacing the terrace. "The idea is ludicrous," he said. "But just out of curiosity, what sort of woman do you think would suit me?"

"That's simple," she said, supremely confident. "Your ideal match would be congenial, sweet, and doting. The sort of woman who lives for the moment when her husband walks through the door in the evening."

"I can see you've devoted some thought to this," he said wryly. "What else?"

"Well," she said, as if broaching a sticky subject, "your ideal woman would need to be patient enough to tolerate your meticulous and sometimes moody nature."

"This is extremely enlightening," he quipped. "Is that all?"

"No, of course not. She'll need to be pretty." She smirked, signaling a final jab was coming. "So that there's at least the possibility that you'll produce attractive offspring."

He glowered at her, and she waved a dismissive hand. "I only tease because you know very well that women find you attractive. I don't want your head to grow too big."

Leo took a moment to digest the compliment—if it could accurately be classified as such. Then he said, "Let me see if I have this correct." He held up a hand, preparing to tick off her list on his fingers. "You think I need a woman who's meek, desperate, and not hideous."

"I was significantly more tactful," Kitty said with a shrug. "But your characterization is also accurate."

Leo started pacing again, beyond frustrated.

"What's wrong?" Kitty asked. She frowned as if she was truly puzzled. "You're not interested in finding a nice woman to court?"

The truth was he didn't want docile or timid. He wanted spirited and passionate. He wanted obstinate and clever. He wanted Kitty.

"You have no idea what I'm looking for in a partner," he said flatly.

"Then why don't you inform me?"

He faced her, propped his hands on his hips, and gazed into her eyes, wondering if she'd recognize herself in the description he gave. "I'm looking for someone with a rapier wit and a saucy smile. Someone who knows what she wants and unapologetically goes after it. Someone who challenges me and who occasionally even drives me a bit mad."

Kitty seemed to consider this for a moment, then clucked her tongue in disbelief. "You're quite certain about that?"

"I am."

"I'm afraid I simply can't see that working," she said, her voice laced with regret.

"Why not?" he asked, incredulous.

Kitty gracefully rose from the wall and began to slowly circle him, as if taking his measure. "Would you like me to be honest?"

He tried not to flinch under her scrutiny. "Yes," he said, though he was fairly certain he wasn't going to like her answer.

"We've already established that you're handsome enough. That isn't the problem."

Leo was grateful she was behind him so that she couldn't see him flush. "I sense there's a *but* coming."

"It's the way you dress and carry yourself, the way you interact with people. You're too predictable, principled, and *nice*."

He resisted the urge to grind his teeth. "Those are bad qualities?

"Not at all," she assured him. "But they're not going to attract the sort of woman you described."

"Very well. What qualities do I need?"

"I cannot give you a list, Leo. It's more complicated than that." She paused in front of him, lifted her chin, and met his gaze. "If you wish to catch the eye of a daring woman, you must be able to walk into a room and command the attention of everyone in it. You must have a dangerous air about you—the sort that makes a lady's heart flutter."

With each word she spoke, his own heart sank. He was nothing like the man she described. And she wasn't finished. Her expression turned wistful, and her mouth curved into a sensual smile—as if she was imagining the man of *her* dreams.

"You should have a sense of mystery or intrigue. A deliciously disheveled look that makes people wonder whether you've come directly from a high-stakes card game or a lover's bed."

He swallowed, and her words hung in the air between them like the aromatic smoke of a cheroot. Once he'd located his tongue, he asked, "Women truly want that?"

"Not all women," she corrected. "But some do." The faraway look in her eyes left no doubt as to which camp she fell into.

Kitty wanted a rogue. A reprobate. A *rake*.

And he knew exactly what he needed to do.

"Fine," he said, keeping his tone light. "Teach me."

She inhaled sharply—as if someone had splashed her with cold water. "What?"

"You asked what I wanted in exchange for helping you with your contest entry. Show me how to be that kind of man."

She opened her mouth, closed it, and opened it again. As if she was having difficulty making her voice work. At last she managed, "Are you jesting?"

"I'm dead serious."

"But there's nothing wrong with the way you are," she said. "You're perfectly fine."

Fine? He'd have rather she called him "perfectly infuriating" or even "perfectly diabolical." Any adjective would have been preferable to *fine*. Except, perhaps, nice.

"That's not the point," he said evenly.

She stalked back to the wall and sat, flouncing her skirts in exasperation. "I don't see why—" Her eyes grew wide and her mouth formed a small *o*. As if understanding had dawned.

Panic clambered up his chest and skittered around his neck. Kitty knew how he felt about her. She'd finally seen through his facade, and he was totally exposed. As vulnerable as a roofless house in a thunderstorm.

"You needn't be embarrassed," she said earnestly.

"No?" He hadn't dared to believe that she might return his feelings. Especially after everything she'd told him tonight.

"You're fond of someone here in Bellehaven," she whispered conspiratorially. "And you want her to believe you're a rake."

Bloody hell.

Her expression was triumphant—as if she'd cracked a secret code. "It's true, isn't it?" she prodded.

"Yes." He saw no point in denying it.

She leaned forward. "Who's the woman you fancy? I must know."

"I'd rather not say." His mouth felt dry as dust. "The question is, can you help me?"

She cast a skeptical glance at his boots, his clothes, his hair. "It would require quite a bit of work, and you'd need to trust me."

"I do trust you," he said evenly.

"I would need to know that you're one hundred percent

committed," she crossed her arms, adamant. "I don't do anything by half measures."

"I know." It was one of the things he adored about her. "I'm willing to do whatever you say."

She arched a brow at that. "You must be quite smitten by this mystery woman."

"I suppose I am."

For the space of several heartbeats, she was silent, and Leo wondered if she'd refuse.

At last, she blew out a long breath. "Very well. You will be my consultant for the design contest. In return, I shall teach you how to be a rake."

He extended a hand to her. "Deal."

She took his hand, and the touch of their palms sent a rush of heat surging through his body.

"Deal," she confirmed. She didn't release his hand right away, but instead searched his face—as if she longed to know his secrets.

He didn't let go, either. When it came to Kitty, he would never be the first to let go. "A fair trade," he said. "I'll help you win the design contest. You'll help me win the object of my affections."

She smiled at that, then slowly uncurled her fingers, releasing his hand. "I should return to the ballroom before the next gentleman listed on my dance card forms a search party." She frowned slightly, then added, "What was it you wished to discuss in the first place?"

He swallowed. "I wanted you to know that even though I'm taking over my grandfather's practice, you are welcome to stay and work there for as long as you like."

She hesitated for a moment, then nodded thoughtfully. "Thank you." As she turned and crossed the flagstone terrace, he watched the subtle sway of her hips and the swish of her gown around her legs, half-mesmerized.

"Oh, and Leo?" she called over her shoulder, mid-stride. "Meet me on the corner of Main Street and Broadneck tomorrow at half past two."

He scratched his head. "What for?"

She paused and rolled her eyes as if praying for patience. "Your first lesson. Don't be late," she instructed. "And be sure to bring your billfold with you."

Chapter 3

When Kitty arrived at the meeting spot the next day, Leo was already there, standing like a soldier at attention. His light-brown hair was so short and well-tamed that it did not move the slightest in the stiff ocean breeze. His brown trousers and jacket were a similar shade as the sandy street, so much so that he almost blended in.

Good heavens, but she and Clara had their work cut out for them.

Clara was Hazel and Uncle Beck's adopted daughter, and Kitty considered her a sister. She'd asked Clara to come along for two reasons. First, because the fifteen-year-old was a lovely companion. The sort who could hold a lively conversation or walk in silence when needed. Second, no one in all of England—or France, for that matter—had a better eye for fashion.

"Hullo, Leo," Kitty said briskly. "I'm sure you remember my sister, Clara."

He shot her a warm smile. "Of course—though you're quite a bit taller now. A pleasure to see you, Miss Clara."

"I've asked her to come along so that she can help us select a few key additions to your wardrobe," Kitty explained.

"My wardrobe?" He looked down at his chest, confused. "What's wrong with it?"

"Nothing," Clara said quickly, alarmed that he might have taken offense.

"I know you were interested in purchasing a waistcoat or two." Kitty shot him a pointed glare, probably because he'd said no such thing. "Clara is a gifted seamstress, and she has a knack for picking flattering colors and fabrics. I trust her implicitly," she added, signaling that he should, too.

"Then I'm fortunate you're here," he said graciously.

"The tailor's shop should have everything we need," Kitty said matter-of-factly. She walked down the pavement toward the store until they arrived at a large bay window where Mr. Danvers had created a display of all the accessories a fashionable gentleman could want, from walking sticks to kid gloves to top hats.

"Now then," Kitty said, "we're looking for a few items that will help Leo cut a dashing figure. To make him look fashionable, but not as though he's trying too hard."

Clara nodded as if she understood the goal perfectly.

Leo's expression was somewhere on the spectrum between confused and annoyed.

"Right," Kitty said. "Let's make our way inside."

A little bell above the shop door trilled as they entered, and Mr. Danvers welcomed them in with a wave. "Good afternoon, ladies and—" The shopkeeper squinted through his spectacles as if he feared they were defective. "Leo Lockland, is that you?"

"It is indeed," Leo said cordially. "Good to see you again, Mr. Danvers."

"Aye, it's been too long, lad. So sorry about your father."

Leo tensed and gave a curt nod. Kitty's chest squeezed,

for she knew the pain of losing a parent. Leo appeared more angry than sad, but she also knew that grief took many forms—sometimes all on the same day.

She jumped into the silence, hoping to lighten the mood. "I told Leo about the newest waistcoats you've received from London—the ones with the bright colors and ornate designs. He wanted to see them for himself."

Mr. Danvers fiddled with the tape measure slung around his neck, clearly skeptical. "Is that so?"

Kitty surreptitiously jabbed Leo with her elbow.

"Yes," he said, clearing his throat. "A bit different from my usual tastes."

"Well then, have a look at the beauties on display over there"—the tailor gestured toward a rainbow of waistcoats spread across a tabletop like a giant fan—"while I take Mr. Rodnick's jacket measurements. I shall check in with you shortly."

"Thank you," Kitty said. A particular waistcoat had already captured her attention, and she went directly to it. She slid it from the pile and held it in front of her for Leo and Clara to see. "What do you think of this?"

From the appalled look on Leo's face, one would have thought she'd suggested a potato sack. "It's purple," he said, as if that immediately disqualified it from consideration.

"Periwinkle, to be more precise," Kitty replied dryly, then turned to her sister. "Clara, what is your expert opinion?"

Clara's perceptive eyes flicked from Kitty to Leo and back again. "It is eye-catching, to be sure," she said diplomatically.

Leo snorted. "Maybe that's because it's covered in grossly misshapen birds."

"I believe you meant to say, 'delicately embroidered swans,'" Kitty corrected. But upon further inspection, the swans' necks *did* look rather tangled. Thank heaven she'd brought Clara.

Her sweet sister did not comment on the swans. Instead, she ran a fingertip over the silk and satin garments folded on the table, as if thoughtfully considering each in turn. Her slender index finger came to rest on an olive-green swath of fabric, which she pulled from the pile.

It looked dreadfully drab to Kitty, and though she was sorely tempted to say so, she bit her tongue.

Meanwhile, Clara unfolded the single-breasted waistcoat and brought it closer to the window to examine it in the sunlight. Lighter green threads shimmered against the mossy satin, creating a subtle yet pleasing pattern across the front panels. Clara had not lost her touch after all.

She approached Leo and held up the garment as if she wished to see it near his face. "May I?"

"Of course," he said affably. Clearly, he already trusted Clara more than he did Kitty, which didn't irk her in the slightest.

Clara draped the vest over Leo's shoulders and stepped back to get the full effect. But Kitty already knew it was perfect.

The lime strands complimented his tanned skin. His eyes, which had never stood out to her before, flashed a brilliant amber-brown. But perhaps the greatest favor that the waistcoat did for him—objectively speaking—was to accentuate his admittedly broad chest and impossibly flat abdomen.

She felt an odd, unsuspected hitch in her throat. It was only a waistcoat, after all. He was still Leo.

"What do you think?" he asked earnestly, directing the question not to Clara, but to Kitty—and catching her off guard.

She swallowed, shoved the purple abomination to the bottom of the stack, and shrugged. "I suppose it will do."

He removed the waistcoat from his torso and handed it to Clara with a grateful smile. To Kitty he said, "If you don't like it, we can try some others."

She exhaled, then closed her eyes briefly. She'd made a deal with Leo, and the least she could do was be honest with him. "The truth is that Clara's instincts are flawless. The waistcoat shows your, er, assets to their best advantage. It will be worth every crown you spend on it." There. She'd even refrained from grinding her teeth.

Leo's eyes crinkled at the corners—as if he knew what the compliment had cost her. "Thank you."

"Our work is far from done," she said briskly. "Mr. Danvers will need to take your measurements for alterations, and then we must select some accessories. Clara, what do you recommend?"

A half hour later, their trio exited the shop with a pair of leather gloves, a jaunty top hat, and a fine cambric shirt for Leo. Mr. Danvers had assured him that the two waistcoats he'd chosen would be ready in a few days.

Leo tucked his box under one arm and paused on the pavement, facing Kitty and Clara. "I have you both to thank for this successful mission, and I'd say celebratory tarts are in order. Can I persuade you to go to the tea shop with me?"

"As lovely as that sounds I must go to the school," Clara said regretfully. "I promised Miss Jane that I'd help her design costumes for the annual play."

"Then I shall make it up to you another time," Leo said with a formal bow.

Kitty refrained from rolling her eyes, hugged Clara, and sent her on her way.

"What about you, Kitty?" Leo asked, his voice deeper than it had been a moment before. "Can I tempt you?"

The image of him in the tailor's shop, his fawn-brown eyes gleaming, flashed in her head, unbidden. She reminded herself that he was referring to *tarts*.

"I don't think so," she said, her voice slightly breathless to her own ears. "I intend to start working on my design this afternoon."

Disappointment flicked across his face, but he recovered so quickly that she might have imagined it. "I can't wait to see your drawing," he said. "I assume you're still not ready to tell me what you're designing?"

"I'm not," she confirmed. "But you shall know soon enough."

He gave her a grudging but good-natured smile. "It doesn't seem fair to keep me in the dark when I'm meant to be helping you."

"I know precisely how you feel," Kitty replied, keeping her tone light. "After all, I am helping you capture the affections of a woman—and I have no idea who she is." Sweet Jesus, she couldn't imagine what had made her say that. She supposed it was only natural that she'd be curious, but Leo Lockland's love interest was clearly no concern of hers.

"It's a little different," he said softly. "But you might find out one day."

She feigned indifference. "I scarcely know how I'll be able to sleep till then."

He chuckled at that. "Good luck drafting your design," he said sincerely.

"It's the most difficult part for me," she admitted. "Before I begin, the possibilities are infinite. I find the number of choices paralyzing."

His eyes went wide, as though her confession surprised him. "I always assumed your ideas popped into your head fully formed. That it was simply a matter of transferring that vision to paper."

"If only it were that easy," she said, a question niggling at the back of her mind. "Is it that way for you?"

"Never," he said with a snort. "But when I'm floundering at the start of a project, I know what I need to do to gain my footing."

She arched a brow, waiting for him to say more, then realized he was going to make her ask. She wouldn't have given him the satisfaction if she weren't feeling a bit desperate. "Would you care to share the secret?"

He cocked his head thoughtfully, as if telling her his silly little strategy was tantamount to revealing secrets of the crown. Then his face broke into a teasing smile. "I suppose it *is* part of our bargain. Come with me."

He began striding down Main Street, and she fell into step beside him. She'd forgotten how long his legs were. How driven he was when it came to his work. And how, despite their obvious differences, they'd always managed to find common ground in their love of architecture.

As they walked down the pavement, townspeople called out friendly greetings, as if they were both surprised and pleased to see Leo back in Bellehaven. And Kitty couldn't help noticing that some greetings were more friendly than others.

As the blacksmith's pretty daughter, Lila Bardsley, approached, she eyed Leo like he was the last delectable scone on a tea tray. "Well, if it isn't Leo Lockland," she drawled.

"Good afternoon, Miss Bardsley." Leo smiled politely, tipped his hat at the statuesque young woman, and strode past her without even registering the disappointment marring her smooth forehead.

Kitty jabbed Leo with her elbow.

He grunted in protest. "What in the devil was *that* for?"

"You missed a prime opportunity." Kitty clucked her tongue. "Lila wanted you to engage in a bit of flirtation."

Leo blinked. "Do you think so?"

"Wasn't it obvious?"

He rubbed his jaw—an idle habit of his that Kitty recalled from the days when they'd shared an office. Usually it meant he was perplexed about a design problem.

"I was cordial," he said as if he was trying to convince himself.

"That's precisely the problem. Lila was hoping for a bit of banter, and you greeted her as if she was the vicar's eighty-year-old grandmother." Kitty groaned. "Turning you into a rake is going to be more difficult than I thought. Whoever your mystery woman is, I hope she's worth it."

"She is," he said confidently. "I'm sure of it."

Kitty ignored a small pang of jealousy in her belly. It wasn't that she wanted Leo to like her. The very idea was preposterous. But it would be nice if some gentleman felt that strongly for her.

Eager for a change of subject, she asked, "Would you mind telling me where we're going?"

Leo planted his feet at the corner of Main and South Streets and swept an arm across the road, toward a shop that had been boarded up for years. "Right here."

Understanding dawned. "Oh," Kitty said. "This is the spot where the winning entry will be erected."

"Right." He set his package on one end of a weathered wooden bench across from the site and invited her to sit on the other. Meanwhile, he walked behind the bench and casually rested his elbows on the back, near her right shoulder.

"I don't have my sketchbook or any tools with me," she said. "I don't even have paper to take notes."

"We're not here to do that kind of work," he said, staring over her shoulder. "We're here to get you unstuck." He made it sound as though she was a carriage wheel mired the mud.

"I'm not stuck. It's more like I find myself at a crossroads. I could choose to go in one of four directions, each full of possibilities."

"Right," he said softly. "Choosing one path means giving up the others."

"Precisely." Perhaps he *did* understand.

"When I'm not certain in which direction to take a project, I go to the site and let it lead me." His mouth was close to her ear, and his voice, deep and smooth, vibrated across her nape.

She stared at the rickety shop that hadn't survived a fierce September storm two years prior. Rotting boards covered the windows. Peeling paint hung from decrepit walls. The roofline sagged like a hammock.

"It's a very practical suggestion," she admitted. "And I can see why you might need to reacquaint yourself with this spot. You haven't been in Bellehaven for some time now. But it's not the same for me. I know this town well enough to find my way from my house to Bluffs' Brew Inn and back again, blindfolded."

"I don't doubt it." He chuckled, sending those odd vibrations shimmying down her spine. "But this is a different sort of exercise."

She frowned, wary. "How so?"

"Close your eyes."

"What?" she asked, not bothering to mask her skepticism.

"Don't worry," he said softly. "Few souls venture this far down Main, and no one is watching."

"I'm not worried about that," she fibbed. "But I scarcely see the point."

"Trust me." His voice was deep and husky. "Close your eyes."

"Very well," she said, squeezing them shut. "But if this is some sort of trick, I shall tell Lila Bardsley that you're afflicted with a heinous and humiliating sort of rash."

"It's no trick. All you must do is listen and feel."

"Listen and feel," she repeated, still cynical.

For the space of several heartbeats, he said nothing, and she did her best to focus on the sounds and sensations around her. Seagulls cawing overhead. The low roar of the ocean in the distance. The salty sea air licking at her ankles. Leo's warm breath puffing close to her neck. The erratic thumping of her own heart.

"Now," he whispered, "imagine the abandoned shop is gone. In its place stands your grand, new structure. Imagine it at sunrise, with the light reflecting off its windows. Envision it during the busiest part of the day, when people are milling about, and at dusk, with a backdrop of turquoise water and orange clouds."

His words floated around her head like effervescent soap bubbles. Fizzing. Popping. Bringing her project into focus.

She could finally envision it clearly. Wide, polished marble steps beckoning visitors to a terrace overlooking the sea. Column-like figures of Poseidon and Aphrodite standing guard at the main entrance. Three stories of glistening stone wrapped in a frieze of sea creatures and topped with shining domed roof.

"Can you see it?" he murmured.

"I can." She swallowed, strangely moved by the beauty of it.

It was the building she'd always wanted for Bellehaven. A place where all the townspeople could gather for entertainment, inspiration, and culture.

It was a theater. And her fingers were itching to bring it to life.

She opened her eyes and faced Leo. He was so close that she could see the whiskey-colored specks in his irises. An odd heat crept up her neck. "I must go," she said abruptly. "I need to draw it before the details fade. I think this building could be . . . amazing."

"I know it will be."

She cocked her head. "How can you be certain?"

"I saw the look on your face just now."

"Oh," she said, standing awkwardly. This interaction was unfamiliar territory for Leo and her. The fact that they weren't sparring, teasing, or competing left her a little off-balance. "I'll need a couple of days to work on the design."

"If you require me for anything, you can find me at the office," he said.

"Thank you." She hadn't been there since he returned and wasn't certain how she'd feel working so close to him again. As she was about to leave, she asked, "Are you playing in the cricket match on Saturday?"

Leo nodded. "I was at the Salty Mermaid last night. Nathan Gutridge asked if I'd be bowler for the locals."

"And you agreed?"

Leo chuckled. "Would you say no to Nathan?" The barkeep had biceps as thick as logs and could stop a pub brawl in its tracks with a single growl.

"Most of Bellehaven will be at the cricket match," Kitty said. "Maybe even the young lady you're interested in."

His gaze flicked away, and he rubbed the back of his neck. "She might be."

Good heavens. The woman—whoever she was—definitely had him under her spell. The mere mention of her had him tongue-tied and flushed. If he were to have any chance of impressing her, he needed to appear confident, self-possessed, and a bit dangerous. Kitty supposed that after all Leo had done for her, the least she could do was to give him a few pointers ahead of Saturday's match.

"Meet me at Peacock Cove the day after tomorrow," she said. "And bring your cricket ball and bat."

He held up his palms, clearly puzzled. "We can't practice with two people."

"We can't practice *cricket* with two people, but we can practice plenty of other things." She strolled back down Main and called over her shoulder, "I'll see you at noon."

Chapter 4

When Leo arrived at Peacock Cove, Kitty was already there, perched on the hull of an upside-down rowboat. She'd discarded her bonnet, and her golden hair glistened in the summer sun as she stared at the tranquil turquoise water.

"I almost drowned here," she said without preamble.

The mere thought was enough to make his heart pound. "When?"

"On the first day I came to Bellehaven," she said conversationally. "But Hazel saved me, and then my uncle saved her."

"You never told me that story," he said, keeping his tone light despite the fact that it cut a little. Back when they'd worked together, he'd shared plenty of secrets with her.

She inclined her head, thoughtful. "If I didn't mention it, that's because it doesn't cast me in the best light. If I'd done the rescuing, trust me, you would have heard about it. I'd have demanded that a statue be erected right here in my honor."

"Fair enough," he conceded with a chuckle. "How is your contest design coming along?"

"Very well. But we're not here to talk about my project." She hopped off the boat, brushed her palms together, and rested her hands on the swells of her hips. "We're here to make sure you're ready for tomorrow's match."

"Right. I came prepared." He propped his bat on one shoulder and pulled the ball from his pocket. "But I still don't know what we're doing here."

"Nathan asked you to be the bowler," Kitty said. "Isn't that an important part?"

"Position," he corrected, idly tossing the ball and snatching it out of the air.

"I never claimed that cricket was my area of expertise," she quipped, but her gaze followed the ball as it sailed straight up, dropped down, and smacked the center of his palm. "But that . . . that's good."

"What, this?" He followed the track of the ball as it momentarily hovered above his head—there was nothing special about it.

"The tossing," she clarified. "It makes you look athletic. Quite masculine."

Jesus. The ball bounced off his chest and plopped sadly onto the sand.

She clucked her tongue. "You must think of tomorrow's match as a stage. It's a chance to perform for the rest of the town and, more important, a chance to impress all the ladies."

"I'm not interested in impressing all the ladies. Only one. And I'm not certain she cares about cricket."

Kitty scooped the ball off the ground, grabbed his wrist, and dropped the ball in his palm. His skin tingled where her fingers had touched him. "You must change your way of thinking. It is human nature to want what everyone else wants. A true rake knows this and uses it to his advantage. He charms everyone."

"How am I supposed to flirt while I'm launching a ball at a wicket?"

"You don't have to flirt." She took a step back, tilted her head, and frowned. "You merely need to look athletic. Display your prowess."

"It sounds as though you insisted on this meeting in order to tell me to play well," he said with a shrug. "Nathan's already promised me free drinks if we win, so it goes without saying that I'll be giving my best effort."

"I should hope so," Kitty said. "Winning is much more attractive than losing. But you need to do more than play well. You must look good while doing it."

Leo grunted, not bothering to hide his skepticism. "Serious cricket players don't give a fig how they look."

She closed her eyes briefly, as if praying for patience. "You'd think I'd asked you to wear a powdered wig, when all I'm suggesting is that you take advantage of the opportunity to showcase your . . . er, assets."

Leo felt his jaw drop.

"Have I shocked you?" she asked dryly. "If so, that is another thing we shall have to work on. Rogues are not easily shocked."

"Fine. Tell me what to do."

"Let's set the scene." She walked back to the rowboat and made herself comfortable on the overturned hull. "Pretend that I am sitting in the main tent along with all the eligible young ladies in Bellehaven. That rock near the water is the area where the cricket match is being played."

"You mean the pitch," he said.

She waved a dismissive hand. "Call it what you will. You've just come from the pub with Nathan and all the other strapping young men representing our fair town, and you're about to begin the game."

Leo nodded despite the fact that he still failed to see the point of this rehearsal.

"Now," Kitty continued, "show me how you'll walk onto the beach."

"You mean before the match starts?"

"First impressions are critical," she said loftily.

Feeling more than a little awkward, he gripped the bat handle in one hand, the ball in the other, and strode toward the rock. When he reached it, he turned and shot her a questioning glance. "How was that?"

"A bit stiff," she said, as if she should be congratulated for her tact. "Do you suppose we could try it again? This time, let your arms sway. But not as though you're marching. Attempt to saunter."

"Saunter," he repeated, trying to remember precisely what that entailed.

"Yes, please."

"Very well." He dutifully stalked back to his starting point and inhaled deeply. It had probably been a mistake for him to agree to this plan. Not only was it damned embarrassing, but there wasn't a chance in hell she was going to turn him into a rake.

The only silver lining he could glean from their agreement was that he was able to spend time with her. He supposed that was enough to offset the humiliation.

He paused and recalled her directions. Then, he walked across the beach again, more slowly this time—the same pace he might use when touring a newly completed building that he'd designed. Whenever he did a walkthrough, he had to balance his eagerness to see every room with the need to slow down and appreciate the finer details. A deliberate, steady perusal was the only way to get a sense of the building's true character, which wasn't knowable from a two-dimensional drawing. He doubted there was anything more satisfying.

"That was better," she said brightly, snapping him from his thoughts. "You looked very . . . in command."

"Good." He released a breath, relieved to have the lesson behind him.

"But we're not finished yet," she said, hopping off the rowboat. "Let me have your jacket."

He swallowed. "What for?"

"You aren't going to wear it when you're playing, are you?"

"Of course not."

She snapped her fingers. "Then hand it over."

He dropped the bat, shrugged off his jacket, and gave it to her.

She tossed it onto the rowboat and stood toe-to-toe with him, casting a critical eye over his clothes.

"Is something wrong with my waistcoat?" Surely, she didn't expect him to wear one of the new ones.

"No," she assured him, pointing to one of his arms. "Let me see your sleeve."

He held it up, wondering if there was a stain or a tear in his shirt. But Kitty didn't stop to examine it. Instead, she deftly loosened his cuff and began rolling the sleeve up his forearm. When she reached his elbow, she tugged at the fabric covering his upper arm until she was apparently satisfied with the way it laid.

"Not bad," she said. "Allow me to fix the other one."

He swallowed and obeyed, savoring her closeness. A few pale blond tendrils around her face waved wildly in the stiff ocean breeze, and the citrusy scent of her hair tickled his nose. Her graceful fingers occasionally brushed his skin, heating his blood without even trying.

Heaven help him if she decided to examine the fit of his trousers next. If she did, she was definitely going to see the effect she had on him.

Fortunately, she directed her attention to his neckcloth. "May I?" she asked, pointing at it.

He nodded. "You don't like the knot?"

"It's not a matter of what I like," she said, oddly adamant. More smoothly she added, "but it should be looser. Even a bit lopsided, as if it were hastily tied."

As she reached up to adjust the knot, it was impossible not to imagine that he was living out the wild fantasy that Kitty Beckett was stripping off his clothes. He'd imagined it hundreds of times, and he was still unprepared for the jolt of desire that hit him. When she slipped a finger between the neckcloth and his throat, he flinched.

Her gaze snapped to his. "Forgive me. Am I choking you?"

"No," he assured her. "I'm . . . er, ticklish."

She smiled as if that made perfect sense, then continued to fiddle with the knot. He relished every second, committing the moment to memory. The thick lashes framing her eyes. The cupid's bow of her lips. The expanse of skin above her neckline, and the lush swells of her breasts. He'd never known someone with her kind of beauty. The kind that made it difficult to breathe.

"There." She patted his chest and took one step back to examine her handiwork. The knot hung two inches below his collar, and one of the ends fluttered in the brisk breeze. "That's a definite improvement. Now you look pleasantly disheveled."

"That's good?"

She gave a firm nod. "The goal is to make it appear as though you haven't given a thought to your appearance."

"I haven't."

"That's why you need me," she said with a triumphant smile. "If I may, I'd like to make one other suggestion."

"Go on." He braced himself for anything from rolling in the sand to dancing a jig. Knew he'd do whatever she asked.

"Refrain from shaving tomorrow morning. It will make women wonder if you've come directly from your bed."

"Why would we want them to wonder that?" he said arching a brow. He had an idea, of course, but he wanted to know what she'd say.

Her cheeks pinkened but she looked directly into his eyes. "Rakes spend an inordinate amount of time in bed."

He arched a brow. "Doing what?"

She narrowed her eyes, signaling that she knew exactly what he was about. "I suppose that they are doing what they do best, Leo. Pleasing women. Alas, I cannot teach you *every*thing. Right now we are simply attempting to master the basics."

Holy hell. He wanted to say that if he were ever given the chance to please her, that he would devote his entire life to it. That he'd make it his personal mission to see that she was drunk on pleasure for the rest of her days. That he'd worship every inch of her body and fulfill her every wanton desire till she was a puddle of sated bliss.

But confessing his feelings for her would ruin everything.

He cleared his throat. "Lucky for you, I'm a quick study. It seems all I must do is make myself look as though I've just woken from a drunken stupor."

"Precisely," she confirmed, then frowned slightly.

"What now?"

"It's your hair," she said tentatively. "Do you think you could run a hand through it?"

He sighed, even though he didn't mind in the slightest,

and swept his hair straight back from his brow. "How did I do?"

"No. It looks even neater than it did before. You need to drag your fingers through, like this." As she reached both hands up, her torso bumped into his. The ripe curves of her breasts pressed against his chest, and when the uneven sand made her wobble, he grasped her waist, steadying her.

She blinked, but continued, undeterred. She speared her fingers through his hair, massaging his scalp in tantalizing little circles and driving him half-mad with longing. Her hands lingered in the crop of his hair, and her face turned thoughtful, as if the texture or thickness surprised her.

Her gaze dropped to his lips. His heart pounded with such force that she had to feel it, too. His arousal strained against the front of his trousers, and he fought the primal urge to grind his hips against hers.

Abruptly, she lowered her hands, pulled away, and shook her head as if she'd momentarily forgotten herself.

She brushed her palms together like she was erasing the last ten seconds from her memory, then said, "Much better. Tomorrow, you must wear your hair like that." She made a circle in the air in front of his face.

He peered through the strands that covered his right eye. "It's going to be difficult to hit the wickets if I can't see where I'm bowling."

"Then I suppose you must decide," Kitty said, entirely unsympathetic. "You can win the match, or you can win the affection of your mystery woman. The decision is yours." She strode back to the rowboat and retrieved her bonnet.

He exhaled as he picked up his bat and shoved the ball

in his pocket. At least he'd have a plausible excuse for the bulge in his trousers. "Will I see you at the match tomorrow?"

"I'll be there to cheer on my uncle," she said breezily, "along with my Aunt Hazel and my sisters."

"Then I guess I should count myself lucky to be on the same team as the earl."

"He's playing for the out-of-towners this year," Kitty said.

Leo gaped, incredulous. "Blade is switching sides? Why?"

"Lady Rufflebum insisted. She said it's become tiresome watching the locals trounce the poor tourists. She's hoping that having Uncle Beck switch will even the teams out a bit."

"I daresay it will," Leo muttered.

"Don't look so alarmed." Kitty slipped her reticule on her wrist and began walking toward the pair of towering rocks at the cove's entrance. "It ruins the air of confidence we're trying to cultivate."

"Wait," he called, "we haven't even talked about your contest design."

"I'll have something to show you after the match," she promised. "That is, if you're not at the Salty Mermaid drowning your sorrows after suffering a humiliating loss at the hands of a ragtag group of vacationers."

Leo chuckled. "Care to place a wager?"

She stopped in her tracks and faced him, eyes gleaming. "I would."

"Name your stakes."

She hesitated for only a heartbeat. "The loser is honor-bound to truthfully answer any question that the winner asks. Nothing is off-limits."

Bloody hell. There was no doubt in Leo's mind as to

what Kitty would ask. She'd demand to know the name of the woman he liked. But he couldn't back down now. "You have a deal."

She smiled like a cat presented with a bowlful of cream. "Prepare to reveal your deepest, darkest secret, Leo Lockland."

Chapter 5

"Gads," Lady Rufflebum proclaimed. "The devil himself would be at home in this heat. Miss Beckett, would you be a dear and fetch my fan? Miss Whitford should have it."

"Of course," Kitty said, scanning the crowd. They'd all gathered beneath the large tent that had been erected on the beach so that the spectators could enjoy the cricket match in the comfort of the shade. The players hadn't arrived yet, but it seemed everyone in Bellehaven had converged in hopes of securing a good seat before the first pitch was thrown.

Kitty had come to the match with Hazel, who was eager to cheer on her husband, Kitty's uncle. Lucy and Clara, Kitty's sisters, were there, too, but they'd already flitted off in search of their school friends.

"I'm going to look for the countess's companion," Kitty said to Hazel with a conspiratorial wink. "Let us hope she doesn't melt before I return."

Hazel smiled weakly. "I can sympathize with Lady Rufflebum. I fear the sun is taking a toll on me, too."

Kitty searched her friend's face, which was pale despite the heat. Even the rebellious little curl at her temple had fallen limp. "You should sit," Kitty urged. "Look, here's a free chair. I'll bring you a lemonade after I fetch the countess's fan. Don't move from this spot."

Hazel, who—unlike Lady Rufflebum—was a stoic sort, sank gratefully onto the wooden folding chair. "This is better," she said, as though she were trying to convince herself. "I shall be much improved by the time the cricket match starts."

But Kitty was not nearly as certain. She quickly located Miss Whitford, the countess's companion, near the large refreshment table and procured the fan. Then she poured a tall glass of lemonade for Hazel.

After delivering the fan, Kitty returned to Hazel, encouraged to find her looking slightly less peaked. "Here," she said, handing her the glass. "Drink this."

Hazel blanched. "I'm not thirsty."

"Come now," Kitty insisted. "'Tis the best thing for you. Please, just a sip."

Hazel eyed the lemonade doubtfully. "Very well." She raised the glass to her lips, forced a swallow, and pressed a hand to her belly.

"It's so peculiar," Kitty said, trying to keep the worry from her voice. "You seemed fine when we left the house earlier."

"I was," Hazel assured her. "It's just a spell. Bound to pass."

Kitty wanted to believe that was true, but her friend's ghostly pallor belied her words. "Let me take you home. I know you were looking forward to watching Uncle Beck play, but you're clearly not well, and the heat will only grow more brutal as the afternoon wears on."

Hazel's shoulders sagged. "Perhaps I should go."

"I'm glad you've come to your senses. I'll let the girls know that we're leaving. They can stay for the match and go home with Uncle Beck."

"I can see myself back to the coach," Hazel said. "You should stay."

Kitty scoffed. "Why would I stay to watch a tedious display of male bravado when you have provided me with a perfect excuse to avoid it?"

"You seemed more interested in the match this year," Hazel said, her eyes far too perceptive for Kitty's comfort.

"Not at all," she fibbed. She'd been looking forward to seeing if Leo heeded the advice she'd given him yesterday. And of course she was eager to watch her uncle lead the Visitors' team to victory so that she could win her bet against Leo—and claim her prize. But none of that compared to Hazel's well-being.

"I would honestly prefer it if you stayed to cheer on your uncle and watch over your sisters," Hazel said firmly.

"We both know Lucy and Clara are more likely to keep an eye on *me*," Kitty quipped. Her younger sisters were angels—the antithesis of what Kitty had been at the age of fifteen. As much as she adored them, she'd always felt as though they were innocent lambs and she, a naughty shepherdess. "Besides," she added more soberly, "I won't be able to enjoy myself while I'm worried about you."

Hazel's eyes shone with affection. "You needn't worry about me. Promise."

Kitty dropped to her knee beside Hazel's chair and squeezed her hand. "How can you be so certain?" Terrible things happened all the time. Suddenly and without warning. A person could be hale and hearty one minute . . . and gone the next. No one knew that better than Kitty. It was the reason she refused to fall in love with any man. Why she needed to marry someone who would never demand her whole heart.

A soft smile lit Hazel's face. "Can you keep a secret?"

Kitty swallowed and prepared herself for dire news. "Yes. Whatever it is, we'll face it together."

Hazel leaned closer. "I'm expecting a babe. I haven't told anyone else yet—not even Blade. I wanted to wait until I was certain."

Kitty sat back on her heels. "You're . . . pregnant?"

Hazel nodded. "After all this time. Isn't it wonderful?"

"It is." It was. Truly. The pit in her stomach made no sense at all. But it was the same gaping emptiness she'd felt after her parents died. After her uncle left her at a boarding school. And after Poppy announced she'd be spending a few months in London. "I'm so happy for you—and for me. I shall be an aunt."

"My morning sickness started a few days ago," Hazel said with a groan. "I think the heat is making it worse."

"Let's take you back to the coach," Kitty said, easing her off the chair.

As they made their way across the dunes, Hazel said, "Please make sure Blade knows there's nothing wrong. I don't want him to worry."

"Nor do I," Kitty quipped. "He must be focused on the match if the out-of-towners are to have any shot at winning, and I have quite a bit at stake." When she'd made the bet with Leo, she hadn't considered the very distinct possibility that *his* team would win and that she'd be at his mercy. Forced to answer any question he asked.

"Kitty Beckett," Hazel said with mock censure. "Did you place a wager on the cricket match?"

"I might have. But don't worry, I don't stand to lose my fortune. Only my pride."

Once Hazel was tucked into the coach and on her way home, Kitty checked on her sisters. Lucy, who wore her red hair in a long, thick braid, was sulking because she'd hoped to play in this year's match.

"Why would the men allow you to play?" Kitty asked rhetorically. "You can hit almost as far as Nathan Gutridge and run twice as fast. They know you'd put the lot of them to shame."

"Kitty's right," Clara said thoughtfully. "But it's not fair. If you'd like, we could stand in the middle of the pitch and refuse to leave until they let you play."

Lucy blinked. "You'd do that for me?"

Clara nodded so solemnly that Kitty's chest ached. "Of course I would. You're my sister."

A broad grin lit Lucy's face. "Never mind the stupid match. If I can't play cricket, I shall find some other worthy endeavor. Maybe I'll decide to follow in Kitty's footsteps."

"Me?" Kitty said, mildly alarmed at the prospect that her sweet, innocent sisters would follow her lead in any matter. "What do you mean?"

"I could enter the regatta and try to win," Lucy said excitedly. "Just like you and the duchess did."

"Poppy had much more to do with our success than I did," Kitty said. "But let me know if you'd like to practice your rowing."

"Oh, look," Clara interjected, pointing to the far end of the beach. "Here come the players now."

The soft murmur of the crowd crescendoed into a boisterous roar as the men jogged toward them. They'd apparently come directly from the Salty Mermaid, where it was tradition to enjoy a pint or two while exchanging insults with the opposing team. All in good fun, of course.

The men playing for the Local team wore blue ribbons tied around their biceps, and the Visitors wore red so that the teams were easy to distinguish. When she saw Uncle Beck searching the crowd, she waved vigorously and called him over.

"Where's Hazel?" he asked.

"It's good to see you, too, Uncle," Kitty teased. "The sun was giving her the touch of a headache."

When he frowned in concern, she quickly added, "But she is absolutely fine. She said she was going to take a cool bath and lie down, but odds are ten to one that she's sitting at her desk working on lesson plans."

He chuckled at that, then looked at Kitty earnestly. "You'd tell me if something was wrong?"

She raised her right hand as if she were taking an oath. "If I'm lying, you can lock me in my room for a month."

"I seem to recall trying that before," he said dryly. "To no avail."

Kitty smiled and kissed him on the cheek.

"What was that for?" he asked.

"Good luck. I need you to trounce the Locals."

"That's the plan." He winked at her before rejoining the rest of the players.

And that's when one gentleman caught Kitty's eye.

The bright sun in the sky behind him meant she could only see his silhouette, but he was tall with narrow hips and an athletic build. His trousers fit snugly, showcasing muscular thighs and a taut backside. His hair riffled in the breeze, and the thin lawn of his shirt, damp with ocean spray, clung to the contours of his shoulders and arms. His waistcoat hugged his broad chest and tapered to a trim abdomen.

Despite the oppressive heat, a delicious shiver stole over Kitty's skin.

She hadn't expected to enjoy watching the match, but perhaps she would after all.

Clara, ever observant, followed the direction of Kitty's gaze. "Who is that?"

"I'm not cert—" Kitty began, but then the man threw a

ball straight up in the air and caught it in his palm. Sweet Jesus.

"That's Leo Lockland," Lucy exclaimed. "I saw him in town this morning. He tried to convince Nathan to let me play."

"Did he?" Kitty said, still trying to recover from the fact that she'd unwittingly been ogling *Leo* of all people. "He must not have tried very hard if you're still sitting here with us."

"He threatened to play for the other team if Nathan wouldn't agree, but then the other team also refused to let me play." Lucy sighed. "But he said he'd help me write a petition before next year."

Kitty stifled a snort. The man had been in Bellehaven for scarcely a week and was already making promises about next summer. There was no telling if he'd still be in town, and the last thing Kitty wanted was for Lucy to get hurt. "We don't require Leo's help. You, Clara, and I are perfectly capable of writing our own petition."

"True, but it *was* a kind offer," Clara said diplomatically.

"Yes, he's quite the knight in shining armor," Kitty said with a dramatic roll of her eyes. "Need I remind you that for this afternoon, he is also the enemy?"

"You mean our opponent," Lucy corrected.

"No. I mean our *enemy*," Kitty said. "Uncle Beck's team *must* win this match." She hadn't an inkling what Leo would ask if he won their bet, but since he possessed an uncanny ability to get under her skin, she could only assume that his question would be terribly personal, utterly humiliating, or both. She could not afford to lose. Especially because she wanted to ask him the identity of the woman who he was trying to impress. The woman he was clearly in love with.

"Why are you frowning?" Clara asked, interrupting her musings.

"No reason." Why should Kitty care if Leo Lockland was in love? "Maybe I'm a bit peckish."

"I'll fetch us something to eat from the buffet," Clara offered kindly. "You two can stay here and watch the match."

"Look, they're starting!" Lucy said, gesturing to the men scattered across the beach.

Leo stood in the middle of them all, gripping the ball in his fist and leveling a glare at the batter several yards in front of him. He took a step, wound up his arm, and hurtled the ball straight at the wickets. The batter missed, and the crowd erupted in applause.

Lucy watched avidly, but Kitty was not interested in the finer points of the game. All she cared about was the score, and the mayor was tasked with posting and updating it on a large tablet propped against a rock in the sand.

Clara returned with a plate of sandwiches for her, Kitty, and Lucy to share, and the three of them perched on wooden stools where they could observe and cheer on Uncle Beck's team. While her sisters discussed strategy and nuances of the match, Kitty surreptitiously watched Leo.

She supposed it was only natural that she'd want to see the fruits of her labor. In the same way that a teacher regularly tracks her pupil's progress, she was measuring his.

And she had to give herself credit. On the surface at least, Leo had come a long way. He'd rolled up his sleeves. His neckcloth was loose. His trousers were snug. She did not recall advising him to wear snug trousers, but she could not fault the way they clung to his backside and thighs.

"Are you overly warm, Kitty?" Clara waved her fan vigorously in Kitty's direction. "Your cheeks are flushed."

"Probably because it's hotter than Hades out here,"

she muttered. "But I'm fine, thank you." She checked the score: 70 to 84, with the Visitors in the lead, thank heaven. But the match promised to be closely fought until the very end.

A thin sheen of perspiration covered every inch of Leo's exposed skin: his tanned forearms and hands, his corded neck, and his chiseled face. Patches of sand stuck to his knees and shoulders. There was even sand in the dark stubble along his jaw and in the hair covering his brow. She'd never seen this disheveled version of Leo, but it was definitely having the desired effect.

Ladies were noticing him, and Kitty caught snippets of their conversations.

"London seems to have agreed with Mr. Lockland," one gossipy matron said with meaning.

Lila Bardsley, the blacksmith's daughter they'd passed in town, chimed in, "I do believe he could pick me up and toss me over his shoulder like a bag of wheat."

And Mrs. Wright, a beautiful young widow murmured, "I may need to pay a visit to Mr. Lockland's office and avail myself of his services."

Kitty blinked at that, wondering if the widow could be the woman Leo was trying to impress. She certainly seemed to fit the description he'd given. Especially the bit about being bold and going after what she wanted.

But Leo was vexingly difficult to read. If he'd glanced at the crowd, Kitty might have followed the direction of his gaze. Other players waved and grinned at the spectators, but not Leo. He seemed to be completely absorbed by the game. Either that, or he was making a concerted effort to avoid looking at anyone—maybe because he feared revealing his feelings.

But that was none of Kitty's concern. All she wanted to do was win the bet and collect her prize. Her gaze flicked to the tablet: 240 to 265, with the Visitors still leading, thank goodness.

"Is the match almost over?" she asked Lucy, hopeful.

"Almost," Lucy said, her eyes glued to the action. "Uncle Beck is bowling, and the last batter is Leo. He's been playing awfully well," she added worriedly.

"Uncle Beck will make short work of him," Kitty said with more confidence than she felt.

The words had barely left her lips when a crack pealed through the air. Leo had smacked the ball, and it sailed over the heads of the players, landing a long way down the beach.

The spectators sprang to their feet, erupting in a cacophony of groans and cheers.

"Oh no," Lucy muttered. "That's not good."

Panic skittered down Kitty's spine. "What do you mean? We're still winning, right?"

"We *did* have the lead," Lucy corrected. "But Leo just scored thirty points. The game is over, and the Locals won again. Poor Uncle Beck."

Bloody hell. Nathan Gutridge and one of his burly friends hoisted Leo on their shoulders. The rest of the Bellehaven players converged, shouting like a herd of marauding Vikings. The crowd applauded enthusiastically, and it seemed Leo's name was the one on everyone's lips.

He laughed as his teammates marched him into the surf for a celebratory dunking. They tossed him into the ocean and dove in themselves. From the way they were splashing and carrying on, one would think they'd slain an evil dragon who'd plagued mankind for centuries, when all they'd actually accomplished was winning a silly little cricket match.

Once the players had sufficiently congratulated themselves on their victory, they emerged from the water, proudly stalking their way up the beach. Some of the matrons attempted to distract their impressionable young daughters so they wouldn't see the men with their clothes plastered to their bodies. Lady Rufflebum pretended to be horrified at the sight, but Kitty caught her gawking at the impressive display of masculinity.

Personally, she failed to see what all the fuss was about. She appreciated the male form, of course, but there was no reason to lose one's mind over—

Good heavens.

Leo made his way out of the water like Poseidon rising from the sea. Confident. Powerful. Virile. Rivulets of water rolled down his face and neck. His skin glistened in the late afternoon sun. And there was no hiding his physique in his soaked garments.

Kitty's breath hitched. Any lingering impressions she had of Leo being the same boy he'd been before he left Bellehaven were shattered. Obliterated by the undeniable proof before her eyes.

He continued his trek up the beach, raking both hands through his hair, just as she'd taught him. The sinewy muscles of his forearms flexed, his biceps bulged, and droplets sprayed around his head like a halo.

That was the moment he looked directly at her and flashed a smile that was easy to read.

It said she should prepare herself for plenty of gloating.

And that he couldn't wait to collect on his bet.

Chapter 6

It was no wonder that Leo had the devil of a hangover the next day. Every bloke in Bellehaven had insisted on buying him a pint to celebrate the local team's victory, and the sun had started to make an appearance before his head finally hit the pillow.

But his mood improved considerably the moment he walked through the door of his office—the one that his grandfather had established two years before Leo was born. He'd spent so much time there as a boy that it felt more like home than his parents' cottage had.

The shop was closed today, but after yesterday's cricket match, Kitty had agreed to meet him there so that she could show him the design she was working on for the contest and give him an opportunity to collect on their wager.

He knew precisely what question he wanted to ask.

But it was risky for two reasons. One, the question itself might reveal the nature of his feelings for her. Two, he might not like her answer.

Light spilled through the large window at the front, where stately black and gold lettering said: SANDFORD BUILDING DESIGN. His grandfather's ancient desk was positioned near the window, opposite two leather armchairs where clients could sit and share their visions, their dreams. That humble wooden desk with the water stains and dented legs had been the place where his grandfather had toiled for hours every day, spectacles propped on his nose, making scores of clients happy. But then his eyesight had started to fail, and he'd decided it was time to move out of the rooms above the office, retire, and hand the practice over to Leo.

And Leo had known that coming home to Bellehaven was the right thing to do.

He set his cup of coffee on his drafting table near the back of the shop and hopped onto the tall stool. He liked an uncluttered workspace, so the only items on his desktop were a small lamp and a tray containing basic tools and his drafting pencil. His current projects were rolled up and tucked away in a basket on the floor.

Kitty's desk, directly across from his, was the same size and style as his.

But it couldn't have looked more different.

Scraps of paper—which she blithely referred to as inspiration—were everywhere. Some were tiny sketches she'd drawn, some were notes she'd scrawled, some were bits of wallpaper or fabric. They were tacked to the wall like a collage, stacked in little towers on her desktop, and spilling out of the drawers. An odd assortment of items formed a line across the edge of her desk that butted against his, delineating her territory.

The makeshift barrier, which included a vase of wilted flowers, a chipped teacup, an old silk fan, and an ivory hair comb, had been there long before he'd left for London. He was glad that she hadn't removed it. It made him think that perhaps she'd believed he'd be back. Why else would she keep the wall that was obviously intended to ward him off?

But it had never really worked. When it came to Kitty, he always wanted to cross the line.

And he couldn't resist doing so now.

He strolled around the end of her table and sat on her stool carefully, so he wouldn't disturb her things. In the middle of her desk, her sketchbook was open to a half-completed but already exquisite drawing of a garden folly. Perfectly proportioned columns flanked the arched entrance to a temple fit for a Greek goddess. A pencil and pastels still sat on the unfinished design, as if she'd just walked away for a quick errand.

But she hadn't been to the shop since he'd returned to Bellehaven.

Back when they'd both been apprentices for his grandfather, they'd spent countless hours on those stools, firing eviscerating looks, savage barbs, and disgusted snorts at each other across the battlefield of their desks. Somewhere between mortal enemies and reluctant friends, they'd often argued about trivial matters, driving Leo's grandfather half-mad in the process.

He'd always said that they brought out the best and worst in each other, and one summer when Kitty was about fifteen and Leo was seventeen, his grandfather tasked them with drafting the design for a new set of stables that would be erected there in town.

Rather than work together, they each developed their own design and individually presented it to his grandfather. But when they pressed him, he refused to say which was better. He steadfastly and wisely refused to take a side— even though one of the sides was his own grandson's.

Instead, he'd left Leo and Kitty alone in the office and told them they could come out when they'd agreed on a plan.

For several awkward minutes they'd glared across their drafting tables in stubborn silence. Of course, it was difficult for Leo to stay agitated while he was looking at Kitty. Even when he wanted to be cross with her, he couldn't help but be dazzled by the fire in her eyes. He found himself wondering how her pouty lips would taste and whether there was a chance in hell that she felt the same way he did.

"I have a proposal," he said at last, sounding pompous to his own ears. "Why don't we exchange drawings? I'll tell you the merits and drawbacks of yours, you can do the same for mine."

She cast a wary glance in his direction. "I'm not certain you're capable of being objective."

"Or maybe you lack confidence in your design."

She twirled a pencil in her fingers. "The only thing I lack confidence in is your capacity to imagine something beyond the ordinary."

"Why not judge for yourself?" He rolled up his design and held it above the wall of her trinkets, challenging her to take it.

"Very well." She took the scroll, then relinquished her sketchbook as if it were a lamb headed for slaughter. "But here are the rules."

He snorted, letting her know what he thought of her rules.

When she reached to take back her sketchbook, he grudgingly relented. "Fine. Let's hear them."

She shot him a triumphant smile. "We must take at least five minutes to silently examine each other's work. At the end of that time, we must agree to say at least one complimentary thing about the other's drawing. Then we may share the rest of our thoughts, giving a fair and honest assessment."

"I suppose I can do that," he muttered.

Her gaze flicked to the clock sitting on his grandfather's desk. "Our time starts . . . now."

Leo flipped open her sketchbook, doing his damnedest to keep his face impassive.

Like all her drawings, this one was extraordinary. It looked as though she'd designed a palace . . . but for horses. Gold stalls were equipped with elaborately carved feeding troughs, and the doors were decorated with lattice work. Large chandeliers were suspended from gracefully arched ceiling beams. These stables were meant for the likes of Pegasus. Hell, this was a stable fit for the gods themselves.

And it wouldn't work in a million years.

Leo grunted and shifted on his stool, earning a scathing look from Kitty.

She returned her attention to *his* design, which was spread across her desk. As her eyes flicked over one part of the scroll and shifted to another, he studied her face, searching for clues. It galled him to admit that he cared what she thought about his work, but he couldn't deny it. Her opinion mattered—and not only because he was half in love with her. She was talented in a way he could only dream of.

Unfortunately, she did not appear to be enamored of his design. She wasn't frowning, exactly, but she certainly didn't look impressed. In fact, if he wasn't mistaken, she was stifling a yawn, damn it all.

Only three minutes had passed. So they stared at each other.

Not exactly a hardship for him. Usually, he was reduced to sneaking glances at her. But now he had an excuse to stare, and it felt different when she was looking back into his eyes. Hotter. Riskier. Fraught with danger.

Lots of boys probably thought she was beautiful, but not for the same reasons he did. Sure, he liked her fancy dresses and her golden hair. And he might have noticed that the blue ribbons she wore were the same brilliant shade as her eyes. But what he liked best about her was the way she made the entire world buzz with possibilities.

It could have been the dreariest, darkest of days, but when Kitty Beckett walked into a room, she lit up everything and everyone around her. She could make Leo annoyed, aroused, or anything in between, but she could never make him bored. Maybe because he never knew what she'd say or do next.

The moment the clock's second hand swept around, completing its fifth rotation, Kitty propped her elbows on her desk and rested her chin on her clasped fingers. "I shall go first."

He wasn't foolish enough to argue. "Go on," he said, with feigned disinterest.

"First, your compliment." She swallowed as if she were trying to keep down a bite of fish that was slightly off. "Your stalls are well-proportioned, and your design makes efficient use of the space. I'm impressed with the way you've made the most of every square inch."

"I'm glad you noticed." He spoke gruffly, so she wouldn't guess that she'd put her finger on the one thing he was proudest of.

He'd spent hours meticulously measuring the site. He'd spent days scouting other stables. He'd interviewed every stablehand he could find to ask about their preferred dimensions and features. Then he'd sat at his desk for heaven knew how long working on a formula to determine which arrangement allowed for the maximum number of stalls to be constructed. More than anything else, practicality had been the driving force behind his design. And Kitty had noticed.

"Are you ready to hear the rest of my thoughts?" she asked, challenging him so that no matter how much he might wish to say no, he couldn't possibly.

"Ready as I'll ever be."

She picked up his design, came to stand beside his stool, and smoothed the scroll across his desk. "Every line is cleanly and precisely drawn," she said, trailing a fingertip beside a pencil mark. "You have measured every wall, window, door, and beam to the nearest thirty-second of an inch. Every feature is drawn perfectly to scale."

Leo was confused, probably because she was standing so close. Her hair smelled like strawberries on the beach. Her dress smelled like sunshine. "You only had to give me one compliment," he said.

"I know," she said with sad sigh. "What I'm trying to say is that *this*"—she swept a hand across the paper—"is not a design. This is the answer to a math problem. Which I'm afraid is a hugely different thing."

He blinked slowly and counted to three. Partly because he needed to recover from the sting of her words. Partly because he knew they were true.

"Well, are you ready to hear what I think about your design?"

She didn't flinch. "Of course. I'm sure you're brimming with compliments. I can hardly wait to hear which one you'll choose," she said dryly.

He exhaled. She'd given him a genuine compliment. He supposed he could do the same. "It's memorable," he began. "Anyone who stepped foot inside these stables would remember the chandeliers and the gold and the elaborate troughs—and they'd know they'd been someplace special.

Your stables would become a treasured landmark in Belle-haven. Maybe in all of England."

For three heartbeats, she said nothing, but her cheeks pinkened.

"Leo Lockland," she said, her tone mildly scolding, but in a good way. His body thrummed as his name tripped off her lips. Every inch of his skin grew hot, keenly aware of her nearness.

"What?" he rasped.

She solemnly turned to face him, and the skirt of her gown brushed against his thigh. "That is quite possibly the nicest thing you've ever said to me. It might be the nicest thing *anyone* has ever said to me."

"It's true." He shrugged so she wouldn't think he'd put too much thought into it.

"All I've ever wanted is to create something special," she said, wistful. "To be known for something other than being an heiress and an orphan."

"I've never thought of you that way." The words had tumbled out before he could stop them.

Her gaze snapped to his, and she swallowed. "How *do* you think of me?"

Holy hell. He couldn't tell her that the sound of her laugh made him drunker than brandy. Or that he dreamt of her every night. Dreams that were hot. Haunting. Wicked. If she had an inkling of the way he felt, she'd run for the door like the office was on fire.

So he settled on something true but safe. "You're fiery."

She inched closer, as if his words were bait, drawing her in. "And?"

"Funny," he said with a smile.

She swayed toward him, probably unaware that her hip pressed lightly against his thigh. "And?" she probed further.

Jesus, it was difficult to think when she was so near. He blew out a long breath, then said, "Ridiculously talented."

She gasped.

Her blue eyes turned sultry.

Her gaze dropped to his mouth.

And she leaned toward him, her expression bewildered. As if she didn't completely understand what was happening.

Shit. God knew Leo wanted her to kiss him. He wanted to kiss her back. Thoughts of kissing her consumed approximately twenty-five percent of his waking hours, and the other seventy-five percent of his thoughts were considerably more scandalous.

He desperately wanted to kiss Kitty.

But *not* if she was kissing him out of gratitude. Or because she was dazed by the headiness of a compliment.

Still, they gravitated toward each other like magnets, their lips a mere breath apart.

"Do you want to know what else I think about your sketch?" he choked out.

She blinked, as if someone had woken her while she was walking in her sleep. "Yes. Of course."

Bloody hell. He had to be the biggest idiot walking the face of the earth. He reached around her and picked up her sketchbook to buy himself some time. "As memorable as your design is," he said slowly, "it's entirely unworkable."

"It's unique," she countered. "But it's not unworkable."

"Gold walls?" He waved a hand at her painted sketch. "They're stables, not the Taj Mahal."

She narrowed her eyes, and all traces of the softness that had been there before evaporated like mist on a summer morning. He'd done that. He'd ruined that moment, and he'd never get it back.

"I wasn't suggesting that we cover the stalls in gold

leaf," she said, speaking to him as if he were a child who was testing her patience. "It's just paint."

"Oh, well then, we might as well add wainscoting and wallpaper," he said, his words dripping with sarcasm. "In case the horses decide to host a tea party. Next you'll be wanting to give them chamber pots." He was aware he was behaving like an ass, but, apparently, he was fully committed at this point.

"Let me assure you that I would rather attend a tea party hosted by horses than by you. I'd rather muck out stables than go anywhere with you." She snatched her sketchbook out of his hands, marched around to her stool, and slapped her design onto her own drafting table. "As for the chamber pots, you should be glad I don't have one at the moment. If I did, I'd be sorely tempted to throw it at your head."

He arched a brow. "I suppose I deserved that." It was a late and probably futile attempt at civility. "All I'm trying to say is that clients don't want to waste their money on paint and chandeliers for horses."

"I happen to think that animals deserve pleasant surroundings, but that's beside the point. *People* will work there," she said. "And clients want a structure they enjoy spending time in. Something they can be proud of."

He dragged his hands down his face and sighed. "I agree," he conceded. "But they also want to make the best use of the space. My design has eight more stalls than yours."

She flipped her hair, and he knew he'd touched a nerve. "Fine. We'll use your layout. But we'll use my finishing touches."

He grunted. "Some of them," he said. "The chandeliers would hang much too low. We can use nice lanterns instead. We'll paint the outsides of the stalls, but not the insides."

"We're keeping the carved troughs," she said firmly.

"They're not practical."

"That's precisely why we need them," she said, matter-of-factly. "Every design needs a bit of whimsy."

With that, she closed her sketchbook, put on her bonnet, and grabbed her reticule.

"Where are you going?" he balked. "We haven't reached a compromise."

She stalked to the front door, hauled it open, and turned to face him. "Nevertheless, I'm through negotiating. We're keeping the carved troughs," she repeated, then let the door spring shut behind her.

In the end, she'd had her way. The troughs were crafted by a carpenter on the outskirts of town, each one a tribute to a different Greek god. They were an outrageous extravagance for a stable.

And they were the best part of the whole damned place.

Leo stared at Kitty's cluttered desk and smiled to himself.

Yes, asking her about the almost-kiss would definitely be risky. She could guess his feelings before he was prepared to reveal them, which would be bad. Or she could laugh at the very idea that she might once have considered kissing him, which would be even worse.

But if she'd been attracted to him once, even fleetingly, perhaps she could be again. He needed the smallest glimmer of hope, and *that* was why he simply had to know.

And soon, he would.

Chapter 7

The bell above the office door trilled, snapping Leo from his thoughts. Kitty breezed into the room, a leather portfolio tucked under one arm. Her gown was the dusky-orange of a sailor's sky, and her skirts swished around her lithe legs as if she were dancing on a beach. The room instantly felt warmer. More alive.

Her gaze flicked to Leo seated at his drafting table, then to his grandfather's desk. "I assumed you'd take over the spot near the window," she said without preamble.

"Good afternoon to you, too," he said dryly. Gesturing toward his grandfather's desk, he added, "I couldn't bring myself to move any of his things. I want him to know that spot is his whenever he drops by."

She nodded approvingly. "As it should be. The office doesn't seem the same without him. He was like a steady, dependable anchor that kept me from floating out to sea."

It was another thing he loved about Kitty: her devotion to his grandfather. She adored him almost as much as Leo did, and the feeling was mutual. "I miss having him here, too," Leo admitted. "But not much else has changed. Your desk looks the same as it did the day I left."

She hung up her bonnet and set her sketchbook and reticule on her desk. "Before you returned I spent almost as much time here as I did at home. It's comforting to have familiar things around me. And nice to know that some things stay the same."

He shifted on his stool. Maybe that had been a subtle jab at him for leaving Bellehaven without warning. Or maybe he was reading too much into her words.

"I know it's an adjustment for you," he said carefully, "not having my grandfather here. But this is still your office, too. It will be for as long as you like."

"Thank you," she said, avoiding his gaze. "I don't intend to be here much longer."

"Why?" he blurted. "Is it because of me?"

She looked at him as if he'd sprouted another head. "No, Leo. I'm much too stubborn to let an annoying office partner drive me away."

"They why would you leave?"

She pressed her lips into a thin line, making him wonder if she'd refuse to answer. Then she said, "It's not widely known, but I'll come into my inheritance soon."

"On your birthday?" he probed.

"Yes. At the end of the summer," she added. As if he couldn't be expected to recall exactly when her birthday was.

It was August twenty-second.

"What do you plan to do?"

"Pursue a career in architecture." She blinked at him, her blue eyes more vulnerable than he'd ever seen them. "It's why this contest is so important to me. Winning would give me some credibility. Something to help launch my career when I move to London."

"London," he repeated, dumbfounded.

"There are far more opportunities there," she said. "Which you know better than anyone."

"Yes, of course," he mumbled.

She idly adjusted the teacup in her row of trinkets. "Isn't that why you moved there?"

It wasn't, actually. But he wasn't ready to talk about the real reason—and doubted he ever would be—so he changed the subject. "Bellehaven is growing rapidly. There's plenty of work here, too."

"That's easy for you to say. You're still working on designs for your London clients," she said with a sniff. "Besides, I want to push the boundaries of architecture. I'm not certain Bellehaven is the best place to do that."

Leo nodded as if he understood perfectly. But his head was reeling. He could scarcely imagine the town of Bellehaven without Kitty in it. It would feel smaller. Duller. Darker.

"I heard about the raucous celebration at the Mermaid yesterday," she said conversationally. "Nathan said he's never poured so much ale in one night. I'm surprised you were able to drag yourself here."

"We set a time to meet. I wouldn't have missed it."

"I suppose you're eager to collect on our bet." She spoke with the resigned stoicism of a queen on her way to the guillotine.

"We can go over your design first, if you'd like."

She exhaled, as if grateful for the reprieve. "These are preliminary sketches," she explained. "I intend to draft more precise drawings once I'm satisfied with the concepts."

"Understood." He slapped his palms on his thighs, keen to see what she'd envisioned. "Are you finally going to tell me what you've designed?"

"No," she said, handing him her sketchbook. "I'm going to show you."

While Kitty fiddled with various items on her desk, she cast surreptitious glances at Leo, waiting for him to say something. He didn't look anything like the man she'd watched on the beach yesterday. His clothes were pressed and buttoned up, his hair was neatly combed, his jaw was clean-shaven.

Clearly, she was going to have to explain to him that being a rake was a full-time proposition. Not a role he could simply step into when it suited him.

But that discussion could wait for another time. Right now, she needed to know what he thought of her sketches. Her theater.

He flipped through the pages of her sketchbook, his expression impossible to read. After several minutes, he sat back and gazed at her, his expression pensive. As if he didn't know quite what to say or quite how to say it.

And as the silence stretched out, her doubts surfaced like dandelions spoiling a lush green lawn. "I wanted to make it bigger," she blurted. "On a scale grand enough for London, but the site doesn't allow for a larger building. And if I made it too tall, I'd block the view of the ocean from the Assembly Rooms, which would be a shame."

"The scale is perfect," he assured her. "You have plenty of seats. Enough for at least a quarter of Bellehaven's population."

"The external walls are brick and lime mortar," she rambled. "Once they're covered in plaster, they'll have a smooth, classical appearance."

He nodded. "A smart choice. Roman cement is cheaper and more readily available than stone."

When he didn't say more, she pointed at the sketch in front of him. "Visitors will ascend the steps in the front or the ramp at the side, then enter through the large central doors leading to the lobby. In the auditorium, the floor slopes down toward the proscenium arch—" She blinked and shook her head. "I don't know why I'm telling you all this. It's clear from the drawings."

"Yes," he said, closing the sketchbook. "It's all there."

"But you haven't told me what you truly think." She folded her arms and braced for the harsh truth. Reminded herself that she'd asked for Leo's help because she needed brutal honesty. And if there was one person who wouldn't hold back, it was him.

He leaned forward on his elbows, halving the distance between them. Her gaze flicked to his interlaced fingers which almost touched his side of the barrier wall.

"What I think," he began soberly, "is that you'll win the contest."

Her heart soared. "You like it?"

"It's beautiful. Elegant. Extravagant."

Her heart dipped, like a kite flying in erratic wind. "You don't like it."

"It's one of the most stunning designs I've ever seen." She could see he was choosing his words carefully. "From what I can tell so far, it's technically sound as well. Your foundation walls are thick enough to bear the load of the building. The roof trusses and joists should provide ample support, even if you use blue slate. I'll take a closer look at all the measurements and help you calculate materials and the costs once you've completed your detailed design."

He was still dancing around the truth. "Why don't you like it?" she pressed.

He sighed. "It's not a matter of not liking it. I think it's brilliant."

"But . . . ?"

"It's a theater," he said reluctantly. "In a town that has neither an acting troupe nor opera singers."

"That's because they have no place to perform," she said, incredulous that she should have to explain such an obvious fact. "Once the theater is built, many acts will come to town, bringing not only entertainment to our residents, but also business to our shops."

"You may be right," he said, his tone annoyingly calm and civil, while her insides were in shambles. She would have preferred one of their old arguments, the kind that was full of fire and passion. At least then she'd be able to unleash the tension coiled inside her.

She gripped the sides of her stool and took a moment to compose herself. "But you still think a theater is a bad idea?" she asked evenly.

"No, not at all." He stood and began to pace the length of the office. "I just don't think it's the most practical idea."

She sniffed. "Forgive me for wanting to bring a modicum of culture to our town."

"It's a noble goal," he said, placating her again. "But there are so many other buildings that Bellehaven needs. We don't have a proper jail, a hospital, or even a lending library."

"We should have those things, and I daresay Mayor Martin will find a way to fund them. But this contest is about giving Bellehaven something beyond the necessary and mundane."

"Your theater does that," he said diplomatically. "I've no doubt the judges will be impressed. Your design is bound to win."

She shot him a pointed glance. "But you don't think it deserves to?"

"Why do you care what I think?" He planted his hands on his hips and exhaled. "I'm not a judge."

"You're quite right," she said curtly. "Your opinion as to

the practicality of my building is irrelevant." She rubbed a spot at the base of her throat, hoping to ease the odd ache lingering there.

"You didn't ask me to advise you on the creative aspect of your drawings. That's your area of expertise. So ignore my opinions. Listen to your own instincts."

"Very well. I shall rely on your counsel solely when it comes to technical issues. As far as all other matters are concerned, perhaps you could be so kind as to keep your negative thoughts to yourself."

"My apologies." He cursed under his breath and looked at her, his brown eyes earnest. "I didn't mean to dampen your enthusiasm for your project. I meant what I said before—it's beautiful."

His last two words echoed in her head, a balm to her nicked pride, but she shrugged as if his opinion mattered naught to her. "I have enough to proceed with the detailed drawings. I'll begin working on them tonight."

"You could work here, if you like." Leo rubbed the back of his neck. "That is, I wouldn't look over your shoulder or bother you. It just makes sense since all of your tools are here. And I'd be on hand in case any questions arose."

She did like working at her drafting table, and though she wasn't certain she'd be able to concentrate with Leo there, she supposed she could give it a try. "Perhaps I will work here. But I need some fresh air before I dive in."

"I understand. Thank you for trusting me to look at your work. I never find it easy to share." He strolled back to his stool, sat, and picked up his pencil, looking relieved to have the ordeal behind him. Almost as though it was *his* work that had been picked apart. "Maybe I'll see you later then."

"I'm not quite ready to go."

He arched a brow. "Suit yourself."

She rolled her shoulders, dreading the next bit. "If it's all the same to you, I'd like to pay up now."

Understanding dawned on his face. "You're referring to our bet."

"Precisely." She lifted her chin and imagined her wrists being bound to a stake at her back. "You may proceed to ask me anything."

For the space of several heartbeats, he said nothing, but the way he tapped his pencil on the desk was not unlike the motion of a torch setting fire to the kindling at her ankles.

"We can do this another time," he said magnanimously.

"No," she said firmly. Flames licked her toes. Heat crept up her body. "I'd rather be done with it."

"Are you certain?" His forehead creased with sympathy. "It seems as though it's been a trying afternoon for you."

"Oh, it has," she admitted. "But never fear. I'm capable of handling any question you throw my way. And waiting just gives you more time to lord it over my head. No, thank you."

"I won't lord it over you," he said.

Kitty snorted. "If the roles were reversed, *I* would."

"I've no doubt you would," he muttered, dragging his hands down his face. "Do you know what? Forget it. You don't owe me anything. I officially absolve you of your debt, Kitty Beckett."

"It's Kat," she said reflexively, even as she struggled to understand him. He had earned the right to ask her a question and was voluntarily forfeiting it. By all accounts, she should have felt a sense of relief, but what she was feeling more than anything at that moment was exasperation.

She slapped her palms on the desk. "This is exactly why you'll never impress your love interest."

"I beg your pardon?" he asked, clearly confused.

"You're too nice," she said. "A rake would never let a woman off the hook."

He crossed his arms and glared at her in disbelief. "I was *trying* to be a gentleman."

"I know," she said slowly, for maximum provocation. "It's why you'll end up with a meek and docile wife in a dull and tedious marriage. It's why you'll never be a genuine rake."

"You don't know what you're talking about," he said with a huff.

"Don't I?" She slid off her stool, walked toward him, and propped an elbow on the corner of his annoyingly pristine desk. "You're like a fencer who has the tip of his rapier pointed at his opponent's throat. You're in control. Victory is all but assured. And at the critical moment, you *flinch.*"

"That's ridiculous," he said dismissively, but the tic in his jaw told her she'd touched a nerve, and it propelled her forward.

A part of her knew she should quit while she was ahead, and yet, she couldn't seem to resist poking him. She needed to know if there was anything fierce or raw beneath that buttoned-up exterior.

"Your problem," she said in a raspy whisper, "is that even when you have a golden opportunity to wield your power, you relinquish it. You lack the will to make your opponent pay. You're . . . soft."

With that one word, she'd altered his entire demeanor. His nostrils flared, his eyes narrowed, and his lips pressed into a thin line.

"Shall I hold your feet to the fire then?" he drawled. "Is that what you're daring me to do?"

An unexpected thrill shot through her. "I suppose I am,"

she said blithely, even though she already suspected that she'd regret her decision. "Do your worst."

"Fine." His eyes turned icy, raising the hairs on her arms. "I feel compelled to remind you that the wager requires you to answer the question honestly."

She shot him an offended look. "Of course."

"I have a question for you, but first I must spark your memory."

"I daresay my memory is better than yours," she said. "But do go on."

He arched a skeptical brow. "Approximately six years ago today, you and I were standing in this very spot."

She swallowed, hoping her nervousness didn't show. Praying he wasn't going to bring up one of the most mortifying days of her existence. "We've spent a great deal of time together in this office," she said vaguely. "Most of it arguing."

"But not all," he said pointedly. "On the day in question, we were comparing designs we'd created for a new set of stables."

Blast. "If I recall, you were less than enthused about the embellishments I envisioned."

"I don't want to ask you about our conversation." He shook his head to let her know that she would not be getting off so easily, and a sly smile lit his face.

"How long do you intend to dance around it?" she taunted.

"Not long. Here's what I want to know. On that day and in that moment when we were standing less than an inch apart, did you want to kiss me?"

Chapter 8

It would have been infinitely easier for Kitty to respond to Leo's question if she weren't standing so close to him.

And if she hadn't been sworn to answer truthfully.

He was staring at her intently. Almost as if he was afraid to blink, lest he miss something telling in her expression.

She did her best to keep her face impassive, but she remembered the day all too well, for the same reason one recalls a snow squall in May.

It was an anomaly. An aberration. An unexpected and disastrous hiccup in the sacred laws of nature.

She'd simply have to explain it to him in the same way she'd attempted to explain it to herself.

"I feel obliged to remind you that our emotions were running high that day," she said.

"I don't disagree."

"I suppose I was feeling quite vulnerable after having shared my stables design with you."

"Understandable."

"And then you said something complimentary, which caught me off guard," she said, vaguely accusatory.

"Clearly, such behavior is out of bounds," he quipped.

She pressed a hand to her chest—a futile attempt to slow the beating of her heart. She dreaded saying the next bit aloud. Indeed, she would have rather strolled down Main Street wearing nothing but a nightgown. But the sooner she said it, the sooner she could shove the memory back into its hole and bury it forever.

"To answer your question," she began shakily, "for that fleeting, bizarre moment in time, I thought about kissing you. Although, perhaps it's more accurate to say that I wasn't thinking at all. It was as though my mind briefly lost control of my body."

"You're not the sort of person who does things she doesn't want to do."

"Agreed." She blinked slowly, searching for the words to describe the highly disturbing phenomenon. "All I can say is that an odd feeling came over me, causing me to forget the myriad ways in which we are completely unsuited. But yes. I almost did it," she said with a helpless shrug. "I almost kissed you."

His eyes gleamed in triumph. "Why didn't you?"

"I'm not certain what brought me to my senses," she admitted, "but I'm forever grateful for it."

He gave a resigned nod, almost as though his victory had lost some of its shine.

But at least the worst was over. She blew out a long breath and managed a weak smile. "Consider my debt paid."

"In full," he said, extending a hand.

She took it, wholly unprepared for the warmth that shot through her as their palms touched. Clearly, something about that spot in the office or that period in time had a mysteriously disturbing effect on her.

He was still holding her hand when he said, "Don't think I didn't realize what you were doing."

She shook her head innocently. "What might that be?"

"Teaching me a lesson," he said with sly grin.

"What?"

"About being ruthless. About being a rake. You gave me an opportunity to go in for the kill, so to speak. How'd I do?"

The intensity of his gaze combined with the sensation of his touch caused an odd flutter in her belly, so she withdrew her hand. "Ah, my lesson on pressing your advantage," she improvised, quickly recovering her wits. "You were admirably merciless. No pulling of punches this time. Bravo."

She moved back to her side of the desk where she was more protected. Less likely to suffer from that strange frisson. "You'll not wield that sort of power over me again any time soon," she added as an afterthought.

"No. I rather suspect the rapier will be at my throat next time." He tugged at his neckcloth as though he was envisioning it. "I only narrowly escaped—and I confess I'm relieved since I know precisely what you would have asked."

"I don't think you do," she said honestly, feeling the echo of an old pang in her chest.

"Please," he said, as if she was insulting his intelligence. "You were going to make me reveal the name of the woman I'm trying to win over."

"No," she said blithely. "I did consider it, but I feel fairly confident I'll eventually figure that one out on my own."

He shifted on his stool. "There's something about me you're more curious about than that?"

"Upon further consideration, yes."

"Then why don't you ask me?"

Why, indeed? "Fine," she said, determined to keep her voice even despite the hurt that was seeping through all her defenses. "I will."

Leo tried to imagine what else Kitty would want to know about him. There wasn't much he'd tried to hide in the course of their relationship, other than the way he felt about her. She already knew that he was hopeless when it came to dancing and that he'd had a fear of heights since falling out of a tree when he was eight. She knew that he'd once retched in the bushes outside his house after a wild night at the Salty Mermaid.

Still, he braced himself for anything.

"What I'd like to know," she began, "is how you could leave Bellehaven without a word to someone you'd worked with for three years."

Shit. "Kitty, er, Kat," he quickly corrected, "I'm sorry about that." He hadn't thought she'd care. Or maybe it had been convenient for him to tell himself she wouldn't care.

"If you were truly sorry, you could have sent a note," she said, uncharacteristically serious. "But in the four years that you were gone, I didn't hear from you once."

Guilt niggled at the back of his neck. "We were always arguing back then. I figured you'd be glad to see me go. And I didn't think you'd be eager to hear from me afterward."

She blinked as if she couldn't have possibly heard him correctly. "Had I not occasionally seen your mother here in town, I wouldn't have had the slightest inkling whether you were alive or dead."

"Well, if there's one good thing about Bellehaven, it's that you may depend on a steady stream of gossip." He chuckled in an attempt to lighten the mood.

But Kitty's expression remained serious. "You went to London to establish your career and pursue your dreams. I don't fault you for that, and if the contest goes to plan, I intend to do the same. But you never gave a thought to the people you left behind. I'll bet you never once wondered how I felt."

"That's not true." He'd thought about her every day.

Missed her more than everyone else in Bellehaven combined. "I should have written, but I'm not good at that sort of thing."

She crossed her arms. "I wasn't expecting Shakespeare or Byron. Just some evidence that you hadn't been kidnapped by highwaymen and tossed into the Thames."

"You're right," he said earnestly. "I wish I'd handled things differently. But the situation was . . . complicated."

"It doesn't seem complicated to me. You were sitting on that stool one day, and the next you were gone. As if it couldn't have been easier for you to walk away."

He swallowed. "There was more to it than that."

"What, Leo?" Frustration flashed in her eyes. "I want to understand."

"I know." But he couldn't reveal the real reason he'd left so suddenly. Not without ripping the bandage off a wound that hadn't properly healed. Besides, exposing it wasn't going to make him whole again.

It was better for everyone involved if he kept the truth to himself. He'd become rather adept at wrapping it up and tucking it away in the far recesses of his mind. That was the real reason he hadn't written to Kitty. He couldn't explain why he'd fled to London, and he wouldn't insult her by giving her some half-truth. So he'd avoided her and anything else that reminded him of home and the way his father had betrayed them. Instead, he'd immersed himself in his work and pretended that he was fine. Everything was fine.

But now Kitty was looking at him expectantly. Asking him to go back to that wretched place where anger, grief, and disgust had almost consumed him. And he couldn't do it—not even for her.

"I wish I could talk about it," he said soberly. "But all I can say is that I had my reasons."

She picked up her sketchbook, reticule, and bonnet, signaling that her patience was depleted. "Then I guess you should count yourself lucky that you didn't lose the bet. Because I would have demanded an answer." With that, she headed for the door.

"Will I see you later?" he asked, hoping he hadn't done irreparable damage to their relationship—if it even qualified as such.

She paused and stared at him. "You will," she said smoothly. "Maybe tonight, maybe tomorrow. But I can assure you that *I* will not remove myself to London without making my plans known. I'm not the sort of person who abandons her friends."

She swept through the door, leaving the bell tinkling in her wake and Leo ruminating at his desk. He wasn't at all certain what had just transpired, but he did know a few things.

Kitty had not forgiven him for leaving.

Despite all indications to the contrary, she'd once considered him a friend.

Their almost-kiss had *not* been a figment of his imagination.

Perhaps there was hope for him after all.

"The Sandcastle Festival is Saturday," Leo's mother announced at dinner that night.

"I believe I heard something about that," he said with a smile. One couldn't walk a block in Bellehaven without seeing a dozen colorful flyers plastered on every streetlamp and on every window.

He'd joined his mother and his grandfather at their cottage, where she'd prepared his favorite meal—shepherd's pie. It was strange to be back in his usual spot at the trestle table, eating the same dish from the same plate he had as a boy. But he hadn't known about his father then. And he'd never look at his childhood the same way.

"It was the highlight of your summer," she said wistfully. "You'd be covered in sand from head to toe at the end of the day, but you always built the most impressive castles."

"Even back then, you had the makings of an architect," his grandfather interjected proudly.

"I daresay you're both a bit biased," Leo said, polishing off the last bite on his plate.

"Well, I hope you'll go to the festival," his mother said. "You're a bit too old to enter the competition, but there are bound to be plenty of eligible young women there enjoying the picnic."

Leo ignored the sly hint and his grandfather's wry snort. Any acknowledgment of her comment would undoubtedly lead to a full-scale inquisition, so he pretended to be oblivious to her machinations as he wiped the corner of his mouth with his napkin. "This is delicious, Mama. I hope you didn't go to too much trouble on my account."

She looked well enough, but there were subtle signs that grief had taken its toll. Her cheeks weren't as rosy as they'd once been, her eyes weren't as bright. Her brown hair, now streaked with gray, was swept into a neat knot at the top of her head.

One of the reasons Leo had returned to Bellehaven was to ensure that she could keep their family cottage and continue to live as comfortably as she always had—especially now that her father, Leo's grandfather, had retired. He didn't know what, if any, provisions had been made for her, but Leo had sent word to his father's solicitor in London, inquiring about what was to become of his property and belongings. Leo hoped to hear back soon so that he could put his mother's mind at ease—as well as his own.

She waved a thin hand. "You know I enjoy cooking. Your grandfather picked up the meat from the butcher's this morning and I had plenty of vegetables from the garden. I'm glad you like it. I'll give you a bowl to bring home with you."

"You're spoiling me," he said sincerely, "but I'm not about to refuse."

"How are things at the office?" his grandfather asked.

"Busy," Leo said. "The mayor came in yesterday. Apparently, the old gazebo was damaged in a storm last summer, so he wants to knock it down and erect a grander one in its place. I'm drawing up a couple of options for him."

His grandfather nodded approvingly. "The old one is an eyesore. Never liked it."

"I visited the South Street site this morning," Leo continued. "The framing for the town houses is done, and they've begun work on the masonry."

His mother stood up to clear the plates, but Leo beat her to it. As he carried the bowls to the sink, she called out, "Has Kitty Beckett been in the office?"

"Yes, Mama," he said evenly. "She works there, too."

"I confess I had my doubts about her at the beginning," his grandfather mused. "I never questioned her talent, mind you, but I wondered if she'd have the courage to back herself in this business."

"Well, you needn't have worried." Leo rolled up his shirtsleeves and began scrubbing the dishes. "If there's one thing Kitty has in spades, it's courage."

"True enough," his grandfather said with an affectionate chuckle. "She's a feisty one, but she also fussed over me like a mother hen. What project is she working on now?"

"Her entry for the Bellehaven Design Contest," Leo said, looking over a shoulder. "She asked if I'd help with some of the technical aspects."

"Better not tell me more." His grandfather held up a staying palm.

"Why not?"

"I'm one of the judges."

The plate Leo was holding plunked into the soaking tub. "You are?"

"Is that so surprising?" his grandfather asked, mildly offended.

"No," Leo said quickly. "But won't it be difficult for you to be unbiased?"

"Not at all. There are three of us, and we each pledged to evaluate the entries according to the criteria and on their merits." His grandfather adjusted his spectacles. "When I agreed to judge last month, I didn't realize you'd be back in town. But now that you are, you should enter. Just don't expect any preferential treatment from me."

"I haven't made up my mind about entering yet," Leo said. But it didn't seem right, going head-to-head with Kitty. Not when the contest was clearly so important to her. Besides, he wasn't at all certain he could beat her.

Almost as if his grandfather could read Leo's mind, he said, "You're one of the most highly skilled architects I've worked with, and this contest could give you an opportunity to share your gift with Bellehaven in a unique way. I hope you'll consider entering—if not for your own sake, then mine. Make your old grandfather happy, won't you?"

"I'll think about it," Leo said, touched by the sentiment. He handed a bowl to his mother, who stood at the ready to dry. "Just out of curiosity, who are the other two judges?"

"I don't suppose it's a secret," his grandfather said with a shrug. "Mayor Martin and Lady Rufflebum."

Leo scoffed. "Neither one knows much about design."

"No, but the contest was the mayor's idea, and Lady

Rufflebum agreed to sponsor it. Both of them want to have their say in the outcome," his grandfather replied.

"Naturally," Leo replied. "But I don't have much faith in their ability to remain impartial." The mayor would have shaved his head if he thought it would increase his popularity, and the countess would have gone to similar lengths in order to enhance her own social standing.

His grandfather nodded sagely. "Then the trick to winning will be to design a structure so spectacular that they can't possibly pass it over." He hesitated, then added, "Are you up to the challenge?"

"I said I'd think about it," Leo said with a chuckle, "and I will."

"Good," his grandfather said, mollified for now. "But don't dally too long. The summer will be over in the blink of an eye."

"He's right," Mama said. She set the stack of dried bowls on a shelf and hung her towel to dry. "It's hard to believe it's almost time for the Sandcastle Festival."

"We're back to that, are we?" Leo teased.

"I thought you'd be eager to go," she said, ruffling his hair like he was a lad of five years. "When you were a boy, you loved it more than Christmas Day. You were so anxious to start building, you'd shake your father awake at dawn, demanding that he walk you to the beach. He was nearly as excited as you were."

Leo gripped the edge of the basin and kept his lips pressed tightly together while his mother, oblivious to his discomfort, rambled on. This was precisely the reason he'd left for London. He couldn't pretend that his father was a saint. Even when his father had followed him to town, hoping to smooth things over, Leo had turned him away. There was no way to fix the mess his father had made. No way to undo it.

"Those castles you built were so elaborate—complete with turrets, battlements, and drawbridges." She smiled fondly at the memory. "And your father loved being your faithful apprentice. Remember all the trips he'd make to the water, just to try and keep your moats filled?"

Leo's knuckles turned white, and his arms trembled. It took every ounce of restraint he possessed to keep from storming out of the cottage.

"He was so proud of you." She stared past Leo, as if she were slipping back in time. "He'd carry you on his shoulders all the way home so that everyone could see the ribbon pinned to your chest."

Leo blinked hard. He loved his mother. Would do anything for her. But he couldn't stand there and listen to her talk about his father like he'd been a paragon or a saint when he'd been anything but.

"I . . . I think I need some fresh air," he choked out.

Her brow furrowed and she patted his shoulder. "I understand, dear," she said, sympathetic. "I miss him, too."

But she didn't understand at all. If she did, she wouldn't mention him in Leo's presence. She wouldn't have his hat still hanging on the hook by the door and his pipe sitting on the table beside his favorite chair.

"Thank you for dinner," he managed. "I'll visit again soon."

"Will I see you at the festival?" she asked, hopeful.

"Sure." He would have said anything to escape the cottage at that moment. "I'll be there."

Chapter 9

The next morning, Kitty popped through the doorway of Hazel's sitting room and held up a sack from the bakery. "I've brought your favorite."

Hazel, who was sitting on a chaise in her nightgown, looked up from the book in her lap. "Cherry tarts?" she asked hopefully.

Kitty grinned as she crossed the room, handed her the sack, and perched on the foot of the chaise. "Does your enthusiasm mean that your appetite has returned?"

Hazel peeked inside the bag, sniffed, and closed her eyes as if she were in heaven. "I'm always hungry—except for when I'm queasy," she added with a chuckle. "Thank you."

"I've been worried about you. Have you spoken with Dr. Gladwell?"

"Not yet." Hazel took a bite of the tart and sighed happily.

Kitty clucked her tongue. "Have you told Uncle Beck?"

"I will tonight," Hazel said, emphatic—almost as if she were trying to convince herself.

"I thought you would have on the night of the cricket match . . . or yesterday. Is there a reason you haven't?"

Hazel swallowed, set aside the tart, and shot Kitty an

affectionate smile. "I suppose I wanted things to remain as they are for a bit longer. Please don't misunderstand—I couldn't be happier about the babe," she said. "But I think I'm also adjusting to the idea that this perfect life we all have—centered around Bellehaven Academy and our patchwork family—is about to change. Does that make sense?"

Kitty's eyes stung unexpectedly. "Yes," she said with a sniffle. "It does."

Hazel slipped an arm around her shoulders. "One thing I can promise you is that the Belles will stick together, no matter what."

"I wish Poppy was here," Kitty confessed. "Does she know?"

Hazel shook her head. "Only you. But it does seem like the sort of secret that the Belles should share. Perhaps we should write her a note together and tell her the news."

"That's a lovely idea, but I do wish we could see her face when she finds out. She's going to be so happy." Especially since it would be something else that she and Hazel would have in common: doting husbands, idyllic marriages, and sweet babies. Kitty didn't necessarily covet any of those things, but she did want to belong, and it felt like the divide between her and the other Belles was only growing.

"We'll have to tell Poppy about the latest with your contest entry as well," Hazel said.

Kitty scoffed. "That's not nearly as exciting."

"I beg to differ." Hazel stood and glided across the room toward her desk. "There's something different about you lately. A gleam in your eye that I haven't seen in some time."

Kitty squirmed on the chaise. "Perhaps it's due to the prospect of becoming an aunt."

"No, no," Hazel said, smoothing a piece of paper on her desk. "The spark happened before you knew about that—on the night the mayor announced the contest. It's as though a part of you came to life."

"I do like a challenge," Kitty admitted, not caring to examine what other reasons could be responsible for her recently attained glow.

"It's a bit more than that though, isn't it?" Hazel mused, tickling the underside of her chin with her quill. "You're on the brink of a momentous time, too. This contest, coming into your inheritance, possibly moving to London . . . after this summer, your life will never be the same. And I predict that you—and your talent—will take the world by storm."

"That's my plan," Kitty said, with more confidence than she felt. "But the first step is winning the contest, and that is not going to happen unless I get to work."

"Will you go into the office today?"

Kitty stood and smoothed her skirts. "I don't think so." Leo was sure to be there, and she didn't need distractions at this stage of her design. What she needed today, more than anything, was the comfort of home. A sense that she belonged. "I'll work in my room. That way I'll be just down the hall if you need me."

"Don't be silly," Hazel said with a dismissive wave. "I don't need a thing, and even if I did, I'm blessed to have Clara, Lucy, and our faithful staff on hand. Go and work on your contest design. Nothing makes me happier than seeing you chase your dreams."

Kitty wrung her hands. "You're certain you don't need me?"

"Not at all." Hazel's pen was already gliding across the page, composing her note to Poppy, but she looked up and smiled warmly. "Blade and I have a dinner party with one of his business partners, so if I don't see you this evening, we can chat more tomorrow."

"Very well." Kitty mustered a smile despite the hollow feeling in her chest. "Then I suppose I will go to the office."

"Thank you for the tart," Hazel said sincerely. "And thank you for understanding . . . about everything."

An hour later, as Kitty walked into town, she was still feeling a bit bruised and raw. She knew in her heart that Hazel wanted to see her thrive and excel. Kitty wanted that, too. But she'd wanted it to be on her terms—when she was ready.

Not by necessity, because the people she loved were moving on without her.

She'd gathered up her sketchbook, tools, and other supplies, then asked Cook for a sandwich to bring with her, reasoning that taking her lunch on the beach would cheer her. She could sit on the rocks and let the sound of the ocean soothe her nerves. But first, she'd stop in the office and drop off her things.

She wasn't eager to face Leo again, but she was prepared to move on, as they always had after their rows. Indeed, sometimes she suspected the problem was with her. Maybe she expected too much from people, or maybe she'd just wanted more from *him*—which was setting herself up for inevitable disappointment.

As she reached the office door, she saw the small sign hanging in the bay window that read, "Will return soon." A glance inside confirmed the shop was empty, and she stepped inside, grateful that she didn't have to face Leo quite yet.

But as she crossed the room, her skin prickled ominously.

She blinked at her desk to be certain her eyes weren't deceiving her.

How dare he.

Her desktop was bare. All her inspiration gone.

Her wallpaper and fabric samples, her sketches and notes had been thrown into a basket like yesterday's rubbish. Her cherished keepsakes—the ones that had marked the boundary between her territory and Leo's—had been tossed into the basket too. As if they were useless trinkets that should be relegated to the attic.

Heat pulsed through her veins. He had no right to touch her belongings, no right to push her out. This would not stand.

She slapped her bag and sketchbook onto her desk, staking her claim once more.

"Leo!" she called, poking her head into the tiny back room. He wasn't there, but the door to the stairs leading to his living quarters was slightly ajar, and she shoved it open.

"Leo Lockland!" she shouted again, stomping up the staircase. The door at the top was closed, so she banged on it with the side of her fist. "Open up now!"

When he didn't, she turned the knob and let herself in.

Only to find him standing directly in front of her, half-naked. He was wearing trousers, thank heaven, but his shirt was most definitely missing, as were his jacket, waistcoat, and cravat. A towel was slung around his neck as though she'd caught him in the middle of his morning shave. Sweet Jesus.

"Kitty?" he said, gaping at her like she had two heads. "What the devil are you doing here?"

Her face turned hot, but she refused to avert her eyes. "It doesn't feel nice, does it," she said dryly, "having someone barge into your space?"

He shrugged helplessly. "I actually don't mind you visiting, but it would have been nice to have some advance notice. I could have prepared some refreshments. Or at least put on a shirt."

"Now that you mention it," she said curtly, "why *aren't* you wearing a shirt?"

"Because I'm in my own apartment," he said deliberately, as if the answer should have been obvious.

"It's the middle of the day, for heaven's sake. Do you always cavort around your sitting room in a state of undress?" She threw up a hand. "Never mind. I'd rather not know."

"I can assure you I wasn't cavorting." His mouth twitched, as if he found her predicament amusing. "The least I can do is offer you a seat."

"This isn't a social call."

"Well, if it was about work, you could have waited till I returned to the office. I left a sign in the win—"

"I saw the sign," she snapped. "I didn't want to wait."

He frowned and gripped the ends of the towel hanging from his neck. "It must be quite important, then," he said earnestly—as if he hadn't the slightest inkling what he'd done to incite her ire.

Leo Lockland was many things. Meticulous. Exasperating. Vexing. But he was most certainly not dense. "You honestly have no idea what you've done?" she demanded.

"Does it have something to do with our argument yesterday—about me not writing while I was in London?"

"No!" She paced the length of his room, just now noticing how abysmally neat everything was. Some might have called it *tidy*. She called it hopelessly devoid of personality and warmth. "I'm upset because you clearly have no regard for me or the space in which I work."

He frowned, clearly insulted by the accusation. "That's

not true. I—" He raked a hand through his hair, and she found herself unexpectedly distracted by the flex of his biceps. His whole arm was rather well formed, blast it all.

"Wait a minute," he continued. "Is this because I moved your things?"

"Yes!" she shouted, as though he'd finally guessed correctly in a grueling game of charades. "You had no right. How would you like it if I . . ." She glanced around the room and fixed her sights on the sofa pillows. There were three square cushions, precisely positioned at regularly spaced intervals, and she picked up the middle one. "How would you feel if I just tossed this on the ground?" She flicked it across the room like an old newspaper.

Leo's eyebrows rose a fraction. "I suppose I'd be mildly confused."

"Mildly confused?" she repeated, incredulous. "Perhaps another demonstration is in order." She picked up another pillow and hurled it toward the dining table, where it toppled a mug and knocked over a bowl of fruit.

His eyes tracked a pear as it rolled haphazardly across the floor, coming to a stop just a few inches in front of his boots. His nostrils flared, and his fingers flexed as though they itched to return the pear to its rightful place.

But instead of bending to pick it up, he flicked his gaze to hers.

"How do you feel *now*?" she drawled.

He rubbed his jaw as though he were giving the matter serious thought, but it was a mockery—an attempt to get under her skin. And it was bloody well working.

At last he cleared his throat and said, "I feel oddly invigorated."

Holy hell. She picked up the last pillow, took a giant step forward, and launched it at his head.

He ducked and the pillow sailed over him, hitting a

framed design hanging on the wall. It dangled precariously from the nail, and Kitty held her breath.

She recognized that design. It was the one he'd created for the Bellehaven stables. The one she'd updated with her decorative accents. He'd had it framed.

A bit of wire on the back seemed to be holding, thank heaven, and she exhaled.

But then the plaster around the nail crumbled.

The frame crashed to the floor.

Tiny shards of glass flew everywhere.

And to her utter horror, she burst into tears.

Chapter 10

Kitty hadn't known the tears were coming, but once she started sobbing, she couldn't stop. It was as if she'd sprung a leak from a place deep inside her, and her stiff upper lip was no match for the deluge.

Leo gently placed his hands on her shoulders and searched her face, his eyes full of concern. "I'm sorry," he blurted. "Are you hurt?"

Intelligible speech was quite beyond her, so she shook her head emphatically.

He exhaled, obviously relieved. "Don't move. There's glass all around you. It'll go right through the soles of those slippers."

She sniffled in a valiant attempt to rein in her emotions. She was not given to blubbering in public, and even if she were, Leo was the last person on earth she'd want to witness an outburst. "I didn't mean to break it," she said raggedly.

"I know." He shot her a teasing grin. "You meant to hit me squarely in the head."

"You shouldn't have ducked," she said, only half jesting.

"Clearly, I'm to blame," he said good-naturedly.

The warm pressure of his hands on her shoulders was

strangely soothing, and her body tingled. "You shouldn't have moved my things," she said firmly.

"I was trying to protect them. I dropped a pot of ink, and it splattered. On my shirt, on my desk, and on yours. I set your things aside while I cleaned up the mess, and I planned to return everything to its proper place. You came in before I had the chance."

"Oh, I . . ." Heat surged to her face, which was undoubtedly already red and splotchy. "I suppose I assumed the worst. I know you dislike the clutter on my desk."

"No," he said with a shrug. "I dislike clutter on *my* desk. I don't mind it on yours."

She blinked, sending a fat tear sliding down her cheek.

Leo released one of her shoulders, absently patted his chest, and grimaced.

"Did you just reach for your handkerchief?" she asked with a hiccup.

He chuckled. "I was trying to be a gentleman."

"And forgot you weren't wearing a shirt, much less a jacket?" Despite her resolve to remain miserable for the foreseeable future, her lips quirked. "It may surprise you to learn that, as a rule, gentlemen wear shirts in the presence of ladies."

"Then your lessons must be working. It seems I'm well on my way to becoming a rake." With that, he unceremoniously scooped her into his arms.

She gaped at him. "What are you doing?"

"Carrying you to the sofa," he said as he took a step, glass crunching under his boots. "So you don't cut your feet."

Her arm instinctively wound itself around his warm, bare neck, and she held on.

The sofa wasn't terribly far away, but it may as well have

been on the other side of the world. Those twenty seconds were an eternity. Molasses in an hourglass.

She was keenly aware of the hard wall of his chest pressed against her side.

The mossy-green flecks in his eyes.

The steady thumping of his heart. But then, perhaps the thumping was coming from her own heart—it was difficult to be certain.

To make matters worse, she had the most peculiar sensation in her belly. Not unpleasant, but disconcerting. And her breath was coming in short little puffs—the aftereffects of her crying spell, no doubt.

"There we are." His voice, deep and low, seeped beneath her skin as he settled her onto the sofa and sat beside her. "Are you feeling better now?"

"I don't know." He still had one arm behind her back, and she was still holding onto his neck. She could have released him—probably should have—but she wasn't feeling entirely steady. "But I'm afraid I do owe you an apology. I shouldn't have assumed the worst."

He scoffed and waved a hand. "Even the best of friends have the occasional row. There's no harm done."

She cast a skeptical glance at the mess on the floor. "I'll purchase a new frame," she said, punctuating the sentence with a hiccup.

"Would you like me to bring you some water?"

She shook her head. "I just need a moment to catch my breath."

His palm made soothing circles at the base of her spine, and her eyes closed of their own accord. She resisted the urge to lay her cheek against his bare shoulder. It seemed impossible that only a few minutes ago she'd been resisting the urge to commit bodily violence against him.

But Leo had always had that effect on her. He could spark her ire one moment and talk her off a ledge the next.

"I understand why you were angry about me moving your things," he said slowly—as if tiptoeing around a minefield. "But I've never seen you quite so upset. Did something else happen today?"

"Hazel's having a baby," she said, painting on a smile.

For several heartbeats, he said nothing. Then, he gazed at her earnestly. "Nothing—not even a baby—will come between you and the countess. You are akin to her sister, daughter, and best friend, all rolled into one person. She'll need you more than ever if she's going to deal with a small, demanding, nappy-wearing human."

Kitty's eyes stung again, but she nodded, grateful that he'd cut to the heart of the matter without making her say the words out loud. "She will, won't she?"

"You'll be the best sort of aunt, too." His arm was still draped around her like a shield protecting her from the outside world. "You'll spoil the baby when they're little. And when they're older, you'll be the one they come to when they're in trouble."

"Trouble happens to be my area of expertise," she said with a reluctant smile.

"I can't think of anyone more qualified."

She met his gaze. "Thank you. For everything."

"You're welcome," he said, exhaling. "I suppose we should clean up this mess and return to the shop."

She clung tightly to his neck. "Wait."

He shot her a puzzled glance. "Wait?"

"I'm not sure why I said that." She only knew that it felt good to be close to someone who understood her. And she wasn't ready to let him go.

In fact, she was feeling rather like she had on that

day in the office when she'd almost kissed him. Like she *wanted* to.

"You can stay here for a while if you need time to collect yourself," he offered.

"Actually," she began, "I was thinking this would be an opportune time for a lesson."

His muscles tensed. "What sort of lesson?"

All of the air seemed to have been sucked out of the room, and a delicious shiver stole over her skin.

She swallowed and blinked slowly. "A kissing lesson."

"I see." His eyes grew dark, and his gaze dropped to her lips, unleashing a whole new host of butterflies in her belly. "I'm not opposed to the idea."

"It would be purely for instructional purposes," she added quickly.

"Tell me more," he urged, sending a shiver over her skin. Those three innocuous words were somehow more seductive than anything whispered in her ear by a rogue or scoundrel.

She cleared her throat and hoped her voice would not betray her nervousness. "We would engage in a kiss with each other. Afterward, I could provide you with an evaluation of sorts. After all, kissing is something you'll need to master if you've any hope of becoming a rake."

His mouth quirked in a half smile. "You're going to critique me?"

"How else can you be expected to improve?" she reasoned.

He nodded, thoughtful. "Well," he drawled, "if I'm going to be given a rating, I'd better do my best."

A frisson of awareness rippled through her. "Yes," she murmured, leaning closer. "Impress me."

The words were barely out of her mouth before he touched his lips to hers. Softly at first, then more insistently, teasing her lips apart. He cupped her cheek in his palm as though he intended to savor every touch, every taste.

With the warm pressure of his mouth, the teasing flick of his tongue, and the sensuous caress of his fingers, he made her feel treasured. Revered. Like she was the center of his world.

She'd been kissed a time or two before. But never quite like this.

Leo didn't attempt to dominate her or stake his claim. Rather, he seemed eager to please. To spark desire in her rather than satisfy his own.

And, against all odds, he was succeeding.

With a ragged breath, she speared her fingers through his hair and let go. Of her worries, fears, and ambitions. She simply let herself feel.

Pleasure buoyed her like a gentle ocean swell. It tickled her chin, lifted her feet off the ground, and left her body tingling with possibility.

She curled her fingers into the hard, smooth flesh of his shoulder, pulling him closer. A soft sigh escaped her throat as she tangled her tongue with his.

It was naught but a kiss, she reminded herself. And yet, its effects traveled well beyond her lips. Her body thrummed, her heart raced, the tips of her breasts tightened to hard little buds.

"Kitty," he murmured against her mouth.

She flinched. Maybe it was the use of her familiar name, or maybe it was the way he'd uttered it—almost like a plea. Perhaps it was the sudden recollection that he was enamored of someone else. Whatever the reason, she came to the unwelcome realization that he *might* not be as consumed by the kiss as she was. And she abruptly drew back.

His eyes were slightly dazed, his expression unreadable. "I hope I didn't overstep."

"You didn't," she assured him, willing her pulse to slow.

He rubbed the back of his neck as if he were trying to recall precisely how they'd ended up kissing on his sofa. "How do you feel?"

"Fine." She couldn't bring herself to confess that she was exhilarated and embarrassed at the same time. That, even now, her lips tingled and her belly fluttered.

He nodded slowly. "You're not angry?"

"Why would I be?" she asked as nonchalantly as she could manage.

"I imagine you were expecting a kiss that was shorter and rather more. . . . chaste."

"I'm tutoring you in the ways of a rake," she said dryly. "I certainly wasn't anticipating a perfunctory kiss on the cheek. Rest assured, I'm far from scandalized."

For several seconds he said nothing but appeared to be pondering her words. Then he frowned. "Should I have taken the kiss further?"

She shrugged philosophically. "A true rake would have."

His mouth curled into a slow, potent smile. "Then I suppose I'll have to try again."

Her cheeks flamed. "I don't anticipate . . . that is, I don't foresee this"—she wagged a finger in the air between them—"becoming a regular occurrence."

He stiffened almost imperceptibly. "No. Of course not."

Awkwardness crept onto the sofa and planted itself firmly on the cushion between them.

Kitty smoothed a few loose tendrils away from her face in a futile attempt to compose herself. "Would you like me to help you clean the mess?"

"No," he said, scoffing. "I'll take care of it."

"Perhaps I should go then," she said, stealing a glance at the door.

"Let me at least sweep up the glass around your feet." He stood, retrieved the broom from a closet, and began clearing a path between her and door while she endeavored not to stare at the flexing of his arm and chest muscles.

Sweet Jesus, she was more depraved than she thought.

"By the way," he said casually as he crouched and picked up a large shard of glass. "What did you think?"

"Hmm?" she asked innocently.

"Of the kiss," he clarified. "How did I do?"

She resisted the urge to slink beneath the sofa. "Oh, the kiss," she said, buying herself some time. "It was . . ." She searched for a suitable adjective. One that would adequately describe it while allowing her to hold on to the precious last scrap of her dignity.

He stood and planted a hand on his hip, expectant. "It was . . . ?"

She swallowed. "Nice," she said, painfully aware that the description didn't do it justice.

Something akin to disappointment flicked across his face. He hesitated for a moment, then said, "That's it? That's the extent of your evaluation?"

"No," she improvised, "I'll have more to say . . . after I've had some time to reflect on the matter."

He opened his mouth as if he wanted to say something in response, but then pressed his lips into a thin line.

It was so like Leo to hold back. To be civil even though she'd barged into his apartment, caused a considerable amount of mayhem, and initiated an ill-advised kiss. She wished *he* would throw a pillow or at least rant a bit. Anything to make her feel as though she weren't the only one who'd completely lost her wits.

She crossed her arms, issuing a challenge. "You can say what you're thinking."

"Actually, I can't." He propped the broomstick against the wall, grabbed his ink-stained shirt off the back of a chair, and stuffed his arms into the sleeves. "But I'll look forward to hearing your full assessment of the kiss once you've had the opportunity to complete your analysis." There was no rancor in his voice, no underlying sarcasm. Just a calm, cool acceptance.

She stood, grateful that her wobbly knees still functioned. "It's probably best if I work on my design at home today—given the state of my desk," she added quickly, lest he think the kiss had something to do with her decision.

"I'll see that it's set to rights before the end of the day," he said soberly. "I hope you know that desk, that spot, is *yours*. For as long as you want it."

"Thank you," she said, tucking his words away for safe-keeping.

As she made her way to the door, he said, "Will I see you in the office tomorrow?"

She swallowed, knowing full well she couldn't avoid him forever. But she wasn't quite ready to spend hours working directly opposite him in such close quarters. "Probably not tomorrow. But if you're going to the Sand-castle Festival, perhaps I'll see you there."

"I'll be there," he said gruffly.

"Most of Bellehaven will be—including Lila," she added, arching a brow.

"Lila," he repeated flatly.

"It's clear she's fond of you." She shot him an

encouraging smile. "All the other eligible young ladies are bound to be there, too. It will be an excellent opportunity to advance your campaign."

He reached down, carefully picked up the old stable design, and looked into her eyes with an intensity that made her shiver. "Maybe you're right."

Chapter 11

"It's not the fairest day we've ever had for the festival," Mayor Martin said. "But it could be worse."

Leo looked beyond the beach, to where the dreary gray sky met the angry blue sea. "It could indeed," he said diplomatically, but the weather had obviously kept a fair number of people home that morning. The crowd was half its usual size.

"No sense in postponing the event." The mayor held out a palm and glanced up at a fat rain cloud. "A few sprinkles won't hurt anyone, and I'd hate to disappoint all our young people."

"A little rain is good for sandcastles," Leo said. It was also notoriously bad for picnics, but he refrained from mentioning it.

"If anyone knows the secret to a good sandcastle, it's you," Mayor Martin said jovially. "You won more than your share of blue ribbons when you were a lad. Perhaps you could give our contestants a few tips," he added with a conspiratorial jab of his elbow.

"I'm not sure I remember the finer points of castle construction," Leo said, making his way down the path leading to the beach. "It's been a while since I've built a moat."

At least two dozen square building sites had been staked out with string along the shore, well out of reach of high tide. From the looks of their structures, several of the contestants had been working for hours.

He could almost remember that feeling of thrusting his hands into a big pile of sand and fashioning it into something magical—something that could protect imaginary inhabitants from fire-breathing dragons, stone-throwing catapults, and arrow-slinging enemies. He'd relished the awed expressions of the townspeople as they circled his masterpiece, marveling at the intricate details and the impressive towers.

The blue ribbons had been nice, but they hadn't meant as much to him as the pride in his father's eyes. At least the ribbons had been real. Leo wasn't certain that anything about his father had been genuine.

Ignoring the pang in his chest, he strode onto the beach looking for Kitty.

It had been two days since he'd seen her. Two days since they'd kissed.

And he had the distinct impression that she was avoiding him.

"Leo!"

He turned at the sound of the familiar voice behind him. "Mama," he said, kissing her cheek. "It's good to see you. I wasn't sure if you'd venture out in this weather."

"I'm not going to stay," she said as she waved to a friend down the beach. "But I wanted to give you this." She handed him a large picnic basket, and he lifted the corner of cloth to peek inside.

"There's enough food in here to last me a week."

She patted his shoulder fondly. "Strapping young men have hearty appetites. And I may have packed a little extra in case you wanted to share with a special someone. No one should picnic by themselves," she added with a wink.

"Thank you," he said, ignoring the shameless hint. "It smells delicious."

She smiled wistfully at a few rowdy boys splashing in the rough surf. "I'm just so happy that you're back, Leo. I want you to be happy, too."

"I am," he assured her, even though it was a bit of a stretch.

"Good," she said, looking unconvinced. "I'm going to meet a few other ladies at the tea shop and share recipes." She leaned closer and whispered, "That's code for exchanging gossip."

"Don't tell stories about me, Mama," he said with a chuckle. "But enjoy yourself."

She waved as she strolled down the shore toward her friends, and Leo tucked the picnic basket in a shady spot between two rocks so he could walk through the sandcastle village—and look for Kitty—unencumbered.

It didn't take him long to find her. Several tendrils of pale blond hair had worked themselves loose from their pins and blew around her face. Even without her canary-yellow dress and bright white parasol, she would have been an antidote to the overcast day.

One glimpse of her brought him right back to the afternoon in his apartment. It was the strangest kiss he'd ever had. And the best, by far.

She stood beside one of the teachers from Hazel's school, looking on while a trio of braid-wearing girls knelt in the sand, building industriously.

"Well done, Olive," Kitty said with genuine enthusiasm. "But pack your pyramid a bit more. If it collapses, it will crush the Sphinx."

The little girl gasped and set about shoring up the sides.

Leo approached the building site and nodded approvingly. "I feel like I've walked into the Egyptian desert."

"Good morning, Leo," Kitty said smoothly—as though they hadn't kissed the last time they were together. "Jane, girls, this is Mr. Lockland, who recently moved back to Bellehaven from London. He won this contest a time or two." She glanced up at Leo. "How many ribbons do you have?"

"I don't know . . . a few," he said, attempting to be modest.

"Nonsense." Kitty crossed her arms and tapped a toe. "How many?"

He shrugged. "Five."

She gave a satisfied smile. "What advice do you have for our intrepid builders?"

"I'm impressed with the sharpness of your edges and the vertex—that's hard to do." He knelt beside the pyramids, taking a closer look. "But if I had to give one piece of advice it would be to build on a grand scale."

"What do you mean?" asked a dark-haired bespectacled girl.

"It you want to win over the judges, make it big. The bigger the better."

"But that's risky," Olive said. "It could all fall down."

"That's true," he said with a smile. "But a sandcastle isn't meant to stand forever. That's why it's best to push the limits. Defy gravity. Make it magical."

The smallest girl sat back on her knees and scratched her cheek with the back of her forearm. "How do you make it magical?"

"Don't ask me," he said, standing and brushing off his palms. "Miss Beckett is the expert on magic."

Kitty arched a brow at Leo, then addressed the girls,

who all looked at her expectantly. "You already have a sphinx, which is an excellent start," she said sincerely, "but I'll wager you can think of something even more magical."

The girl with dark braids scrunched her freckled nose. "More magical than a sphinx?" she asked, incredulous. "How?"

Kitty shot her and her cohorts a mysterious smile. "You tell me."

Olive rubbed her hands together. "We could make our own mythical creature. I think she should have the head of a woman . . ."

"And the body of a hawk," the small girl piped up.

"And the tail of a fox," shouted the last.

"There you are," Kitty said, holding up a palm. "My work here is done. But the lot of you need to get busy if you've any hope of finishing your magical creature before Mayor Martin rings the bell."

Leo greeted the teacher, Miss Jane, and inquired after her family. He gave the schoolgirls a few more words of encouragement. And when he'd ticked all the boxes that good manners required, he leaned under Kitty's parasol. "Do you think we could talk?" he asked.

She gave a resigned sigh and opened her mouth to reply when—

"Mr. Lockland!"

Lila Bardsley hurried down the path to the beach, waving a handkerchief.

Kitty jabbed him with her elbow. "Look, you're in luck."

"Actually, I was hoping that you and I could finish our discussion from the other day."

"We will," Kitty whispered. "But you mustn't disappoint Lila. A true rake makes every woman feel like the center of the—"

"Can you believe it?" Lila said, slightly breathless from her walk over the dunes. "What a stroke of good fortune. My younger brothers are working on their castle right here." She waved at the stringed-off square next to the Bellehaven Academy girls, who looked up from their work to cast fierce glares at their competition.

"It's nice to see you again," Leo said cordially. Well aware that Kitty was rolling her eyes at his lackluster greeting, he searched his brain for something suitably witty or suggestive. Something a rogue might say.

"I'm glad the rain didn't keep you away," he continued. "Your smile has already brightened up this corner of the beach."

Kitty, who was on his right, clucked her tongue and muttered under her breath, obviously underwhelmed by the attempt.

Lila seemed happy enough, though. "You'll make me blush," she said, playfully swatting his arm with her fan. "I came down to check on my brothers—and to make sure they weren't fighting each other, as usual." She frowned at the pair of boys beside her. "Where's Liam?"

"He was bored," said a towheaded boy with a wild cowlick. "I think he went swimming with the other lads."

"You're supposed to be looking after him," Lila scolded.

"The only way we'd be able to keep track of Liam is if we kept him on a leash, and you weren't keen on the idea," the other gangly-limbed brother said with a shrug. "I'm sure he's fine."

Lila shielded her eyes from the glare and gazed out at the frothy surf, trying to pick Liam out of the half dozen heads bobbing in the waves. "I can't see him."

"Shall we walk down and find him?" Leo offered. "Maybe we can lure him out of the water with the promise of a pastry."

Lila nodded and shot him a grateful smile. "The only thing he'll be getting from me is some extra chores."

Leo turned to Kitty, intending to let her know he'd return shortly to continue their conversation. But the next thing he knew, Lila had attached herself to his arm and was pulling him in the opposite direction. He looked helplessly at Kitty, who surreptitiously shooed him toward Lila. Almost as if she were glad for the reprieve.

"He's a pint-sized boy," Lila was saying, "but he has a knack for finding big-sized trouble."

"Some people do," Leo mused, still thinking of Kitty.

Before long, they were at the water's edge, and Lila was shouting to the boys splashing in the white-capped water. "Have you seen Liam?"

"Aye!" a boy called back. "He's just over there, by the rocks."

Lila and Leo walked a bit farther, but there was no sign of her little brother.

Until one of the older boys, who was at least thirty yards offshore, started shouting and waving his arms wildly.

The hairs on the backs of Leo's arms stood on end, as he cupped his hands around his mouth. "Are you all right?"

The boy pointed toward a white dot in the vast gray sea behind him.

Lila cried out and waved wildly. "Liam!"

A thin arm surfaced then disappeared.

"The current must have dragged him out," Leo said, already pulling off his boots.

"Oh my God." Lila covered her mouth with her hand, horrified. "He's so far out there. He'll drown."

"Call the other boys to shore," Leo said, shrugging off his jacket. "I'll bring back Liam." And he ran into the surf.

* * *

Unless Kitty's eyes deceived her, Leo was diving into the menacing, wind-whipped waves—and she was fairly certain he wasn't going for a leisurely swim.

"It looks as though something's happening in the water," she whispered to Jane, trying to keep the worry from her voice. "I'm going down there to see if I can help."

Jane craned her neck, attempting to see the commotion. "I'll stay with the girls. If the sky turns any darker, I'm going to get them off the beach—at least until the storm passes."

As if on cue, a bolt of lightning crackled on the horizon. An ominous buzz raced through Kitty's limbs, and the beach erupted in gasps.

"We're going, girls," Jane said definitively. Turning to Kitty, she added, "You should come with us. It's going to start pouring any minute now."

"Don't worry about me," Kitty said, already striding toward the water. "Once I see what's going on, I'll head to the office and wait out the storm."

As thunder rumbled in the distance, Mayor Martin picked up his megaphone and addressed the crowd. "In the interest of safety, I regret to inform you that this year's contest is officially cancelled. Hurry someplace safe, everyone."

The young contestants groaned as fat raindrops pelted their sand creations, ruthlessly melting hours of work. Adults attempted to herd them toward the dunes and off the beach.

But the small group near the water's edge didn't heed the mayor's warning.

Kitty rushed toward them, angling her parasol against the wind. "Lila," she called, "did you find your brother?"

She looked at Kitty, her face pale with fear. "He's out

there," she sobbed, pointing at the murky ocean. "But I've lost sight of him." She looked as though she might be sick.

Kitty swallowed and slipped an arm around Lila's shoulder. "Leo won't give up," she said confidently. "He'll find Liam and bring him back."

"I want to believe that." Lila's voice quavered, and her body trembled. "How can you be sure?"

"No one's more dependable. He may not be the fastest swimmer or the strongest. But when he sets his mind to something, he does it," she said firmly, trying to reassure herself as much as Lila.

"I think I see him in the water by the rocks," Lila said.

Kitty turned to the boys who'd been swimming. "Go fetch Dr. Gladwell," she said. "Hurry."

While they sprinted up the beach, Kitty and Lila walked parallel to the water, tracking Leo. His arms cut through the water with steady, solid strokes, but his progress was painfully slow—as if he was battling for every yard.

Kitty began to worry, too. Leo *was* dependable. And stubborn to a fault.

He was intent on saving the boy—and if he couldn't do it, she feared he'd drown trying.

A sudden gust of wind whipped off the water, tugging at her parasol and snapping the delicate ribs like twigs. She tossed it on the ground and linked arms with Lila as they shivered helplessly on the shore.

Leo seemed to be treading water in one spot.

"I think he's got him!" Lila cried hopefully.

"Yes, I see his head next to Leo's," Kitty said.

But they both knew the hardest part was yet to come. Leo was surely exhausted, and he still had to fight the wicked current while hauling Liam back.

For a full minute, he didn't seem to make any headway,

and Kitty wanted to crawl out of her skin. "Come on, Leo," she murmured. "You can do it."

At last, he began to inch closer to the shore, pulling Liam along. Every so often, they'd disappear beneath a large swell and Kitty would hold her breath until they surfaced again. She could feel Lila doing the same.

"Liam's moving his arms," Lila exclaimed. "That's a good sign."

It was. But Kitty was focused on Leo, and the strain on his face worried her. Every stroke required Herculean effort. Every kick sapped his strength. She didn't know how long a person could exert that much energy.

And she couldn't bear to think what would happen to Leo if he stopped swimming.

She dropped her reticule and bonnet in the sand and untied her bonnet.

"What are you doing?" Lila asked with alarm.

"I'm going in." She kicked off her slippers and waded waist-deep into the churning surf. "I think Leo needs help."

"Wait!" Lila cried. "What if you're swept away, too?"

"I'll be careful," Kitty called over her shoulder. She was not an expert swimmer by any means, and she could already feel the current pulling on her heavy skirts. But the thought of Leo struggling, fighting to keep his and Liam's heads above water, propelled her forward.

The white-capped crest of a large wave loomed over her head, and she dove beneath it, then surfaced, looking around for Leo.

She spotted him several yards away, sputtering as water sloshed around his face. "Hold on—I'm coming!" she called out.

Leo looked in her direction. "Go back," he rasped.

Liam was coughing like he'd swallowed several mouthfuls of the ocean. "Help! I . . . can't . . . breathe."

Kitty dove again, kicking through the cold, murky water until she reached them. She surfaced, gasped for air, and reached for Liam. "Let me take him," she pleaded. "Get yourself to shore."

"No," Leo said, panting. "I've got him."

She wanted to argue the point but realized it was futile. "You don't have far to go," she said, grabbing a fistful of his shirt.

She drew a deep breath, headed for the beach, and kicked with all her might. She held on tight to Leo and fought her way, inch by inch, closer to land.

When at last her feet hit the sand, she wanted to cry with relief. "We made it," she gasped, dragging Leo and Liam forward.

A few seconds later, Lila was pulling her out of the knee-deep water, then running past her to Liam.

Leo handed the boy over to his grateful sister, then staggered into the surf beside Kitty and collapsed.

"Come on," she urged, hooking an arm under his shoulder. "You made it this far, there's no sense in drowning here."

With her help, he managed to crawl onto the sand.

Lila carried her brother out of the water and started making her way up the beach toward the boys and Dr. Gladwell, who were running to meet them.

Meanwhile, Kitty and Leo sat on the sand in the rain, trying to catch their breath.

"You shouldn't have come after me," he said raggedly.

"You would have preferred that I sit on the beach and watch you drown?"

"Rather than risk your life?" He dragged his hands down his face. "Yes."

One of Lila's brothers came charging down the beach, a quilt tucked under one arm. He handed it to Kitty.

"Dr. Gladwell said to give this to you. He wants to know if you're both all right."

"I'm fine," Kitty assured him.

"As am I," said Leo. "Tell him not to worry about us. He can focus on tending to your little brother."

"Yes, sir," the boy said, already running toward the dunes. "Thank you!"

Leo looked at Kitty and gestured toward the quilt in her lap. "You should wrap up. Give me a moment, and I'll see you home."

"I thought you wanted to talk," she said.

"I do. But this . . ." He looked up at the angry sky and lifted his chin toward her soaked gown. ". . . isn't the ideal place. You'll catch your death's cold."

"Then we'll go someplace dry." She started to stand—a bit awkwardly due to her clingy, sopping skirt—and he scrambled to his feet to help her. She took the hand he offered, and a shimmer of warmth traveled through her palm despite the wind and rain swirling around them.

"The office?" he asked, skeptical.

"No." She pointed down the beach. "Pirate's Cave is closer. We can dry out there and have a chance to talk privately."

He looked into her eyes then, as if he were recalling the times they'd explored there when they were younger. "I'm surprised you remember it."

Of course she remembered it. "The sooner we go, the sooner we can get out of the storm."

"Run ahead and take shelter. I'll gather your slippers, my boots, and our clothes—and I'll meet you there."

Chapter 12

Despite its name, Pirate's Cave was not a true cave, and
Leo would have bet his favorite square rule that no pirate
had ever set foot there.

It hadn't changed much in the decade since he'd last visited. Hidden at the base of a cliff, it was about eight yards
wide and half as deep. It was far enough from the water
that it never flooded, and the ceiling was tall enough for
him to stand upright. The sand floor was soft and mostly
free from rock and shells, thanks to generations of boys
and girls who'd imagined the spot was everything from a
dragon's lair to a palace ballroom.

When he arrived, Kitty stood on the far side of the shelter. Her hair hung in dark golden waves around her shoulders; her yellow dress clung to her torso and legs. Clumps
of sand stuck to her arms and feet.

Anyone else would have looked disheveled. Not her.
Like a demigod, she was both hauntingly ethereal and
imperfectly human. And as always, she took his breath
away.

Her back was to him as she ran her fingers over one of
the rock walls.

"Looking for your initials?" he asked, depositing the
armful of items he'd brought.

"Still here," she confirmed.

He frowned at the folded quilt sitting on the ground by her feet. "Why haven't you wrapped up in that?"

"It seems pointless as long as my gown is still drenched." She crossed her arms and rubbed them. "I'll give it some time to dry out."

"I think I found all your things." He deposited the items he'd brought from the beach near one wall and began laying everything out—her bonnet, slippers, and reticule; his boots, waistcoat, and jacket.

She walked closer to inspect the pile. "Is that a picnic basket?" she asked, incredulous.

"Compliments of my mother," he said with a chuckle. "I almost forgot I'd left it on the beach earlier."

"How is she?" Kitty asked, and the tenderness in her voice made his chest ache.

"Still reeling a bit," he said, deftly dodging any mention of his father. "But improved enough to want to match me off with an eligible young lady."

"That's good," she said with a sly smile. "Your heroic efforts today will certainly make a few more women sit up and take notice. You'll be pleased to know that Lila was dazzled by your courage."

"Lila seems like a fine person," he said. "But I'm not interested in pursuing her."

"Oh," Kitty said, obviously taken aback. "Well, no matter. Word will travel fast, and the woman you fancy will soon realize that you are highly sought after. It can only help in your campaign to win her heart."

He nodded slowly, wishing that were true.

When he'd finished laying out the items, he brushed off his hands and stood. "I'm not certain your parasol can be repaired, but at least you'll have a good story to go with it. You sacrificed it to save me," he joked.

She waved a hand. "I have plenty of parasols. I have far fewer friends."

The sentiment warmed his chest. Of course he'd have preferred to be something more than a friend to her, but this was progress. "Thank you for coming to my aid," he said sincerely, "even if it was risky and ill-advised."

"You're welcome."

"Did you work up an appetite after that vigorous swim?" He gestured toward the picnic basket. "We could eat something."

"Maybe later."

"I suppose we should talk," he said. They couldn't pretend that the kiss hadn't happened. He needed to know if she'd felt even an iota of what he'd felt. Because if she hadn't, there was no sense in continuing his pursuit. Nothing would change the way he felt about her, but if she could never return his feelings, he had to respect that. He'd have to move on.

"Yes," she said, lifting her chin as if she were Marie Antoinette on her way to the guillotine. "Let's sit at the back where we'll be protected from the wind."

Leo swept the sand at the base of the rock wall, making a smooth spot for Kitty, and she eased herself to the ground beside him. But even there, in the driest, warmest part of the cave, she couldn't stop shivering. "You need to warm up. I'm getting the quilt," he said.

When he tried to drape it over her lap, she held out a hand. "Wait," she said through chattering teeth. "It won't do any good unless I get out of these clothes."

Leo blinked at her, disbelieving. "Do you have a change of clothes hidden somewhere?"

"Of course not," she said, standing. "The quilt will do for now."

"I'm afraid I don't follow."

"Open it up and hold it between us like a curtain," she instructed. "I'll strip off my wet clothes and wrap up in the quilt while we talk."

"You're going to take your dress off . . . *here*?" he asked.

"There's not a soul on the beach," she said with a shrug. She was already reaching behind her back, loosening the laces of her gown.

"*I'm* here," he said pointedly.

She arched a brow, issuing a silent challenge. "Will it offend your delicate sensibilities if I disrobe in your presence?"

There was zero chance of him being offended. There was every probability, however, that he would be tempted. Knowing she was undressing on the other side of a quilt and not being able to see or touch her sounded like the worst kind of torture.

And he was about to subject himself to it. Eagerly.

"Not at all." He scrambled to his feet, shook out the quilt, and held it like a dressing screen in front of her. He immediately heard movement and the rustle of fabric.

"Aren't you going to tell me not to look?" he asked.

She went still for a moment. "I trust you."

He closed his eyes and wondered if she had any inkling as to the wicked direction of his thoughts. "You wouldn't trust a rake," he said gruffly.

"No. But we've already established that you're not a rake, haven't we?"

"I don't know," he mused. "The transformation is underway. I'm becoming more depraved by the day."

"Mmm," she said distractedly—as if he were a lady's maid instead of a warm-blooded male.

"And I have you to thank for that," he added.

"There," she said, apparently free of her soaked clothes.

"I'm going to take the quilt from you, on the count of three. One, two, three."

He released the blanket and heard her sigh as she wrapped it around her.

"That's so much better," she said blissfully.

"Good," he said, still averting his gaze.

"You can look at me," she said with a chuckle. "The quilt is more modest than the gown I was wearing. Promise."

He cast a cautious glance in her direction and found that she'd wrapped the soft blanket around her shoulders like a cape. It was large enough that there were no gaps at the front, a circumstance that was both a relief and a disappointment.

A pile of clothes littered the ground behind her, and it included more than her gown. Apparently, she'd stripped off her corset, stockings, and underclothes as well. The thought of her naked beneath the blanket sent a shot of pure desire through his body, and he stifled a groan.

"Could I ask another favor?" she said sweetly.

"Go on," he choked out.

"Would you mind laying out my clothes to dry? I'd do it myself, but it's difficult to move freely in this quilt."

He swallowed. "I don't mind."

As he untangled her silk stockings, he tried not to think about peeling them off her lithe legs. As he laid out her lace-trimmed corset, he tried not to imagine untying the satin ribbon at the front. And, as he untwisted her thin petticoat, he tried not to imagine seeing her lush curves through the transparent fabric.

His body, however, did not cooperate with the plan, and he was grateful that Kitty seemed too distracted to notice his state of arousal.

She returned to the spot at the back of the cave, and gracefully lowered herself to the ground, the quilt billowing around her. "Now then, where were we?"

They needed to talk about the kiss, but it was hard for Leo to think clearly when all the blood in his body had rushed south. He needed to take his mind off of their kiss and her nakedness, so he steered the conversation in a safer direction—for now.

"How are your drawings for the theater progressing?" he asked.

"Fairly well, I think. I changed the orientation of the building by a few degrees to maximize the area with a view of the ocean."

He nodded approvingly.

"Now I'm considering reducing the size of the auditorium in order to increase the square footage allotted for the backstage area." Her forehead creased. "But there may be another solution that I haven't thought of."

"Maybe I can help," he offered.

"It would be much easier if I were able to show—" She stopped abruptly, then said, "I have an idea." She looked on the ground around her, then reached an arm through the opening of the quilt to grab a stick.

"Here's the stage." She used the stick to draw a sweeping arc in the sand. "Here is the auditorium, with boxes here and here," she said, adding those elements to the floor plan.

"And the lobby?" he asked.

"All along the east side," she said, marking its location in the sand. "With the entrance here."

"So, the backstage is this area, on the west?"

"Yes. But I only have about ten yards of depth here, and I'm afraid that all of that will be needed for backdrops and sets." She frowned at the drawing and tapped her stick on the ground in the same way that she normally tapped her pencil on her desk when she was perplexed.

"I see what you mean," he said, scratching his chin. "That doesn't leave much space for changing rooms."

"I thought about putting the dressing rooms along the south wall, but that's farther from the stage, which makes it more difficult for the actors and actresses to do quick costume changes."

"Agreed." Leo hesitated, then said, "What about putting them under the stage? The performers would have easy access to both sides of the stage from below."

Kitty tilted her head and studied the floor plan, trying to imagine it. Then her gaze met his, and her mouth curled into a wide smile. "That's brilliant!"

She dropped the stick and moved toward him as if she was going to hug him—then quickly thought better of it. Her cheeks flushed a rosy-pink. "Thank you for the idea."

"Glad I could help," he said gruffly. "Anything to hold up my end of the deal."

"Right," she said flatly. "The deal."

"Are you regretting it?" he asked, bracing himself for her answer.

"No," she said without hesitation. "Are you?"

"No." At least not yet. He might feel differently once it was all over. Once she'd won the contest, moved to London, and left him brokenhearted in Bellehaven.

"Well," she said, nervously licking her lips, "I promised that I'd give you my opinion of our kiss, and I've had some time to dwell on it."

"You've had sufficient time to draw up a treatise on it," he quipped.

But her expression remained serious. "I'm going to be honest with you."

"I know." Every instinct told him that she'd enjoyed

the kiss. He'd felt her rapid pulse, heard her soft moans, seen the desire in her eyes. But he could never be certain where Kitty was concerned. It was hard to be objective when one was head over heels in love.

She cleared her throat slightly. "The mechanics were fine."

He scratched his head, deflated. "Would you care to elaborate?"

"I cannot fault your technique, but . . ."

"Just say what you're thinking," he urged.

"I found the kiss to be . . . unsettling."

"Unsettling," Leo repeated with trepidation. "In what way?"

"I felt things," she said. "Things I didn't expect to."

"Good things . . . or bad things?"

She closed her eyes briefly before responding. "Your kiss had the intended effect on me, the recipient. Thus, I think we can conclude that you are quite accomplished."

"At?"

She shrugged beneath the blanket. "At the art of kissing."

His chest warmed. His heart soared. But he knew better than to gloat. It couldn't have been easy for her to admit such a thing—and yet, he needed more from her. He needed her to be honest not only with him, but with herself.

"That is good to know," he said, "but you didn't answer the question. Did you like the way the kiss made you feel?"

"No," she answered quickly. "And yes. I was hot and achy and full of an odd sort of longing. I think that what I was feeling was . . . desire. Trust me when I say that it's the last thing I expected or wanted to feel."

"If it's any consolation," he said, "I was feeling it, too."

She blinked at him. "You were?"

"When it comes to kissing, you are also rather adept."

She nodded sagely, as if unsurprised by his admission. "I suppose it's only natural that we would feel a spark," she said. "We're human, after all."

Leo cast a curious glance at her. "You would have felt that spark with anyone?"

"With anyone who was somewhat attractive and reasonably proficient at kissing." Her brow creased. "Yes, I believe so. Wouldn't you?"

"I'm not certain." But that wasn't true. He'd kissed at least a dozen beautiful women over the course of his adulthood and never felt a fraction of the desire he felt for Kitty. "But I agree that it's only natural—and perhaps unavoidable—to feel aroused in certain circumstances."

"Precisely!" she said, leaning forward. "We cannot control our bodies' physical responses to stimuli. Even when we are with a person who is clearly not a suitable match."

He nodded in agreement—as if he wasn't gutted by the fact that she considered them incompatible. "You needn't feel embarrassed, in any event," he said. "Desire is normal. Perfectly healthy. And you deserve to feel . . . pleasure."

A strawberry stain crept up her neck and over her cheeks. She looked at him, quizzical. "Do you really think so?"

"Yes." If it were up to him, he would make it his life's work to please her. To indulge her every fantasy. To see that she was completely and utterly satisfied.

"I have an odd confession to make." She exhaled, then looked directly into his eyes. "I'm feeling that ache again. Right now."

Leo went very still. All the air seemed to have been sucked out of the cave, for it was difficult for him to breathe, much less talk. "What would you like to do about it?" he managed.

"I wouldn't mind kissing again." She paused and looked at him earnestly. "I wouldn't mind trying . . . other things as well."

His heart tripped in his chest. "Other things?" he repeated.

"I've kissed a few gentlemen," she said soberly. "During a stolen moment on a terrace, or while taking a private stroll in the park. But I've never experienced anything beyond a chaste kiss. Perhaps it's time I rectified the matter."

"With me?"

"Why not you?" she countered.

"You don't care for me in that way," he said.

"That's why you're the perfect candidate. There's no danger of my feelings becoming engaged."

"Right," he said, rubbing the ache in the center of his chest.

"Moreover," she went on, "you admitted that you felt a modicum of desire for me as well. It would be a mutually beneficial arrangement."

"What do you hope to gain?"

Her gaze turned wistful. "I would like the chance to experience . . . carnal pleasure."

His mouth went dry. "I'm certain you have no shortage of opportunities."

"I can see how you might think that," she said with a thoughtful sigh. "But the truth is that all the gentlemen who pursue me are driven by ulterior motives. Half of them are after my fortune. The other half are intrigued by the challenge I present."

He arched a brow, puzzled. "Challenge?"

"They are familiar with my reputation for flouting convention, and they seek to be the man who eventually tames me. Who sweeps me off my feet and turns me into a docile, biddable wife."

"Then they are fools twice over," he said, not bothering to hide his disdain. "First, for thinking they can change you, and second, for wanting to."

She shot him a winsome smile that made him want to pull her into his arms and kiss her—if only to make her believe that there was at least one man who loved her for precisely who she was.

"Nevertheless," she said, "I think you can see the predicament I'm in."

He nodded.

"There are few men I trust," she said slowly. "But I do trust you."

"Thank you," he said—even though he wanted more than her trust. He longed for her whole heart.

"So if you feel attracted to me in the slightest, perhaps we could recreate the kiss . . . and take it a bit further." She looked at him quite earnestly and added, "It would also be an excellent opportunity to hone your rakish skills."

"I've already told you I find you attractive," he said—in what was obviously the understatement of the century. "And I would be willing to engage in a dalliance with you." Correction: *That* was the understatement of the century. "But only if you're certain it won't create awkwardness between us."

She frowned at that, and he desperately wished he could stuff his words back in his mouth. Only an idiot would sabotage his chance to be with Kitty Beckett. "I see what you mean," she said slowly. "However, I think we've known each other too long to feel unease in each other's company. You're much more likely to make me feel annoyed or vexed."

"And vice versa," he said.

She smiled as if he'd paid her the highest compliment. "Then we're in agreement?"

"I have no objection," he said, as if she'd suggested an innocent walk on the beach instead of an illicit tryst in a cave. He gazed deep into her clear blue eyes. "How do you propose we begin?"

For the space of several breaths she said nothing. Beyond the mouth of the cave, rain drops pattered on the sand. Frothy waves whooshed along the shore. His heart pounded in his chest.

At last, her mouth curled into a sultry smile, and she gracefully rose to her feet.

He stood too, giving her time. Waiting for her to make the first move.

A wicked gleam lit her eyes.

A flush stole across her cheeks.

And she shrugged off the quilt, letting it fall to the ground.

Chapter 13

Despite the lousy weather and the near-drowning, Leo could say with one hundred percent certainty that this was shaping up to be the best Sandcastle Festival he'd attended. Ever.

Kitty was an arm's length away. Completely naked. And she wanted to experience pleasure—with him.

It was the stuff of his fantasies. Only it was real.

She stood before him, her chin held high, her arms at her sides.

"You're beautiful," he rasped, committing every lush curve to memory.

"You are wearing far more clothes than I am." Her gaze flicked over his wet shirt. "Perhaps you should take that off." She tilted her head as if a thought had occurred to her and added, "Unless you'd prefer me to?"

He swallowed. Maybe he *had* died in the ocean because this . . . this was surely heaven. "Do whatever pleases you," he said.

She nodded thoughtfully and took a tentative step forward till only a few inches separated them. They were so close that he could see the dark-blue flecks in her irises and the tan beauty mark on her shoulder. He could smell the ocean in her hair and hear the faint hitch of her breath.

He could feel the potent attraction swirling around them, heating the cave like a blaze.

The hem of his shirt hung loosely around his hips, and she reached for it, lifting it up and over his head and raised arms. She tossed it aside and made a slow circle around him, shamelessly examining his torso from every possible angle.

"You're beautiful, too," she said with a frown—as if this were a most unwelcome development. She reached toward him as if she'd touch his shoulder, then hesitated. "Do you mind if I . . . ?"

"Not at all," he assured her, doing his best to remain still under her scrutiny.

With smooth fingertips, she slowly traced the line of his collarbone from one side to the other. And though she'd scarcely touched him, his whole body thrummed in response.

She followed a path back to the hollow at the base of his throat, then moved her palm down to his sternum, making small circles in the patch of springy hair there.

Her unabashed curiosity was almost as arousing as her nakedness. She studied him freely, letting her fingers wander around his nipples and over the ridges of his abdomen.

Blissfully unaware that every touch seared his skin like a brand, making him forever hers.

But when she reached the barrier of his waistband, she froze and lifted her gaze to his. "I'm not certain where to go from here."

He barely refrained from growling. "Maybe I can help."

Leo reached for Kitty's hand with a tenderness that was unexpected—and oddly arousing.

He let her hand rest in his while he uncurled her fingers and traced slow, sensuous circles on her palm. A sweet frisson of awareness vibrated through her body, taking up residence in her core. Her body arched toward him of its own accord, but vexingly, he didn't haul her close.

Instead, he bent his head over her lifted palm and kissed it, letting his lips linger there. Tickling her skin with the tip of his tongue.

Her knees wobbled.

Her nipples puckered.

A sigh escaped her throat.

Leo lifted his eyes, and the heavy-lidded sensuousness in his gaze took her breath away. He brushed his lips over the inside of her wrist and left a trail of kisses from there to her elbow.

His mouth teased the sensitive skin of her forearm with the finesse of a feather, with the warmth of a hot spring.

Dizzy with desire, she speared her fingers through the thick crop of hair at his nape. Gasped when he flicked his tongue over the tip of her breast. Swayed on her feet as he took the taut peak into his mouth and hummed softly, as if his pleasure matched her own.

A shimmer of pure bliss radiated through her, and she clung tightly to his broad shoulders.

It was hard to imagine that Leo could make her body take flight in this way.

At the very same time, it was hard to imagine that anyone else could.

The sounds of the rain outside mingled with little cries of ecstasy—and it took a moment to realize they came from her. Her back pressed against cool, rough rock as he worshipped one breast, then the other. His warm, sure hands skimmed over the curve of her hips and squeezed her bottom.

But his caresses only seemed to stoke her hunger, exacerbating the incessant pulsing at her core. And when he finally captured her mouth in a scorching kiss, he seemed to be filled with the same desperate longing. As though he wanted—nay, *needed*—more of her.

None of the scandalous texts Kitty had read, none of the shocking pictures she'd studied, had prepared her for the potent need that swirled inside her. She longed to throw caution to the wind and surrender to that desire.

But a small voice at the back of her mind wouldn't let her forget the inherent dangers. Losing control was risky—even with Leo.

Maybe *especially* with Leo.

Slowly, she lowered the temperature of the kiss. Gradually pulled back.

He searched her face, his forehead creased in concern. "Are you all right?"

"Yes." She sank onto the quilt and exhaled in the hope her heart would resume its normal rhythm. "I just need a moment."

He collapsed onto the sand beside her. "As do I," he said, panting almost as hard as he had after rescuing Lila's brother.

For a while, they said nothing, but she could feel him looking in her direction. He could have been trying to read her expression, but she suspected his intent was somewhat less noble than that—and that he was more intrigued by her nakedness.

She could not fault him for that; she was similarly mesmerized by his bare torso. It was odd to feel such a strong, strange attraction to him, but she could no longer deny it. Not even to herself.

He dragged a hand through his hair and leaned back against the cave wall. "I apologize if I crossed a line."

"We both crossed a line. Actually, we jumped headlong over it. But I don't have any regrets." Her stomach sank as she thought about Lila—or whomever his love interest was. "Do you?"

"No," he replied, as if the very idea were preposterous.

A chilly breeze off the ocean swirled inside their refuge, and Kitty pulled the quilt around her shoulders. "That's good," she said conversationally. "And we were each able to successfully accomplish our goals."

He scratched his head. "Remind me what they were, precisely?"

She chuckled. "Mine was to engage in a dalliance. Yours was to hone your rakish skills."

"Right," he murmured distractedly. "How did I do?"

She swallowed. "I was duly impressed," she said sincerely. "Even though I pressed you into service, you made me feel as though . . . it was something you wanted, too."

His gaze snapped to hers. "I did want it. I wouldn't have done it otherwise."

"Regardless," she said, waving a hand. "It was a lovely experience. I give you high marks."

She'd thought the compliment would please him, but he appeared confused. "For what?"

After a moment's hesitation, she said, "For sweeping me away. It's just what a rake would endeavor to do, and you have somehow managed to master the technique without an iota of coaching from me." She paused, trying to decipher his guarded expression. "The woman you admire is bound to fall under your spell."

"I'm not certain about that," he said flatly.

"You must trust me," she said, managing a bright smile even though the mention of Leo's love stole some of the afternoon's magic. "However, there is one area I do think we can improve upon."

He arched a brow. "Do tell."

She made a circle in the air between them. "This."

"This?" he asked, obviously perplexed.

"For lack of a better word, we shall call it the aftermath." She tilted her head in order to meet his lowered gaze. "Please, do not take offense, I merely want to help you as you've helped me."

He scoffed. "I'm not offended—yet. I do confess, however, to being quite curious as to my failings with regard to the aftermath." His dry tone left no doubt that she'd unintentionally hit a nerve. Which only served to make her point.

Poor Leo. He needed her even more than he knew.

"Let's refrain from calling them failings," she said, doing her best to be gentle.

"Would you prefer shortcomings?" he quipped. "Tragic flaws?"

She rolled her eyes at his dramatics. "I've already said that the dalliance exceeded my expectations," she said, congratulating herself on her remarkable display of patience. "But in the aftermath, a rake would not be so solicitous. And certainly not so sensitive. Such men avoid sentimentality, preferring to live in the moment without regard to consequences."

He snorted at that. "All actions have consequences. Only a fool would pretend otherwise."

"I don't disagree," she said. "But if you wish to convince someone that you're a rake, you must imitate all of the associated foibles. Remember what we said at the outset," she reminded him.

He looked deep into her eyes, inadvertently resurrecting an echo of the pleasure she'd felt before. "I said I'd trust you."

She nodded. "And that you'd commit yourself one hundred percent."

"What would you have me do then?" he said. There was

an earnestness in his voice that made her wonder if he was talking about something other than his transformation, and yet, she couldn't fathom what that might be.

"My advice is that you keep the mood light. Refrain from discussing serious matters. And above all," she said solemnly, "promise nothing beyond the pleasure of the present."

"That's really what women want?" he asked wearily.

"I would never purport that my views represent those of all women," she clarified, "but yes, one of the most alluring things about a rake is that while he is the consummate charmer, he never gives his whole heart to one woman."

Leo dug the heel of one boot in the sand and shook his head dolefully. "I shall never understand the fairer sex. Why would a woman wish to be with a man who seduces her and then casts her off?"

"She doesn't," Kitty said quickly. "And I suppose this is where we come to the biggest secret of all . . . which I will share with you now."

He shot her a questioning glance from beneath a thick lock of hair, which only proved how well his lessons were progressing. "I'm all ears."

She paused, half wondering if lightning would strike her for giving away such sensitive information. But she owed Leo, and she knew him well enough to know he'd never intentionally hurt a woman. "The true appeal of a rake is wrapped up in a fantasy," she said slowly. "Women secretly hope that they will be the one to finally make the rake change his ways. They think they will be the one to reform him . . . and make him fall in love."

He narrowed his eyes at her. "But that never happens?"

"Not to my knowledge," she replied firmly. "No."

He heaved a frustrated sigh and rested an elbow on his bent knee, giving her an excellent view of his biceps and the contoured planes of his torso. She reminded herself that none of this was real and made a valiant attempt to refrain from staring.

"May I ask you something else?" he said.

She swallowed. "Of course."

"I've known you for a long time," he began. "And while we may not have always seen eye to eye, I know you to be a kind, intelligent, and thoughtful sort of person."

Her chest warmed, and she squirmed beneath her quilt. "Thank you."

"My question is this: Why would someone with so much to offer seek out a man who could never return her affections?"

It was a question Kitty didn't even like to ask herself, and her spine tingled in warning. But she saw no reason to withhold the truth from him. "Your question presupposes that I am looking for a rake."

"Aren't you?"

"As it happens, yes." She tossed her hair over her shoulder and raised her chin. "But I have no wish for him to fall in love with me."

He stared at her, incredulous. "Why not?"

Why, indeed? It took every ounce of restraint Kitty possessed to resist the urge to flee the cave and the conversation. "Because," she said, choosing her words carefully, "I do not wish for a love match. I can see that marriage would afford me a greater degree of freedom. And I should very much like to have children someday. But I am not looking for a love for the ages. I want someone who does not pretend to be anything other than who he is. Someone who does not make promises he can't keep. Someone who is charming, witty, and amusing, and who does not interfere with my plans for a career or my dreams."

"And you think that a rake is just that sort of person?"

She nodded slowly. "There's no chance that a rake will fall in love with me and no chance that I would fall in love with him . . . which is why he's the perfect candidate."

His gaze snapped to hers. "You have someone in mind?"

"Not yet," she said, shaking her head. "But I have my eyes open. I feel certain I shall find the right one soon."

"I find it hard to believe that your uncle and your friends approve of this plan," he muttered.

"They don't know," she said, lacing her words with warning. "Besides, they wouldn't understand. They're different from me." They had suffered loss, too, but not in quite the same way. They weren't constantly left behind. Abandoned. Alone.

"Yes, but they care about you. They'd want better for you."

Kitty gazed out at the ocean. Leo was right—her friends *would* want better for her. She'd once dreamed of more, too. But she'd set aside those childish fantasies. Part of becoming an adult involved adjusting one's worldview so that it aligned with reality.

And her reality was that everyone she cared about eventually left.

She didn't blame them. Sometimes it simply couldn't be helped. Death took people away with chilling capriciousness and dreadful finality. But there were other circumstances, too. People moved to marry, to start families, to begin new careers. Sometimes they trotted off to London without so much as a goodbye or a note.

The only thing that was certain was that in the end, she had to rely on herself. And that's what she intended to do.

"Everyone else may *think* they know what's best for me," she said. "But the decision is ultimately mine. I will chart my own course."

"That much, I've never doubted," Leo said with a

thoughtful nod. "All in all, I'd say it's been an enlightening afternoon." He arched a questioning brow. "Would you agree?"

She pretended to ponder the question, but the truth was that her body was still buzzing from that brief but blissful taste of passion. "Enlightening is an apt description," she said at last.

"For my part," he replied smoothly, "I've learned that in order to be a respectable rake, I must live solely in the moment, thinking of nothing but satisfying every desire." The deep timbre of his voice sent an echo of pleasure shimmering through her. "Do you want to know what I desire right now?"

Her gaze dropped to his full lips. She shifted closer to him and prepared to let the quilt slip from her shoulders.

"Wine," he said decisively. "That is, wine and food."

While Kitty tamped down a twinge of disappointment, he sprang to his feet, retrieved the picnic basket, and began unpacking a mouth-watering selection of fruits, cheeses, nuts, and sandwiches. She hadn't realized till that moment quite how ravenous she was, and she eagerly sampled a bit of everything. Meanwhile, Leo uncorked a bottle of wine and poured a generous glass for each of them.

"A toast," he said, handing her a goblet. "To my transformation: from boring, dependable gentleman to daring, pleasure-seeking rake. Thanks to your guidance, I know exactly how I must proceed."

She raised her glass and smiled like a proud teacher. "I'm glad," she said, trying her best to sound convincing. Now that she saw the changes taking place in Leo—both outwardly and inwardly—she wasn't certain that she was entirely in favor of this new version of him.

And she hoped she wouldn't regret losing the man he'd been.

"By the way," he said, snapping her back to the conversation. "If you should find yourself in want of someone to . . . experiment with again, I'm more than happy to oblige."

She froze and met his gaze over the rim of her wine glass. "I shall keep that in mind."

Indeed, she suspected it might be quite difficult for her to think of anything else.

Chapter 14

No less than a half dozen different townspeople had popped into Leo's office the next morning in order to congratulate him on rescuing Lila's brother. The story had apparently been embellished as oft it was repeated, and Leo found himself clarifying a couple of points.

First, that he had not fought off a shark while pulling Liam to shore.

Second, that he had not saved Kitty as well. In truth, she had saved him.

It didn't matter how many times he reiterated that bit of information though . . . no one seemed inclined to believe him. Which only proved how much they underestimated Kitty—and the entirety of the fairer sex.

He stared across his desk at Kitty's cluttered workspace, wishing that she was perched on her stool. After all that had happened in Pirate's Cave yesterday, there was bound to be some awkwardness between them, but avoiding each other would only make matters worse. The best way to proceed was to go on as if nothing earth-shattering had happened.

Even though he'd dreamed of her all night long.

A movement outside the large picture window caught his eye, and his heart leapt.

But when the door swung open and the bell suspended from the ceiling trilled, a tall man wearing a bright plum jacket and waistcoat sauntered in.

He was a talented rival architect from London—and the last person Leo expected to see in Bellehaven.

"Victor Kirkham," Leo intoned, warily extending a hand. "To what do I owe the pleasure?"

The dark-haired man gave his hand a curt shake, then strode farther into the office, craning his neck to look around. "Good to see you, too, Lockland. You've got great light in here," he remarked with practiced casualness.

"I can't complain." Leo crossed his arms, taking the other man's measure. They'd been on friendly enough terms before Leo moved home. The second son of an earl, Kirkham had attended the best schools and moved in the most elite circles. But he was a skilled architect, and Leo respected that.

Kirkham propped his hands on his hips and stared out the front window where puffy white clouds sailed across a sea of blue. "The view offers plenty of inspiration."

Leo arched a brow. "Was there a shortage of inspiration in London?"

Kirkham chuckled and stroked the cleft in his chin. "Just taking a well-deserved holiday, old chap. Staying at a quaint establishment . . . the Bluffs' Brew Inn, is it?"

"Best lodgings in Bellehaven." Leo walked back to his desk, sat, and twirled a pencil in his fingers. "I take it you're planning to stay and attend the regatta like the rest of England?"

Kirkham shrugged. "Seems only polite to participate in the local customs . . . and competitions," he added meaningfully.

Shit. "What sort of competitions?" Leo asked—though he suspected he already knew the answer.

"The design contest, of course."

"Why waste time on a contest entry? Your practice already has more clients than you can handle."

"Ah, but the practice isn't mine—yet. I work for my uncle, and he's rather peeved with me at the moment due to an unfortunate incident."

"Related to work?"

Kirkham winced. "Tangentially. I was discovered in a somewhat compromising position with the daughter of our biggest client, who happens to be engaged to my cousin."

"Good God, Kirkham."

"My uncle was less than pleased, as you can imagine. He sent me here to keep me away from Town during the happy couple's nuptials. And he told me that if I don't win the design contest, I shouldn't bother returning to the practice." Kirkham glanced up at Leo. "I assume you're entering?"

"I am," he said impulsively. As much as he disliked the thought of competing against Kitty, he couldn't let Kirkham waltz into Bellehaven thinking the contest would be an easy win. Besides, his grandfather seemed eager for him to enter, and Leo hated the thought of disappointing him.

"I'd love to take a look at your design," Kirkham drawled.

"I'm sure you would."

"I knew this would be fun," Kirkham said with a grin. "There's nothing like a worthy adversary to stoke the competitive fires."

"True," Leo said. "You might be surprised at how competitive the field is."

"That's what I like to hear." He approached Kitty's desk, cast a curious eye at her trinkets, and reached for her chipped teacup.

"Don't," Leo warned, stopping him dead in his tracks.

Kirkham held up his palm as if he'd meant no offense. "I actually came to ask a favor."

Leo arched a questioning brow.

"I need a place to work for the next couple of weeks. It looks like you have plenty of space here," he said, gesturing toward Leo's grandfather's desk.

"You can't work there," Leo said, adamant. He pinched the bridge of his nose, suspecting he'd live to regret his next words. "But I suppose you can use my desk. I'll use my grandfather's for the time being."

Kirkham gave Leo a grateful slap on the shoulder. "Good man. I'm happy to pay a fee for the use of the facilities."

Leo waved away the offer. "You can buy me a few drinks at the Salty Mermaid."

"Consider it done."

They shook hands again, and Leo began moving his tools and basket of projects to his grandfather's desk at the front of the shop.

Kirkham tested out Leo's stool and lifted his chin toward the cluttered desk across from him. "Who sits there?"

Just as Leo opened his mouth to answer, Kitty burst through the door and drew up short. Her gown was the soft pink hue of a conch shell, and the tails of her silky white sash fluttered behind her like streamers. Her gaze flicked to Kirkham, then to Leo, expectant.

"Miss Beckett," he said reluctantly, "allow me to introduce Mr. Victor Kirkham, a fellow architect from London."

Kirkham quickly stood and made a gallant bow.

"A pleasure, sir," she said with a gracious tilt of her head.

Kirkham's eyes lit up as if he were a child in a sweet shop. "I assure you, the pleasure is all mine, Miss Beckett."

Kitty cast a surreptitious look at Leo, and though it may have been wishful thinking on his part, it seemed her cheeks flushed as she walked by him.

"Forgive me for being forward, Mr. Kirkham," she said rather unapologetically, "but why were you sitting at Leo's desk?"

Kirkham's mouth curled into a wicked grin—as if he couldn't have been more delighted to discover that Kitty was not only beautiful, but feisty as well.

Leo began to think that this arrangement was ill-advised at best.

"I'm staying in Bellehaven Bay for the next few weeks," Kirkham answered. "I intend to enter the architectural design contest. Perhaps you've heard about it?"

Kitty arched a brow. Leo *almost* felt sorry for poor old Kirkham. "I am quite aware of the contest," she said smoothly, depositing her reticule on her desk. "As it happens, I intend to win it."

For several beats, Kirkham merely gaped at her. To his credit, he recovered faster than most men would have. "Consider me duly impressed, Miss Beckett."

"I've given you no reason to be impressed—yet. But I do believe that my work will speak for itself."

Leo decided to take pity on Kirkham and fill in a few details. "Miss Beckett and I both learned the trade from my grandfather. We were apprentices at the same time."

Kirkham propped an elbow on the corner of Leo's desk and nodded thoughtfully. "I begin to understand why you were eager to return to Bellehaven, Lockland."

It was merely an idle observation and, moreover, an attempt to flatter Kitty. But Kirkham's patronizing tone rubbed Leo the wrong way. "You should not presume to understand anything about me or my relationship with Miss Beckett."

It was Kirkham's turn to arch a brow. "Forgive me," he said dryly. "I did not mean to give offense."

Kitty rolled her eyes as if she found the entire exchange tiresome. To Kirkham, she said, "If you are going to be working at Leo's desk, please kindly refrain from touching anything on mine."

Kirkham chuckled again. "I wouldn't dream of it."

"Then I don't anticipate we shall have any problems," Kitty replied, opening her sketchbook. She picked up a pencil and briefly closed her eyes as if another thought had just occurred to her. "You don't talk excessively, do you?"

"I shall endeavor to keep my tongue-wagging in check, Miss Beckett."

"Excellent."

Leo sat at his grandfather's desk and ran a finger over his engraved nameplate before tucking it into the top drawer for safekeeping. He was already kicking himself for putting Kirkham in such close proximity to Kitty. While he might have looked the part of a gentleman, he was always skating on the edge of impropriety. Pushing the limits of good behavior just as far as he could without getting himself banned from polite society.

Leo didn't doubt that Kitty could hold her own against Kirkham—or anyone.

But he did worry that Kirkham might be precisely the sort of man Kitty was looking for.

He was pondering what that could mean for Kitty and him, especially given the recent intriguing developments in their relationship, when the front door opened again.

"There is the man of the hour!" Lady Rufflebum bustled

into the office, followed by her faithful companion, Miss Whitford. The countess clasped her hands together and beamed at Leo. "By now, all of Bellehaven has learned of your heroics, but I simply had to come and express my thanks in person."

"It wasn't only me," Leo demurred. "Miss Beckett was instrumental in saving Liam, too."

"Good heavens," the countess exclaimed. "The story grows more interesting by the minute."

Kitty waved a hand. "Leo is the one who risked life and limb to save the lad. I merely helped pull him to shore at the end."

"Regardless of the details, I feel that this is cause for celebration." Her gaze flicked to Kirkham, who stood, awaiting an introduction.

Leo obliged. "Lady Rufflebum, Miss Whitford, this is Mr. Victor Kirkham, an architect from London. He's staying in Bellehaven for a few weeks while he works on an entry for the design contest."

"How wonderful," the countess said, preening. "I told the mayor that the contest would encourage more tourists to visit our town—and you have proven me correct. For that reason alone, I am already fond of you, Mr. Kirkham."

"I am gratified to know that I'm in your good graces," Kirkham said smoothly, "and I shall do my utmost to stay there."

"It's not so very difficult," Lady Rufflebum said with a girlish titter. "In fact, you may begin on the right foot by making an appearance at my croquet tournament tomorrow. I shall have an opportunity to introduce you to all of Bellehaven's most esteemed residents. And, of course, we will raise a glass in honor of Mr. Lockland and Miss Beckett, who managed to save a young boy from the clutches of a stormy sea." She turned to her companion and whispered, "That sounded quite good, did it not? We must write it down when we return home so I can use it during the toast tomorrow."

Leo winced. "It's very kind of you to host a gathering, but there's no need to make a fuss on my account. In fact, I'd prefer it if we simply moved on from the incident. Everything ended well—that's all that matters."

The countess gaped at him as though he'd suggested that she set her wig on fire.

Kitty clucked her tongue. "Leo, you mustn't be so humble. The countess wishes to honor you with a party, and it won't kill you to be in the spotlight for a few minutes. Besides," she added meaningfully, "a celebratory gathering could be the perfect opportunity to further your campaign."

Kirkham narrowed his eyes. "What sort of campaign?"

Sweet Jesus. "Never mind," Leo said quickly. To Lady Rufflebum, he said, "I appreciate your generous offer and will, of course, be delighted to attend."

"That's more like it," the countess said, obviously pleased that natural order had been restored. Her eyes flicked over his waistcoat—one that Kitty and Clara had picked out for him. "There's something different about you lately," she mused. "I can't quite put my finger on precisely what it is, but I daresay you'll turn some heads now that you're back in Bellehaven."

Kitty's mouth curled into a smug smile. Kirkham looked away as if he were trying valiantly not to burst into laughter. Leo wanted to crawl beneath his grandfather's desk, but instead he made a polite bow in Lady Rufflebum's direction.

"This summer is proving to be even more entertaining

than the last," she said with relish. Waving a hand at her companion, the countess added, "Come, Maude. There's much to be done before tomorrow's festivities."

Leo waited until the ladies had departed and the door closed behind them. Turning to Kirkham, he said, "I imagine there's much you wish to say right now."

"Oh, there is."

"Have a care," Leo warned. "Or you might end up drafting your contest entry on the bar at the Salty Mermaid."

"Understood." Kirkham shot Kitty a conspiratorial grin, which only added to Leo's misery.

After what had transpired in the cave between Kitty and him, he'd hoped she'd give up her quest for a rake. At the very least, he'd thought she might look at him differently. That she'd realize they could be more than rivals. More than friends.

But she seemed more determined than ever to help him win the heart of another woman.

To make matters worse, Kirkham had a gleam in his eyes that worried Leo.

Maybe it was time he told her about his feelings.

Before it was too late.

Chapter 15

"You didn't have to come with me today," Kitty said to her uncle. She sat opposite him in the coach as he bounced a knee and looked out a window distractedly. "I know you're worried about Hazel."

Blade's gaze snapped to hers, and he winced guiltily. "Forgive me. I confess I was concerned when she said she wasn't feeling well this morning, but she assured me it's quite normal. She wouldn't fib about that, would she?" he asked, his expression anxious.

"No," Kitty said. "She wouldn't."

He exhaled and managed a smile. "In any event, I promise to be a better escort from here on out. Hazel truly wants you to enjoy yourself at the croquet match—probably so that you can tell her all about the afternoon in excruciating detail when we return home. And I . . . well, I am sorry we haven't spent more time together lately."

"I am, too. But I understand," she said. Blade had been busy overseeing construction on their new house and Hazel's school, and other business often called him back to London as well. "You aren't the only one to blame. I've been spending quite a bit of time at Mr. Sandford's office," she admitted.

In truth, she'd spent many hours with Leo *outside* of

the office. Sparring with him on the beach. Kissing in his apartment. Stripping off her clothes in Pirate's Cave. Her cheeks heated at the thought.

"Well, I've missed you," Uncle Beck said soberly, but then his eyes twinkled. "I even miss the way you used to nick the brandy from my study. At least then we had reason to talk."

"You mean you had reason to shout at me. But I've turned dreadfully boring of late, dear uncle," she teased. "Or perhaps I've simply become more skilled at avoiding being caught."

Blade chuckled, and Kitty relished the rich sound. No one could make him laugh quite like she could. "True. Tell me what mischief you've been up to," he said.

She batted her eyes innocently. If Blade had even an inkling of what she'd been doing with Leo, he'd lock her in a tower and find a fire-breathing dragon to guard it. "No mischief," she said breezily. "I've turned over a new leaf. I'm the picture of industriousness now, devoting all my time and energy to a pair of projects."

He arched a dark brow. "What projects might those be?"

"My contest entry, for one. Don't tell anyone, but I'm designing a theater." She closed her eyes for a moment and imagined the lines and curves and colors in her sketchbook, all blending together in perfect harmony. "I've never undertaken anything quite like it. But if I can manage to convey the vision in my head, I think I could win."

"I know you can," Blade said proudly. "You're one of the most talented people I know, Kitty. And I don't even need to see your drawings to know your theater would be the jewel of Bellehaven Bay."

She shot him a grateful smile. "I expect the competition to be fierce. One of Leo's colleagues from London arrived in town yesterday. He plans to enter, too."

"You can hold your own against anyone," Blade said with a shrug. "Just remember that."

"I shall try."

"What's your other project?" he asked.

Kitty blinked. "Hmm?"

"You mentioned that you had a couple of projects."

Right. But she couldn't very well mention that she was teaching Leo to be a proper rake. "The other one is more personal in nature. I'm helping a friend achieve a rather ambitious goal."

"How philanthropic of you," Blade said dryly.

Kitty glanced out the window at the brilliant blue sky. "You know me too well."

"If there's one thing I know, it's that you'll do anything you set your mind to. I believe in you."

It was a lovely sentiment, and he'd said it with such conviction that she couldn't doubt it. But it wasn't quite the message she longed to hear.

"What if I *do* fail spectacularly?" she asked. "What then?" She wanted him to say that it didn't matter a whit to him. That he and Hazel would always be there for her no matter how many cute babies they had. No matter how many orphans they took in. No matter how awfully she disappointed them.

"You won't fail." He reached across the coach, took her hand, and sandwiched it firmly between his. "You, Kitty Beckett, are a survivor. You've endured more adversity in your lifetime than anyone should have to. It's made you stronger than you know."

She swallowed the lump in her throat. The truth was that she was weary of being strong. All she wanted was to lean on someone else for a while and know that they wouldn't go away. That they wouldn't leave her alone in this unpredictable, chaotic world.

If she asked Blade to make her that promise, she had no doubt he would. But even if she swallowed her pride and begged for that assurance, it wasn't quite the same as him offering it of his own accord. And after he'd just waxed on about how strong she was, she couldn't bring herself to look so pathetic and needy.

"In fact," Blade added tentatively, "I was hoping to ask you a favor."

Kitty summoned her courage and smiled. "Go on."

"After today's party, I'm heading to London for a week or so. I hate to leave Hazel when she's not feeling well, but it can't be helped. I wondered if you'd keep a close eye on her and summon me if you have any concerns about her or the baby."

"Of course," she said, giving his knee an affectionate pat. "I will keep her company while you're gone. And before you ask—yes, I'll make certain that she doesn't over-tax herself."

"Thank you." He smiled, his eyes conveying a mix of warmth and pride that hit her with a startling punch of sadness.

Because it was precisely how her father had looked at her when she was a girl.

Even though Blade didn't closely resemble her father, there were certain times—like just then—when the similarities in their expressions were uncanny. And it always sparked a sharp, unexpected pang in her heart.

Blade frowned. "You look a little pale. Are you feeling well?"

"Perfectly fine," she said with a scoff. If there was one thing that she'd learned over the years, it was that if she could convince others that she was fine, she could some-times convince herself. At least for a while.

"There's something else I wanted to discuss before we

arrive at Lady Rufflebum's," he said pointedly, raising the hairs on the backs of her arms.

"That sounds rather ominous."

"Not at all," he said with a chuckle. "But as your uncle and guardian—as someone who cares about you—I feel obliged to ask whether you still intend to marry."

Kitty swallowed. She'd known this conversation was inevitable. "Clever of you to ask while we're in a moving coach. I can't very well fling myself out the window."

"I'm not giving you an ultimatum, if that's what you're worried about," Blade said. "You'll come into your inheritance at the end of the summer, and you'll have the means to live your life however you wish. But it's something you should consider before . . ." His voice trailed off.

"Before I'm on the shelf?" she provided.

"Before your options become more limited," he clarified.

She arched a brow at that. "I've always wanted children, so yes, I do intend to marry."

Blade exhaled as if he were preparing to vault over another daunting hurdle. "And is there a certain gentleman you have in mind?"

"There is a certain *sort* of gentleman," she said. "Someone who is not overly sentimental and who does not pretend to be anything he is not. Someone who respects my work and will not interfere with my pursuit of a career."

"That's it?" Blade asked, incredulous.

Kitty ran through the checklist in her head. "Those are the most important qualities, although I should also prefer it if he were good-looking and amusing company. Perhaps a bit of a rake."

Blade scratched his head. "You didn't mention anything about love."

No, she had not. And the omission was quite intentional.

She hesitated and prepared herself for the well-intentioned advice which was, no doubt, in store for her. "I hope you're not terribly disappointed," she said soberly. "I've realized I'm not destined for a love like Hazel's and yours or like Poppy's and Keane's. I don't need to be swept off my feet. In fact, I would rather not be. A marriage of convenience would suit me very well, and I'd be perfectly content if my future husband and I lived separate lives."

Blade frowned. "Have you spoken to Hazel about this?"

"Not in any detail," she replied, gratified to see that they'd finally turned into Lady Rufflebum's drive.

"I think you should," he urged. "I am not going to attempt to tell you how to live your life. I've known you long enough to realize the futility in that. But I do think you deserve more, Kitty, and I'm certain Hazel would agree."

"Ah, look," she said, as the carriage rolled to a stop. "We've arrived at last."

Blade grunted. "This conversation isn't over."

Perhaps not, but Kitty intended to avoid it for as long as possible.

She and Blade alighted the coach and made their way around the back of the countess's sprawling house. Beyond the terrace, clusters of ladies in pastel gowns and gentlemen in brightly colored waistcoats dotted the vast lawn. A large white tent near the lake was adorned with yards of daffodil-yellow bunting, and the croquet hoops and pegs were planted in the ground nearby at perfectly spaced intervals. A trio of minstrels wandered through the crowd playing lively music.

"Lady Rufflebum doesn't do anything on a small scale, does she?" Blade murmured.

"Apparently not." Kitty spotted Lila mingling with a group of young women near the tent and seized the opportunity to escape her uncle's watchful eye. "I see some friends just down the hill. Would you excuse me?"

He rubbed the back of his neck and cracked a smile. "Enjoy yourself, Kitty. I'm going to pay my respects to the countess and locate a brandy. Not necessarily in that order."

She gave him an impulsive, fierce hug before flitting across the lawn toward Lila.

"Kitty!" The redheaded young woman exclaimed, waving enthusiastically. She held a clipboard in one hand and a pencil in the other. "I'm so delighted you're here. You must allow me to sign you up for the tournament."

"Certainly," Kitty said, taking a peek at the brackets on Lila's paper. "You are at liberty to write down my name wherever you like."

Lila's forehead creased. "Well, it's not quite that simple. You must have a partner."

Kitty shrugged. "Would you like to be my partner? I'm not a master of the sport by any means, but I think I can hold my own."

Lila shook her head, her expression one part regret and one part delight. "Lady Rufflebum has decreed that all the pairs must consist of one lady and one gentleman."

"Of course she has," Kitty said with a groan.

Lila leaned forward. "I'm partnering with Leo Lockland," she said in a conspiratorial whisper, "though I'm not certain he was enthused at the prospect."

"That's just Leo," Kitty said, rolling her eyes demonstratively. "He's rarely enthused about anything unless it involves complex calculations. Perhaps if you pressed him to keep score?"

Lila grinned. "I shall do that. In the meantime, we must find a partner for you."

"I may be able to prevail upon my uncle," Kitty said with a shrug.

"I was rather hoping you'd allow me to be of service," a smooth, masculine voice interjected.

Kitty whirled around to find Victor Kirkham standing behind her, shamelessly flashing the dimple in his chin. "Mr. Kirkham," she said. "I see you've made good on your promise to Lady Rufflebum."

"I do my utmost to avoid disappointing ladies whenever I can, Miss Beckett," he said with a gallant bow.

"Lila, allow me to introduce Mr. Victor Kirkham, who worked with Leo in London. Mr. Kirkham, this is Miss Lila Bardsley."

"A pleasure," Mr. Kirkham crooned.

"How perfect," Lila said, scribbling on her clipboard. "I shall list your names in the bracket opposite Leo and me so that we play each other. It's bound to be an exhilarating match."

"May the best couple win," Kirkham said, raising his glass in a mock toast.

"Couple?" Leo strode up to their trio and scowled. "I believe the correct characterization is *partners.*"

"Right, old chap," Kirkham said in a slightly patronizing tone. "That's what I meant."

Leo nodded as if mollified—for now. He wore the moss-green waistcoat that made his eyes glow, but he was terribly disheveled, at least by normal Leo standards.

Perhaps he had been paying more attention during her rake lessons than she'd initially given him credit for, because he certainly looked the part today. Dark circles ringed his eyes and a full day's worth of stubble covered his jaw. His hair was thoroughly tousled—as if he'd driven to the party on a curricle at breakneck speed. His cravat appeared to have been hastily tied, raising all sorts of questions in Kitty's mind.

But she quickly shoved them out.

Despite his disheveled state—or perhaps because of it—there was no denying the attraction she felt toward Leo.

Indeed, it had been difficult to stop thinking about him and the time they'd spent in the cave. She supposed it was only normal. After all, it was the first time she'd ever experienced such intense physical sensations.

Tingling skin.

Wobbly knees.

Sweet pulsing.

Every aspect of their encounter had been eye-opening and thrilling. For her.

But it wasn't the same for Leo. He'd presumably done all those things before with other women and was capable of engaging in a dalliance without thinking about it incessantly. Without wanting to do it again.

"The four of us will play after the current group finishes," Lila said in an official-sounding voice. "If you'd like to practice a bit beforehand, there are a few extra mallets and balls on the other side of the tent."

"What do you say, Miss Beckett?" Mr. Kirkham asked, arching a brow. "Shall we perfect our swings and strategize?"

Kitty tried valiantly to drum up a bit of enthusiasm. "Perhaps we should. The last time I played croquet I was still wearing braids."

He offered his arm, and she placed her hand in the crook of his elbow.

"Strategizing for a friendly croquet match?" Leo scoffed. "Seems a bit excessive."

Kitty blinked, wondering why Leo was particularly ornery today. "There's no harm in being prepared. I happen to know you pride yourself on being prepared for every eventuality."

He frowned. "That's ridiculous."

"You don't go anywhere without your straightedge," she pointed out.

"*That* is different." He scowled again and patted the chest of his jacket. "Besides, I don't have it with me today."

"A circumstance that could prove disastrous," she teased, clucking her tongue. "What if you need to calculate the optimal angle in order to hit the ball through a hoop?"

"I'll manage," he shot back. His gaze flicked to the spot where she rested her hand on Mr. Kirkham's sleeve before he turned to Lila. "I'm going to find a drink," he grumbled. "I'll be back before the start of our match."

"Very well," Lila called after him, looking mildly confused. "It won't be long!"

Mr. Kirkham chuckled as he escorted Kitty toward the practice area. "Oh, I almost forgot." He reached inside his breast pocket and produced a slightly wilted sweet pea flower. "This is for you."

Kitty lifted the pink and purple blooms to her nose and inhaled. "How thoughtful."

"It's just the start," he said meaningfully, "of my campaign to win you over."

She cast him a sidelong glance. "Are you always so forthright?"

"No," he admitted. "But you would have figured it out either way. Perhaps you already had."

She nodded, keeping her face impassive. "I don't mean to sound ungrateful, and I appreciate a romantic gesture as much as anyone."

"But?" he probed.

"But I am not looking for a gentleman to sweep me off my feet."

He pursed his lips and stared at the ground, contemplative. When they arrived at the practice area where several mallets rested on a table beside a basket of balls, he turned to face her. "What *are* you looking for, Miss Beckett?"

She rolled the stem of the sweet pea between her thumb and forefinger. "I suppose I could tell you, but what would be the fun in that?"

He chuckled, and she hastily pinned the flower in her hair before accepting the mallet he offered. She selected a yellow ball from the basket, tossed it into the air, and let it land in her palm with a satisfying slap.

"There is one little-known fact about me that I shall voluntarily divulge," she said. "Only because it's particularly relevant at this juncture."

"Do tell." His eyes gleamed with anticipation, and he leaned a shoulder close to hers.

"I like to win," she said earnestly.

She hadn't felt particularly competitive when they arrived, but after her brief exchange with Leo, she wanted to win more than anything. She had the devilish urge to drive his ball into the next county.

"Have no fear." Mr. Kirkham picked up a mallet and took an impressive practice swing at an imaginary ball in the vicinity of his feet. "Victory shall be ours."

Chapter 16

Leo was not entirely certain how his croquet ball had ended up miles away from the hoop he'd been aiming for. All he knew was that every time he'd hit his ball today, it went considerably farther than he'd intended.

He seemed to have an excess of pent-up energy that manifested itself as he swung his mallet and whacked the ball without any finesse whatsoever.

And that energy centered around Kitty.

Since the day they'd spent in Pirate's Cave, he'd been waiting for an opportunity to finally tell her how he felt, but it seemed like Kirkham was always in the way, seizing on the chance to flirt with her whenever he could and tossing out compliments like chicken feed. *You look ravishing in that bonnet, Miss Beckett. You're pretty as a rose in that pink gown, Miss Beckett. Your smile lights up the whole office, Miss Beckett.*

Sometimes, it was all Leo could do to keep from grunting in disgust. And as if that wasn't bad enough, yesterday afternoon Kirkham had left a blueberry tart from the tea shop on her desk.

As Kitty bit into it, she'd closed her eyes like she was in ecstasy.

Kirkham had grinned smugly.

And Leo had kicked himself for not making that sort of gesture first.

He'd thought he might be able to whisk Kitty away from the crowd for a short time today—at least long enough to reveal how he felt. But the moment he'd arrived at Lady Rufflebum's, Lila had insisted he partner with her, and now Kirkham was leaning close to Kitty, whispering in her ear.

"It's your turn, Mr. Kirkham," Lila called.

He lingered near Kitty a few seconds more before sauntering toward his ball and hitting it with infuriating precision. It rolled through a hoop and stopped in the optimal location for his next shot, which he proceeded to take, setting himself up perfectly for his next turn.

"That is how it's done, Lockland," Kirkham taunted. "Don't fret. You'll get the hang of it eventually."

Leo snorted and watched as the play continued. He tried to be a good partner to Lila, making polite conversation and offering the occasional word of encouragement. But he was undeniably distracted by Kitty.

She looked effervescent in a light, airy gown that seemed to float around her legs when she walked. Several bouncy golden curls hung in front of her shoulder, reminding him of how it had felt when he'd run his fingers through her hair and held her in his arms.

She'd been soft then, with a dreamy look in her eyes—as if she was drunk on pleasure.

But today she had a different temperament altogether. Her brows were knitted, her lips straight, and her expression serious. Odd as it seemed, he found this determined, driven version of her equally mesmerizing.

She stood to one side of her ball, aligned the head of the mallet behind it, and hit it with a blow so forceful that it sailed across the lawn as if it had been fired out of a cannon—directly toward him.

He jumped out of its path just in time. Muffled a curse as her yellow ball thudded on the ground and continued rolling, inch by relentless inch. Watched with horror as it approached his black ball and hit it with a menacing *click*.

Damn.

She propped her mallet on her shoulder and strolled toward him, a triumphant smile on her face. When she reached him, she glanced down at their kissing balls, then met his gaze. "Whoops."

"We both know that wasn't an accident," he said dryly.

She bent over and moved her ball, preparing to drive his even farther off course. "All's fair in love and croquet."

"If you hit my ball into the lake, you could end up hitting your own in, too."

"That's a risk I'm willing to take," she said, surveying the lawn as if this were serious business.

Since reason was getting him nowhere, Leo decided to try another tack. Perhaps it was time to put his rake lessons into practice. "You look pretty today," he murmured.

She fumbled her mallet and blinked at him, annoyed. "What are you doing?"

"I like the way your gown dips low there." He let his eyes linger on the delicate lace trim at her neckline. Watched the rapid rise and fall of her chest. Listened to the hitch of her breath. "It reminds me of Pirate's Cave," he added smoothly. "And the things we did."

"I see precisely what you're trying to do, and it's not going to work." She tossed her hair over her shoulder in the same way she always had, unintentionally confirming that his tactic *was*, in fact, working. Encouraged, he redoubled his efforts.

"I like the flowers in your hair, too," he said softly. "They make me think of you lying in a field of soft, fragrant blossoms, just like those."

A flush stole over her cheeks and she frowned at the head of her mallet. "This is neither the time nor place to practice your rakish banter—which, I feel compelled to inform you, still requires a considerable amount of work."

"You were the one who decreed that rakishness had to become second nature. Besides, any self-respecting rogue needs to master the art of innuendo."

"Fine," she said, clearly exasperated. "We'll plan a lesson—later."

He moved closer and touched the sprig of flowers at her temple. "Did you know that the pale pink of these petals is the same exact shade as—"

"Leo!" she interjected, clearly flustered.

"If I didn't know better," Kirkham called out as he strode toward them, "I'd think you were trying to disarm my partner."

Leo shrugged, pretending innocence. "I wouldn't dream of it," he shouted back.

"Now look what you've done," Kitty muttered as Kirkham approached.

He shot a suspicious look at Leo and turned to Kitty. "I assume he was begging you to have mercy on him?"

"You needn't worry," she replied. "I can be ruthless when necessary."

"That, she can," Leo confirmed.

"I'll consider myself warned," Kirkham said with a grin. "Between the three of us, the design contest is sure to be interesting."

"The *three* of us?" Kitty repeated, arching a brow in question.

Bloody hell. Leo rubbed the back of his neck and opened his mouth to explain, but Kirkham beat him to the punch.

"Didn't Leo mention it? I assumed you were aware . . . he's entering the contest, too."

Kitty blinked slowly and glared at Leo. "Is he?"

"I decided to throw my hat into the ring—as you urged me to," he added as a reminder.

"Goodness. I believe that's the first time you've ever heeded my advice," she said dryly.

"That's not true," Leo countered. He'd listened to all her guidance, at least on becoming a rake.

She glanced at him and Kirkham. "You gentlemen might want to stand back."

They scarcely had time to move out of the way before she took a vigorous swing at her ball, which collided with Leo's and sent it flying into the lake with a dismal *plop*.

Leo cursed under his breath. Kirkham let out a long, slow whistle. Kitty exhaled, and her satisfied expression held not a hint of remorse.

She walked to her ball which had stopped a few yards away from the water's edge and lifted her chin toward the ripples on the lake's surface. "According to the rules, you're permitted to return your ball to the course."

"If you can find it," Kirkham added.

Leo trudged to the muddy shoreline and peered into the murky water.

Meanwhile, Lila scurried across the lawn to join them. "Oh dear," she said as she approached Leo. "I'm afraid we don't have many extra balls. Do you think you'll be able to fish it out?"

"Yes," he said, raking a hand through his hair. But it wasn't going to be easy. The way he saw it, he had two options for retrieving his ball. First, he could wade into the thigh-deep water, which would leave his boots water-logged and three-fourths of his clothing soaked. Alternatively, he could lie down in the mud on his stomach and use the head of his mallet to pull the ball out, which would ruin a new, expensive waistcoat.

Neither option was particularly appealing, but he could feel Kitty's eyes on him, waiting to see how he'd handle the situation. And that's when everything became clear.

He had to ask himself what a rake would do.

If there was one thing he'd learned from Kitty's lessons, it was that substance wasn't nearly as important as style, and even a potentially humiliating scenario like this one presented an opportunity to turn on the charm.

So he smiled as if he didn't have a care in the world as he proceeded to methodically unbutton his jacket and shrug it off.

Lila eagerly held out a hand. "Oh, I can hold that for you."

Kitty sniffed and pursed her lips as he casually walked past her and strode through the reeds right into the cold lake.

He ignored the mud squishing beneath his bootheels. Pretended not to notice the water pouring into the tops of his boots. Didn't flinch as he plunged an arm into the cloudy depths and felt around for his croquet ball.

When he found it, he grasped it in his palm, stood, and marched out of the lake as if soggy boots and drenched clothes didn't bother him in the slightest.

Lila began clapping in appreciation, and a couple dozen onlookers followed suit. With a sly grin, he tossed the ball in the air, caught it behind his back, and made a self-deprecating bow, sparking a fresh wave of applause.

"Good show, Lockland," Kirkham said with a chuckle.

"Bravo!" cried Lila.

Kitty rolled her eyes. "Can we finally proceed with the match? I still need to take my extra shot."

Leo scooped up his mallet and propped one end on the ground like it was a cane. "By all means," he said, moving his arm in a sweeping gesture. "Please do."

"I'm going to see if I can fetch you a towel," Lila said, still holding his jacket as she fled toward the tent.

Kirkham tipped his hat at Kitty, turned, and strolled toward his ball.

Kitty glared at her own ball and prepared to hit it toward the next hoop.

Leo's trousers were dripping, his feet were submerged in water, and he now had no shot at winning, but it didn't matter. He'd gotten under her skin.

He stood a short distance away as she lined up her shot. "I'd hoped we could talk today," he said.

"About what?" She pulled back to swing her mallet.

"About . . . us," he said.

She shanked the ball instead of hitting it squarely, and it skipped along the ground a fraction of the distance it should have.

"Blast," she muttered, then met his gaze. "There. I had an awful turn. I suppose you're happy now."

"No," he said earnestly. "Not as long as you're angry with me."

She exhaled as if she were praying for patience. "I'm not angry with you for entering the contest. I'm disappointed you kept it from me."

"I can explain," he said.

"Not now," she said firmly. "Everyone—including my uncle—is watching us."

"When then?" he asked.

"You're the rake," she said with a shrug of her shoulders. "You figure it out."

Chapter 17

The news that Leo had decided to enter the design contest had come as a shock to Kitty. If she'd heard it from him instead of Kirkham, she wouldn't have felt so blindsided. But now that she'd come to terms with it, she was glad to compete against Leo. Because it fueled her determination to win.

After she and Blade left the croquet tournament and returned home, she went directly to her bedchamber, plopped down at her desk, and pulled out her plans for the theater. She'd worked on them all evening, through dinner, and long past nightfall. A couple of hours ago, Hazel had knocked on her door to check on her, say goodnight, and urge her to go to bed.

But Kitty was still at her desk, sketching, refining, enhancing. Watching in wonder as her theater evolved from a two-dimensional drawing into a building that felt as real to her as the one she was sitting in. She could close her eyes and walk beneath the crystal chandeliers in the grand lobby. She could hear the musicians tuning their instruments in the orchestra pit. She could feel a frisson of excitement as the cerulean-blue velvet stage curtains parted, giving the audience a peek at the wonders that lay in—

Tap.

Kitty froze and cocked an ear toward the French doors at the rear of her room. The house was silent now, but she could have sworn she heard—

Tap, tap.

She drew in a sharp breath and turned down the lamp on her desk. Perhaps a gust of wind had picked up a twig and tossed it against the windowpanes, but the tapping seemed less random and more deliberate. It sounded like someone was outside her doors.

But that was impossible. During her teenage years she'd attended three boarding schools—and been expelled from two. She considered herself something of an expert on sneaking in and out of bedrooms, and she happened to know that despite the French doors, her current second-story bedchamber was *not* easily accessible.

The balcony beyond the doors consisted of a waist-high iron railing and was so narrow that it was purely decorative. There were no trees outside to climb, no bushes below to cushion a landing. And the smooth facade of the exterior wall was impossible to climb.

Tap, tap, tap.

Sweet Jesus. Someone was out there, concealed by heavy velvet drapes in front of the doors.

Heart pounding, she whirled around, scanning the room for a weapon. She grabbed a flimsy parasol first, then traded it for the heavy candlestick beside her bed. Girding herself, she took two steps toward the door.

But as she reached a hand toward the door handle, the skin between her shoulder blades tingled and she halted. This was madness.

She should run for help. Alert the household. Wake her uncle.

Her mind made up, she turned and headed for the bedroom door.

"It's me, Leo." His words were muffled by the glass panes and velvet drapes, but the voice was all too familiar. She exhaled and set down the candlestick.

"Please, let me in, Kitty."

She shoved aside the curtains and hauled open the door. "It's Kat," she said curtly.

"Apologies," he said with a devil-may-care grin. "Kat."

He was sitting on the iron railing, one arm braced against the wall of the house. His hair hung over one eye and his collar hung open with no waistcoat, jacket, or cravat in sight. A thick rope wrapped around one of the balustrades dangled to the ground below.

If the dictionary entry for rake had an illustration, surely it would look like Leo did in that precise moment.

Which proved either that she was an excellent tutor or that he was an apt pupil—or both.

Whatever the case may be, it seemed his transformation was complete, and that was cause for celebration.

Clearly, Leo didn't need her anymore.

She rubbed at the pang in her chest, not caring to examine the cause.

"You're going to break your neck," she said, as if it was a foregone conclusion.

He peered over his shoulder to the ground below and grimaced. "That is a distinct possibility—unless you invite me in."

"I'd prefer that you avoid serious injury until after you've reviewed my plans for the theater," she said blithely. "Come in."

He hopped lightly off the railing and strolled into her bedroom like the crown prince promenading through Hyde Park. "It's dark in here. I thought I saw a light earlier."

"I extinguished it just before I prepared to bash your

head with a candlestick," she said matter-of-factly. "What are you doing here, Leo?"

He walked to the tall footpost of her bed and leaned against it, looking far more tempting than she cared to admit. "I needed to talk with you," he said.

She turned up the lamp slightly, glided to the soft armchair near the dormant fireplace, and tucked her bare feet under her. "Surely it could have waited till tomorrow when we'll be in the office."

"I could have," he conceded, "but Kirkham is always around. Besides, you encouraged me to do what a rake would do."

Kitty nodded sagely. "It seems the student has become the master."

"Hardly. But I could tell you were cross with me, and I . . . I didn't like the feeling."

"After all the years we've spent sparring? I should think you'd be accustomed to it."

"Maybe I should be," he said earnestly. "But the circumstances are a little different now."

Much as she hated to admit it, Leo was right. Their relationship *had* changed. They couldn't fairly be classified as enemies, friends, *or* lovers.

Perhaps they were all three.

All she knew is that it was considerably more complicated than it had been at the start of the summer.

"I wasn't upset about your decision to enter the design contest," she said simply. "But I didn't like finding out from Kirkham, especially after I've shared everything with you about my plans. Why couldn't you have just been forthright with me?"

He walked closer, lowered himself onto a footstool opposite her chair, and propped his elbows on his knees. His shirtsleeves were rolled to his elbows, and her gaze strayed to the sinewy muscles of his forearms.

"Kirkham goaded me into entering," he explained earnestly, "but the second I told him I would, I realized that I truly wanted to. Partly for my grandfather's sake but also for my own. I felt an excitement, a drive, that I haven't felt in my work for quite a long time."

"That's good," Kitty said, meaning it. His participation would undoubtedly decrease her chances of winning, but she still liked her odds. Especially after the work she'd done on her theater drawings that evening.

"I didn't have the chance to tell you before the croquet match, and I wasn't certain how you'd feel about it. I know how important the contest is to you."

"I've already told you that I don't want to win by default. Perhaps I'll rue the day I said this, but I want to compete against the best—and prove that I can come out on top."

"You can." His hazel eyes were dark, his expression serious.

Blade had offered similar encouragement, but as her uncle and guardian, he was almost obliged to spout such things. Leo wasn't, and he'd spoken the words with such conviction that warmth bloomed in her chest.

"Am I forgiven?" he asked, hesitant.

"I can't very well hold a grudge after you risked life and limb to come here and explain, so yes—I forgive you. But I need to be able to trust you. Please don't keep any more secrets from me."

For several heartbeats, he said nothing. Then he swallowed and met her gaze, his face sober. "I won't."

"Good." She went to the chest at the foot of her bed, opened the heavy lid, and dug through layers of linens until she located her silver flask. She returned to her chair, un-screwed the lid, and handed it to him.

He held the flask beneath his nose and sniffed. "Brandy?"

She nodded, and he took a long draw before handing it back.

"Where did you get the flask?" he asked.

She took a sip herself before answering. "I won it in a wager with a classmate, who had nicked it from her older brother. I keep it filled for occasions such as this."

He arched a brow. "For when men scale your balcony and knock on your bedroom door?"

"One must prepare for every eventuality." She shot him a smile and the grin he shot back made her belly flip.

It seemed impossible that Leo, the boy who'd once been the bane of her existence, could now affect her so. Never-theless, she found herself transfixed by the patch of bare skin above his shirt collar. Her fingers itched to reach out and trace the line of his collarbone.

In an attempt to distract herself she said, "What will you design for the contest?"

The mere question made his whole countenance light up. "A new inn and pub," he answered proudly.

She made a valiant attempt to keep her expression neu-tral. "Interesting," she said in the most diplomatic tone she could manage.

His forehead creased. "Why are you making that face?"

Blast. "What face?"

He chuckled. "Like you have a tough piece of meat in your mouth that you intend to spit into your napkin when no one is looking. You can tell me what you truly think."

No, she couldn't. At least not without dampening his obvious enthusiasm. But the truth was that Bellehaven needed another inn and pub about as much as it needed a moat. A moat would have been preferable, actually, as it at least had an element of whimsy and imagination.

"I have no doubt your design will be technically impressive," she said, proceeding with caution.

"But?" he prompted.

"But we already have the Bluffs' Brew and Salty Mermaid," she blurted. "Wouldn't you rather bring something new and exciting to our town? Something like an art museum, a clock tower, or even a botanical garden? An inn and pub just seem so . . . uninspired." She handed him the flask as a peace offering. "I'm sorry."

His expression inscrutable, he took a swig and used the back of his hand to wipe his mouth. She had to give him credit—he'd proven quite skilled at adopting the mannerisms of a rake. So much so, that she wasn't entirely certain he was playing a part any longer.

At least he didn't seem offended by her confession. His eyes gleamed with confidence as he leaned toward her. "My pub isn't likely to fill anyone with awe—I'll grant you that. But it will be a place where people can share a bit of gossip, play a few rounds of cards, or toast a cricket match victory. And at the end of the night, they'll have a place to lay their heads."

"Bellehaven *has* an inn," she reminded him for the second time.

"We do," he conceded. "But there are never enough rooms to handle the flock of tourists during the regatta. And once our town has a theater to rival anything seen in London, we'll have even more visitors. They'll come from far and wide to attend performances here . . . and they'll need a place to stay."

"Only one entry can win the contest," she reminded him. "It will be either my theater or your inn."

"Maybe the countess will host the contest again next year," he mused.

Her belly fluttered happily. He'd talked about her theater like it was more than a dream in her head. He'd spoken of it as if it were a foregone conclusion. "I hope you're right."

"Of course I am."

Maybe it was his self-assured manner, or perhaps it was the way his thin shirt clung to his broad shoulders, but Kitty felt *it* again. The undeniable pull. The irresistible attraction. The need to take a part of him . . . and give him a part of herself.

"There's another reason I was cross at the croquet tournament today," she admitted.

He arched a questioning brow.

"I'm not proud of it, but I was annoyed that you were partnered with Lila. I realize that I have no right to be"— she swallowed, forcing herself to say the word—"*jealous*, but I think that all the time we've been spending together must have affected my emotions."

A myriad of reactions flickered across his face. Shock, wonder, and something akin to relief. "I don't mind that you were jealous."

"Well, *I* mind." She sprang from her chair and began to pace. "For one thing, it isn't fair to you. You've been honest with me ever since you returned to Bellehaven. I know that your feelings are engaged elsewhere."

He exhaled nervously. "I actually wanted to speak to you about that."

"Please," she said, holding up a hand. "Allow me to get this off my chest first."

He nodded. "If it will make you feel better."

She walked back and forth in front of the fireplace, collecting her thoughts. "Our arrangement was intended to help both of us, and you've held up your end of the bargain."

"So have you," he interjected.

"At the beginning, perhaps. Teaching you how to be a rake was supposed to work to *your* benefit. To enable you to impress the woman you love. But somewhere along the way, the lessons took a turn. I think I've been getting far more out of this arrangement than you have."

"No one's keeping a ledger, Kitty."

"Perhaps not, but you seem to have forgotten that I drove your croquet ball into the lake."

He chuckled. "I won't forget that—trust me."

She threw up her hands. "I don't think you need me anymore."

He went to her and gently squeezed her shoulders. "That's not true."

She closed her eyes briefly so that she wouldn't be distracted by the golden flecks in his irises or the fullness of his lips. "I fear I'm becoming a detriment to you."

"You don't have the full picture," he said earnestly.

She nodded. "I know, and you can tell me everything if you'd like, but before you do . . . I'd like to ask one more favor."

"Of course. Anything."

"This is not a usual sort of request. It involves rather more than fetching me a cup of tea or lending me your pencil." Perhaps it was even selfish of her to ask. All she knew was that the idea had taken root and she couldn't stop thinking about it.

"I'm listening," he assured her.

"It may seem shocking." She wasn't entirely certain she could bring herself to say the words aloud. But she *was* sure that she wanted it. It would be a memory to hold close to her chest when all of this was over. A chance to feel something real before she resigned herself to a love-less marriage.

"I've known you for too long to be shocked by anything you say," he said confidently.

She reached up and skimmed a fingertip along his jaw. "I want you to spend the night with me, in my bed. I want us to kiss and explore each other . . . and finish what we started that day in the cave."

"Kitty." He gaped at her, his expression incredulous. "What are you saying?"

She swallowed and met his heated gaze. "I want us to make love."

Chapter 18

Leo tried to recall what he'd eaten for dinner that night. Wondered if there was something other than brandy in Kitty's flask. Because clearly, he'd ingested or imbibed something that had caused him to hallucinate.

Either that, or Kitty Beckett had just asked him to make love to her.

She blinked up at him, her blue eyes huge and pleading, her expression serious.

"Why?" he asked. Not the most eloquent of responses, but a one-syllable word was the best he could manage.

"I want my first time to be with someone I trust." She slid her hand down the side of his neck and traced the hollow at the base of his throat. "Besides, I cannot deny the effect you have on me. When I stand this close to you, my body thrums in the most disconcerting way. I think that spending the night with you would cure me of these vexing symptoms."

His cock strained against the front of his trousers, and he barely resisted the urge to press his hips against hers. "I desire you as well," he said. "But it's not that simple. There's risk involved."

"Then we'll be careful," she said soberly. "I know that I'm asking a great deal, and I know your heart belongs to another. She will notice you soon—if she hasn't already—and you will have the woman you've dreamed of."

"About that," he began.

"Please." She pressed a finger to his lips and closed her eyes. "If it's all the same to you, I'd rather not dwell on it now."

"Why not?"

Her forehead creased. "It only stirs up that ugly feeling inside me. The one that resulted in you fishing your croquet ball out of the mud."

"You don't need to be jealous, Kitty," he said, willing her to believe it.

"I wish I could extinguish it as easily as a lit candle, but it doesn't seem to work that way."

"Would it help if I told you I was jealous, too?"

Her eyes narrowed, and the corner of her mouth quirked. "Were you?"

Leo nodded. "Of Kirkham."

"It doesn't feel nice, does it?" she asked earnestly.

He scowled at the memory. "No."

"Perhaps this will make us both feel better." She wrapped her arms around his neck, leaned against his chest, and brushed her soft lips across his.

Growling, he slid a hand behind her and squeezed her bottom.

"Let's take this night for ourselves," she rasped. "To satisfy our curiosity. To douse the flames of desire."

Sweet Jesus.

He covered his mouth with hers, hoping his kiss told her everything he hadn't. That she was the only woman he'd ever wanted. That he'd gladly spend the rest of his life trying to make her happy if she'd let him. That he loved her.

She pulled at the hem of his shirt and hauled it over his

head. He spun her around to loosen the laces of her gown. Couldn't resist kissing the column of her neck.

Making a mental note of every little moan and sigh she made, he slowly eased the sumptuous silk lower. Over her breasts. Over her hips. All the way to the floor.

With a sultry smile, she stepped out of the circle of fabric at her feet. She held his gaze as she untied her corset, pulled at the ties, and removed it, leaving her thin chemise skimming her body.

She glided back to the chair, sat, and reached for the top of one stocking.

"Wait." He dropped to his knees in front of her. "Let me."

She sank back into the cushions and extended a long, lithe leg. "Be my guest."

He cradled her stockinged foot in his palm, massaging the arch and kneading the heel. Slowly, he skimmed a hand up her ankle. Over her calf. Behind her knee.

When he reached the hem of her chemise, he slipped his hand under, gliding over the supple flesh of her thigh till he reached the delicate tie at the top of her stocking. He stroked the soft skin above, heard her sharp intake of breath, and met her gaze.

"Is this all right?" he asked.

She nodded. "Don't stop."

He swept his thumb over her skin, making a series of small circles. "What if I said I wanted to kiss you here?"

She bit her lip, making his cock even harder. "I would say . . . you can kiss me anywhere you like."

The words were scarcely out of her mouth before he lowered his head and brushed his lips over her inner thigh. He started slowly, but when a soft moan escaped her throat, he increased the pressure, alternately sucking and nibbling.

"Kitty." He murmured her name like a plea. He wanted to taste her. Touch her. Make her his.

As if she knew, she speared her fingers through his hair and looked directly into his eyes. "I want this," she said. "All of it. If you don't feel the same way, I understand. But if you *do*, take what you want . . . and know that I will, too."

Like a peasant who'd just been granted a treasure chest of riches, he didn't question his good fortune.

He began by touching her. By gently stroking the soft, slick folds at her entrance. By circling the center of her pleasure with the pad of his thumb.

She whimpered, grasped the arms of the chair, and let her head fall back.

God help him, he couldn't wait any longer. He lifted her legs over his shoulders and bent his head, flicking his tongue across her most sensitive spot. Stroking and sucking until her back arched.

He savored every second of it. The taste of her. The mewling noises she made. The way she thrust her hips, urging him on. He could feel her muscles coiling, her body reaching. She was on the precipice. About to soar.

He redoubled his efforts, coaxing her closer. "That's it," he murmured. "Come for me."

And she did.

He grasped her bottom, staying with her as she pulsed all around him. As she cried out in ecstasy. As she rode out every last wave of pleasure.

"Leo," she gasped, her expression a mix of wonder and gratitude. "That was . . . better than I'd imagined."

She probably didn't have any idea what her words meant to him, but if he never succeeded at any endeavor for the rest of his life, he'd still have this triumph. He'd helped Kitty experience earth-shattering pleasure, and he couldn't think of any accomplishment he'd rather have to his name.

He gently lowered her legs to the floor, sat back on his heels, and pulled down the hem of her chemise. Several tendrils of her hair had come loose from their pins. Her cheeks were flushed, her eyes dazed.

"You're beautiful," he said soberly. "Always, but never more so than now."

"It's odd, isn't it?" she said, still catching her breath. "How one can know a person for years and then, all of a sudden, see them in an entirely different light?"

He opened his mouth to tell her that he'd felt this way about her for as long as he'd known her but held his tongue.

Because even though it was almost more than he dared hope for, he couldn't help wondering if she was seeing *him* in a different light. And whether tonight would mark a turning point in their relationship.

"I know what you mean," he replied as he carefully removed a stocking. "I meant to do this earlier but was understandably distracted."

"Mmm," she said huskily. "When you're done, I wonder if I could ask another favor."

"Anything you want, Kitty."

Her blue eyes shone as she leaned forward and touched her forehead to his. "Carry me to bed."

Leo scooped Kitty into his arms, strode across her bedchamber, and placed her gently on the mattress. He sat beside her and shot her a smile that made her belly flutter. "Are there any other favors you'd like to request?" he asked in a voice that was deep and full of promise.

"I hate to impose," she said with a cheeky grin.

"Since when?"

"But since you so generously offered," she continued, "you could remove your clothes."

He didn't hesitate a beat. He made short work of his boots then turned his attention to his trousers.

Kitty did, too.

She was mesmerized by the ridges of his abdomen and the little patch of fuzz above his waistband. Her fingers itched to touch him. To see if she could please him the way that he'd pleased her.

He unbuttoned the front of his trousers, shoved them over his narrow hips, and let them fall to the ground.

For the space of several breaths she said nothing. In fact, she doubted she could form a coherent sentence. She'd thought that she knew all there was to know about Leo. He was supposed to be practical, predictable, boring. But there was so much more to him.

So much more.

Leo stood barely an arm's length away. The dim light of the lantern flickered over his skin, casting the angles of his face and the contours of his body in stark relief. His sinewy arms hung at his sides, and his bemused, open expression invited her to study him to her heart's content.

"I want to touch you," she said, her voice raspy to her own ears.

"You don't need to ask. Ever." He paused, then added, "But I have a request too."

"Tell me."

He reached for her shoulder. Tugged on the thin strap of her chemise. "Take this off. Please."

She loosened the tie at her neckline, slipped her arms free of the sleeves, and pulled the thin lawn over her head. The few hairpins left in her hair lost their battle, and a mass of curls tumbled around her shoulders.

She looked into his eyes, and the raw hunger she saw in

them sent a delicious shiver over her skin. "Come here," she said, patting the pillow behind her. "Lie next to me."

They stretched out across the smooth satin of her counterpane and reached for each other. He kissed her neck, caressed her breasts. She let her hands roam over his broad shoulders, down the smooth skin of his back, and over the taut muscles of his backside. Tentatively, she stroked his long, hard length. He moaned in response.

"Show me," she urged. "Show me what feels best."

"You're doing fine," he assured her.

"I want to be better than fine."

"Very well," he said raggedly. "But all your instincts are correct. Trust me."

He guided her, just enough to give her confidence that she was pleasing him. Any remaining doubts she had were erased by the wickedly encouraging words he murmured in her ear.

"I can't resist you," he rasped. "I've tried. But tonight . . . tonight you're mine."

"Yes." She kissed a path down the center of his chest. "And tonight, you're mine." She traced the ridges of his abdomen with her tongue and brushed her lips over his arousal.

"No," he said, his voice laced with regret. "If you do that, it will be over before it even starts."

She lingered a moment longer before returning to her spot beside him. With a blissful sigh, she nestled against his big, hard body. She draped a leg over his thick thigh and slid an arm around his waist, amazed that being with him felt so right. And for two people who couldn't have been more different, she had to admit that they fit together perfectly.

As if he knew precisely what she was thinking, he rolled toward her, capturing her mouth in a scorching kiss. His hips nudged against hers, his arousal pressed against her core. The pulsing she'd felt before started anew, and her body ached with need. She wrapped her legs around his and pulled him closer.

He paused at her entrance and pressed his forehead to hers, his face a mix of torment and ecstasy. "You're sure?"

"I want you to be my first," she said. The physical attraction was tangible. Undeniable. More important, she couldn't imagine trusting anyone but him.

He stared down at her so earnestly that her chest squeezed. "I would never intentionally cause you pain—physical or emotional. But this may hurt."

Perhaps it was the desire coursing through her veins. Maybe it was the tender way he was looking at her. But she wasn't afraid in the slightest. All she felt was anticipation—and the need to be as close to Leo as she could possibly be.

He positioned himself between her legs and thrust, gently at first. Gradually filling her. Teasing her. Making her want more.

She raised her hips to meet his and took him deeper. Claimed him for her own. At least for tonight.

He laced his fingers through hers, pinned her hands above her head, and kissed her until she could barely recall her own name. All the while, he moved inside her, stoking her desire. Kindling her passion. Imprinting himself on her soul.

They moved together, rocking slowly. Then faster. Spiraling higher and higher.

He was everywhere. His lips on her neck, his hand in her hair, his hips pressed to hers.

She wanted the feeling to last forever.

"I knew it," he whispered, more to himself than to her.

"What?" she said, panting. "What did you know?"

He braced himself above her and looked into her eyes. "That it would be like this with you."

"Like what?" she managed through the haze of desire.

"Perfect."

The tenderness in his voice, in his expression, touched her deep in her soul and made her believe tonight was about more than passion for Leo.

Perhaps it meant more to her, too.

She closed her eyes and opened herself to the possibility. That maybe she *could* let somebody love her . . . and open her heart to him as well.

"What if," he whispered, echoing her thoughts. He eased himself deeper and rocked against the center of her pleasure, driving her wild. "What if we were meant to be?"

She clung to him, but any reply she might have made died on her lips. The pulsing in her core spiraled higher and higher till there was nowhere left for it to go.

And she shattered into a million beautiful droplets, shimmering from the top of her head to the tips of her toes.

Leo tensed but stayed with her, murmuring her name over and over.

As the last sweet echoes of pleasure faded, he pulled away, rolled to his side, and exhaled as he spent himself in his hand.

She let her palm glide over the muscles of his back. Pressed her lips to his shoulder blade. "That was . . . lovely."

He chuckled softly. "Agreed."

"Don't move. I'll fetch a cloth for you." She slid off the bed, padded across the floor to her washstand, and returned with a damp hand towel. "Here," she said, gently wiping his palm clean.

"I thought it best to be careful," he explained.

She swallowed. "I'm glad." Especially since she seemed to have momentarily lost her wits.

He laced his fingers behind his head and stared at the ceiling, thoughtful.

She crawled onto the bed and nestled against his side, feeling sated and sleepy. Leo reached for the blanket at the foot of the bed and spread it over her. Her eyes fluttered shut, and she basked in the glow of warmth, affection, and intimacy.

"We still need to talk," he said.

"Yes," she agreed, stifling a yawn.

"It's about the deal we made. There's something I haven't told you."

"I know." But she didn't want to spoil the moment with serious conversation—especially if he intended to bring up the other woman that he fancied. "Do you think we could rest for a few minutes first?" She trailed her fingers through the fuzzy patch of hair in the center of his chest.

He hesitated. "I've always had a hard time telling you no."

"Good," she said with a soft chuckle. "I much prefer it when you say yes."

"Close your eyes for a bit." His palm caressed the length of her arm, leaving her skin tingling in his wake. "We'll talk after a quick nap," he said firmly.

She smiled to herself, confident that as long as he was in her bed, she could find another—quite pleasant—way to distract him.

Chapter 19

Dreaming of Kitty was nothing new for Leo. He saw her almost every time he closed his eyes. But this . . . this was the most intense, erotic fantasy he'd ever had.

He was in her dimly lit bedchamber, lying on sumptuous silk sheets, naked. Even better, she was, too.

She knelt beside him, so beautiful that she took his breath away. Her luminous skin glowed in the candlelight. Her swollen lips begged to be kissed. The rosy tips of her breasts hardened under his gaze.

He reached out, caressed one supple thigh, and heard the subtle hitch of her breath.

Holy hell. This was no dream.

She moved between his legs, the ends of her long golden tresses tickling the tops of his thighs, her breath warm on his cock. Her wicked, wet tongue licked a path from his stones all along the length of him, circling the top. Taking him in her mouth.

Sweet Jesus. He was so aroused that he was in agony—the kind he wished could last forever.

With every wicked flick of her tongue, with every soft moan in her throat, she made him harder, driving him closer to the brink. Desire thrummed in his veins. Blood pounded in his ears.

"Kitty," he panted. "I can't hold back any—"

She sucked, drawing him in deeper, and he was gone. Release thundered through him like wild horses galloping across the beach. Powerful. Breathtaking. Free.

He bit his lip and fisted his hands in the sheets while his body shuddered.

And as he slowly surfaced from his pleasure-induced haze, Kitty sat up and shot him a heavy-lidded, triumphant smile.

"How did you know how to . . . ?"

"The way I know about most things." She shrugged adorably. "I have a book."

He arched a brow. "Maybe you could show it to me one day."

"Perhaps," she said, snuggling against his side.

"What time is it?"

"Almost three in the morning," she said, her voice laced with regret.

"I must leave soon. I won't risk your reputation."

"I appreciate the sentiment, but if you're caught here, my reputation will be the least of your concerns. What you should fear most is my uncle's wrath. He'd wring your neck."

"He would," Leo agreed. "And if he does, death will have been a small price to pay for tonight."

She laughed and draped a leg across his, like it was the most natural thing in the world. He couldn't recall ever feeling so happy. So hopeful.

Maybe when he told her how he felt, she'd be overjoyed— and give up the notion of marrying for convenience rather than love.

"I know you will need to leave soon." She reached for his hand and laced her fingers through his. "In the few minutes we have left, could we stay just like this?"

Leo frowned. "You needn't worry, Kitty. I'm not going anywhere."

"That's not true," she murmured, her voice tinged with sadness. "Everyone is going somewhere. But you're here now, and that's enough," she added—as if she were trying to convince herself.

She pressed her cheek to his chest, and he kissed her forehead, hoping that this night was the first in a lifetime of nights. That he might be imprinting himself on her heart the way she was already imprinted on his.

"What I've been wanting to tell you," he began slowly, "it can't wait any longer."

She tensed but gave an almost imperceptible nod.

It was time. To speak the words he'd locked away in his heart.

The prospect terrified him, but he took a fortifying breath and let all the emotions swirling inside him spill out.

"It's you," he said simply. "It's always been you."

She lifted her head, frowned, and met his gaze. "I don't understand."

He swallowed. "You're the one, Kitty. The one who constantly fills my head. You're the one who's captured my heart and the one I dream about at night. It's you and it's been you for as long as I can remember."

She shook her head and sat up, clutching the sheet to her chest. "You're not in love with someone else?"

"No." He paused and searched her face. After the night they'd shared, surely she felt something for him.

"It was all a lie," she whispered, her expression a mixture of disbelief and hurt.

Holy hell. "Not a lie," Leo rushed to assure her. "I did fall in love with someone. I fell in love with—"

"Stop." She turned her back to him and slid off the bed,

pulling the sheet with her. "You needn't spell it out for me. I believe I see the way of things."

"What?" He rubbed the back of his neck, perplexed.

"Our deal was nothing but a ruse—a way for you to manipulate me into doing your bidding."

He cursed under his breath, angry with himself. "I can see why you'd think that, but it's not the case at all."

She scoffed and stalked the length of her bedchamber, the sheet tucked beneath her arms. "When I think of all the *stupid* lessons I gave you . . . What kind of waistcoat to wear. How to look rakish during cricket. How to be cavalier and ruthless. How to kiss. I fell for the whole diabolical scheme," she said, incredulous.

He instinctively fell back on what he knew best: logic. "No, this wasn't some sinister plan I concocted. You came to me on my first night back. It was you who wanted to make a deal." Leo hopped out of bed and hastily donned his trousers. "I merely agreed."

She snorted at that and tossed her hair over her shoulder—the old, telltale sign that proved he was right. But the victory felt abysmally hollow.

She scooped up her nightgown, strode behind the dressing screen, and continued to talk as she wriggled into the lacy lawn garment. "Do you know what the worst part is?" she asked rhetorically. "I pride myself on being able to sniff out a rake from across a crowded ballroom, and yet, I took the bait. I fell prey to the *worst* sort of rake—the kind who pretends he isn't one."

Her words hit him like a right hook to the chin. "Kitty, I'm sorry. I never intended to hurt you."

"No, you intended to *seduce* me. And you succeeded. Congratulations."

He dragged his hands through his hair, willing her to understand. "Can we please talk about this?"

"No," she said curtly. "Not now, at any rate."

"I love you," he said, his voice hoarse to his own ears. He'd waited forever to confess his feelings, and now that he had, he wished he could go back in time and undo the whole conversation. He wished she was still curled up beside him, her soft cheek nestled against his chest.

Instead, Kitty stuffed her arms into her dressing gown as she walked to the door of her bedchamber. "I'm going downstairs to the library so that you may gather your things and finish dressing," she announced flatly. "Please be gone before I return."

Chapter 20

Later that morning, Kitty breezed into the office looking impossibly composed in her fashionable pale-green gown and straw bonnet. "Good morning, gentlemen." Her gaze flicked to Kirkham, already sitting at the desk across from hers, then to Leo, seated at his grandfather's desk.

Her eyes met Leo's for the briefest of moments, and he read a myriad of emotions on her face. Distrust. Hurt. And perhaps just a touch of curiosity.

He hated that their first meeting after spending the night together was in the office. Most mornings at this time Kirkham was still in bed, sleeping off a few too many pints at the Salty Mermaid. Not today. He was staring at Kitty like she was a dish of ice cream on a summer day.

She hung up her bag, sat at her desk, and began sorting through scraps of fabric and wallpaper, occasionally pinning a sample to a large board. And it was impossible to tell what was going through her head.

Kirkham craned his neck toward Kitty's desk, examining her board with undisguised interest. "Beautiful colors," he mused. "What are the samples for?"

"My contest entry," she said without looking up.

"I gathered that," Kirkham said smoothly. "I wondered where you planned to use the blue velvet."

"I haven't decided yet," she replied.

Undeterred, Kirkham stood and boldly wandered closer to Kitty's desk. "I must say, it looks exquisite next to the flocked sapphire wallpaper you have there. I realize you didn't ask for my opinion, but it would be a shame if you didn't pair them in some way."

She blinked and finally looked at him, her face impassive. "Do you recall, Mr. Kirkham, what you told me on the day we met?"

"Not precisely." He rubbed his chin, thoughtful. "I do like this game though. Let's see, if I had to guess, I probably paid you a pretty compliment. At least I hope I did. If not, you must tell me so that I may rectify the matter at once."

She rolled her eyes heavenward, then exhaled. "You said that you would not talk excessively."

"Ah." He clamped his lips shut and took a step backward. Leo wanted to cheer.

"I don't mean to be rude," she explained, "but it was part of the deal we made when we agreed to share the office."

"You're right." Kirkham raised his hands guiltily and slunk back to his desk. "My apologies."

"Thank you," Kitty said sincerely. "When a gentleman tells me something, I want to be able to take him at his word." She shot a pointed glance at Leo.

"You *should* be able to rely on the word of a gentleman," Kirkham agreed.

"And yet," Kitty said, picking up a pin, "that's not been my experience." She jammed the pin into the board with a good deal more force than was necessary, and Leo had the feeling that the conversation was no longer about Kirkham's propensity for incessant chatter.

Kirkham cleared his throat and nervously smoothed a hand down the front of his waistcoat. "Well then, you must allow me to apologize on behalf of my entire sex. I regret that we have let you down."

"You are not responsible for the misdeeds of all men, Mr. Kirkham." Kitty arched a brow. "You cannot repair the damage that another has caused. Wouldn't you agree, Mr. Lockland?"

He swallowed. "Maybe if the gentleman in question had the chance to explain his actions."

Understanding finally dawned on Kirkham's face, and he nodded, clearly relieved. "You know, I think I'll take a stroll to the tea shop. Shall I bring something back for the both of you?" Before they could answer, he held up a finger. "Actually, you should let me surprise you. It will be more fun that way." He grabbed his hat and made his getaway with impressive alacrity.

The moment the door closed behind him, Leo went to Kitty and searched her face. "There's much we need to discuss."

She set down a scrap of fabric and turned to him. "I agree," she said frostily.

He glanced over his shoulder at the big picture window. "I wish we could talk somewhere more private, but I suppose this will have to do for now." He paused, then said, "Can we go back to the way things were before?"

"You lied to me." There was a hitch in her voice. An unmistakable hurt.

"I shouldn't have let you believe that I was in love with somebody else. But I never explicitly said that there was another woman."

Kitty scoffed. "What about all the lessons? You didn't need any of them, not really."

"I did if I was going to have any chance of impressing you."

She crossed her arms and raised her chin. "I'll bet you were having a good laugh at my expense."

"Never," he said solemnly. "I *did* want to learn to be a rake, because I knew that was the type of man you were looking for. If you'd said you wanted a sailor, I would have joined the navy. If you'd said you wanted a highwayman, I would have robbed a bloody coach. I would have gone to any lengths to try and capture your heart, and now I'm terrified. Terrified that I've ruined everything."

For several heartbeats she said nothing. His entire world was reduced to a dying ember that she could either blow back to life or stamp out forever. He held his breath and prayed she could forgive him. That she would give him another chance.

"I don't think you've botched it completely," she said, and his heart soared.

"Thank God."

"But I am still wary," she hastened to add. "I'm questioning everything that's happened between us. I don't know what was real and what was a charade."

"The connection we have is real," he assured her. "I'm sorry that I let you think there was someone else. I shouldn't have. But the deal we made that night on Lady Rufflebum's terrace gave me an opportunity to spend more time with you . . . and I couldn't pass it up. And then I was afraid that if I told you the truth, you would want nothing to do with me."

One corner of her mouth curled reluctantly. "The lessons were rather diverting."

"Far more enjoyable and edifying than any of my previous scholarly pursuits," he said with a grin. But he was still on pins and needles. Still waiting to hear how she felt about his declaration—and about him. "Do you think you can forgive me?"

"I will try." She looked at him earnestly. "But going forward there can be no more lies, no more secrets. I need to be able to trust you, Leo."

"I know." He wanted to pull her into his arms, crush her to his chest, and plunder her mouth. He settled for squeezing her hand. "I won't let you down. I promise."

She managed a smile. "Good. See that you don't," she added.

He looked at their joined hands, wishing he never had to let go. "Now you know how I feel and what I want. But you haven't told me what you feel. Where do we go from here?"

Her forehead creased slightly. "We need to talk, but this isn't the ideal time or place. The street is already bustling with tourists. Someone could walk in at any time."

"Shall I come to your room tonight?" He didn't relish the thought of climbing the rope up to her balcony again.

"No. It's too risky. I still don't know how you managed to leave this morning without breaking your neck."

"I didn't leave the same way I came," he admitted with a chuckle. "I slipped out through the house."

"Leo!" She released his hand and gave his shoulder a playful swat.

"No one saw me. I used the back staircase." He shot her a grin. "I suppose that detracts from my rakishness."

"Actually, it's precisely what a rake would have done." Kitty clucked her tongue. "You're lucky you didn't run into my uncle."

"Agreed. It would have been difficult to explain the rope." He met her gaze and turned serious. "Since your bedchamber is out of the question, where would you like to meet? There's my apartment, the beach . . . we could return to Pirate's Cave."

Her eyes widened, as if she'd had an idea. "I know a spot. I haven't been there in ages, but it's very private and surprisingly comfortable."

"Where?" he asked, intrigued.

"On the beach, several miles from town. I'll write down the directions and slip them to you before I leave the office today. Meet me there at sunset."

"How will you get there? Won't Hazel wonder where you've gone?"

"I have a plan, of course," she said, a secretive gleam in her eyes. "Just make sure you're there on time."

Later that evening, Leo offered the apple in his palm to his mare and tied her to a tree bough where she wouldn't be seen from the main road. He grabbed the bag that he'd tied to his saddle and plodded through the brush and beyond the reeds till he reached the sandy path that Kitty had described. The one that led to their meeting spot.

As he walked farther down the winding trail, it seemed as though he was leaving Bellehaven—and the whole world—behind. The evening breeze riffled his hair, the salty air tickled his nose, and the low roar of the ocean filled his head.

It felt as though he'd waited his whole life for this night.

The chance to make Kitty his. Forever.

When he came to a fork in the path, he veered left, parallel to the beach, until at last he came to a clearing, where a small, idyllic lean-to was nestled between two trees.

As he ambled toward it, he spotted Kitty sitting on a large, flat rock overlooking the sea, her knees tucked to her chest. Her golden hair hung loose down her back, and she gazed out at the horizon where the sun had painted fiery-red streaks across the sky.

Her skin glowed in the twilight—as though she was soaking up the beauty of the night and reflecting it back.

So much so that, for a moment, he found it difficult to breathe.

She must have sensed his presence because she turned, greeting him with a soft, serene smile. "You found me."

"I did indeed." He walked closer, hopped onto the rock, and sat beside her. "You can see to the end of the earth from here."

"There's something magical about this view," she mused. "The first time I came here I was running away from my troubles. But now I come here to read, to be alone with my thoughts, and to heal."

"I can see why."

"You're the only person I've ever brought here."

Warmth blossomed in his chest. "Thank you for sharing it with me."

"This isn't even the best bit," she said as she slid off the rock. "Follow me."

She led him toward the shelter between the trees. Half cozy cottage, half enchanted hut, it looked like it had been ripped from the pages of a storybook. Though it had been built primarily from wooden planks and pieces of driftwood, Mother Nature had embellished it with a blanket of moss, ivy, and flowering vines. A faded blanket hanging at the front served as a door.

As a structure, it was as messy as it was improbable. There were no straight beams or square corners. It appeared to be held together with nothing more than a few odd nails, random pieces of rope, and dried mud. It lacked any sort of uniformity in the materials and exhibited a complete disregard for the principles of design.

And it was perfect.

"You built this?" he breathed.

"No," she said wistfully. "But I wish that I had. It belongs to Poppy."

"The duchess?" he asked, incredulous.

"She made it years ago. It was her private sanctuary, but after she married, she bequeathed it to me." Kitty swept aside the curtain at the entrance. "Come inside."

Leo ducked through the door, pleasantly surprised to find the shelter more spacious on the inside than he would have guessed. A lantern on an overturned crate gave the interior a warm glow, and a round window at the rear allowed for a mellow cross breeze. The ceiling wasn't tall enough for him to stand upright, but he was able to sit on the quilt that covered the floor and stretch out his legs with room to spare.

"I wouldn't have been surprised to find this place inhabited by elves or fairies," he quipped.

"No magical creatures. Just us." Kitty smiled and gracefully sat beside him. "Unfortunately, I cannot stay for long. I told Hazel I was visiting Poppy's father, whose cottage is nearby. I popped in on him and told him I was going to take a walk on the beach before I left. The coach is waiting for me at the cottage, and Hazel will expect me to return within an hour or so."

"Then we shouldn't waste any time." He reached for her hand, uncurled her fingers, and pressed a kiss to her palm. "I need to know exactly what's in your head and heart, Kitty. Tell me everything you're feeling. Tell me what I can do to make you happy."

She swallowed and looked deep into his eyes. "I will be honest with you, because you deserve the truth. And I hope that you can understand."

"I want to understand," Leo said. Now that he sat across

from Kitty in the beach shelter, it seemed even more en-
chanting than usual. More intimate. "Help me."

She tucked her bare feet under her, trying to remember the explanation that she'd practiced and recited in her
head. But the words floated out of the window like smoke
up a chimney, and she could only tell him the truth in its
rawest, unpolished form.

"When we made love last night, I thought it would be
the last time we were together. I thought you were in love
with someone else, and I intended to step aside. So that
you could pursue her and have your heart's desire."

"I wanted to tell you before," he said.

"I know." Kitty closed her eyes, recalling the moment.
"You tried. I asked you to wait."

"Are you disappointed, then? Would you have preferred
that I *did* love someone else?" There was no sarcasm in his
voice, no censure. Just a genuine desire to know.

"No," she replied quickly. "That is, I don't think so. I
was jealous of the woman you were smitten with, but at
the same time, knowing you loved someone else made
you . . . safe."

His forehead creased in puzzlement. "You're always
safe with me. I can promise you that."

"I know you would never hurt me physically," she assured him. "What I meant is that you were safe because
you were unavailable. Off-limits."

"That was a good thing?" He scratched his head, clearly
still at a loss.

"In a way, yes." She struggled to admit it to herself, so
she understood why he was grappling with it, too. "I felt
as though I could spend time with you, even experiment
with physical intimacy, without worrying that we would
form an attachment."

"But I have," he said quickly. "I was hoping that you

might have, too. That you might see a future with me—
the way I dream of one with you."

He looked at her with such undisguised affection that
her chest ached. She longed to kiss him, to lie with him,
and recreate the magic of the night they'd spent together,
but she'd promised herself she wouldn't indulge in a single kiss until she'd told him everything. He deserved to
be in full possession of the facts before they picked up
where the lessons had left off.

"If you'd told me at the start of summer that I'd be
contemplating a future with you, I'd have said you were
mad. I thought I wanted a relationship that was easy and
superficial, a husband who was undemanding and distracted. I thought a rake would fit the bill nicely. He'd
be happy to have me pursue a career, leaving him free to
dally with whomever he liked."

Leo shook his head, adamant. "You deserve more.
Surely you can see that."

"I do," she agreed. "Everyone does. But what if I don't
want a love for the ages? What if I don't want to give myself up to something so overwhelming? To something so
powerful that it could consume me and spit me out in the
blink of an eye?"

He reached for her hands and gazed at her, his brandy-
colored eyes heartbreakingly earnest. "Loving someone
doesn't mean losing yourself. It means giving and growing. Together."

"I know how love is supposed to work," she said, frustrated with herself for not being able to adequately convey
her fears. "The problem is that it can be snatched away
from you at any minute. You imagine that a person will
be in your life forever, that nothing could separate you. But
fate intervenes, and . . . they're gone."

"I'm not going anywhere," he said firmly.

"I believe you mean that. But everyone leaves eventually. Uncle Beck left me at three different boarding schools. Poppy and Keane left for London. My parents left me at home one day and never, ever came back. It wasn't their fault, but even they abandoned me . . . leaving me utterly alone." Her voice cracked on the last word, and her eyes burned. She didn't want Leo to pity her, but she didn't know how else to make him understand that she couldn't love anyone so fully, so completely, ever again.

"This is different, Kitty," he promised, resolute. "I'd never leave you."

She swallowed the knot in her throat. "You already did. You left Bellehaven—and me—without so much as a goodbye. You still haven't told me why."

His eyes shuttered, as if he were closing off a part of himself. Locking the door of an unused room and burying the key. "I've apologized for that. It won't happen again."

"You don't know that."

"I do," he insisted. "The last time . . . had nothing to do with you."

"Then why *did* you go?"

"It was a family matter," he said stiffly. "Ugly and unpleasant. I don't talk about it."

"I see." She'd thought that over the last few weeks she and Leo would have progressed beyond vague, cryptic answers. She'd thought that he'd finally be willing to let her into the chilly, shadowy places in his heart, the same way she was trying to open up to him.

Regret washed over his face, and he swallowed nervously. "It's not that I don't trust you. I do. But I don't want to spoil this night with talk of something distasteful. Especially since it doesn't involve or affect us."

"I'm not certain I agree. Whatever it is, it obviously still has some power over you."

"Not anymore." He shook his head, adamant.

God, how she wanted to believe him. "Do you want a future with me?"

"More than anything," he said soberly. "I want us to share our lives together."

"But you won't share this part of you."

"It's not part of me." He raked a hand through his hair, frustrated. "It's part of the past, and you don't need to be concerned about it because you are my future."

Kitty couldn't imagine what sort of deep, dark secrets Leo's family might have. But she suspected two things. First, that it involved his father, and second, that it had wounded him deeply. So deeply that he couldn't bring himself to talk about it with her—someone he claimed to love.

It seemed she was destined to want more than others were willing to give. More than they were able to share.

But perhaps, in this case, it was for the best. As long as Leo held back a piece of himself, she could, too. She wouldn't make the mistake of thinking that he would always be there, by her side. She wouldn't set herself up for the sort of heartbreak that could completely devastate her. She wouldn't let herself fall utterly and completely in love with Leo Lockland.

Even if it would be terrifyingly easy to do.

"Very well," she said, deliberately cool. "We needn't talk about that."

He exhaled, not bothering to hide his relief. "Thank you for understanding."

"The question is, where do we go from here?"

"In case there's any doubt, I shall be completely clear: I want to marry you, Kitty. I want us to build a life together, make a family together. That's all I've ever dreamed of. I just need to know if you want it, too."

Chapter 21

The raw hopefulness in Leo's eyes gave Kitty pause, because the last thing she wanted to do was hurt him. "I think that maybe I could marry you," she said slowly.

Disbelief and joy flicked across his face. "You won't regret this, Kitty. I swear I'll make you happy."

"I know you'll try, and I shall try to make you happy, too. But in the end, we're each responsible for our own happiness. We can't count on anyone else to make our dreams come true."

He blinked, obviously confused. "Maybe not, but what if my dream is to make you happy?"

The question was so spontaneous, so genuine, that it made her chest ache. "There's something I need you to know," she said soberly. "I shall never fall head over heels in love with you. Or with anyone, for that matter. It pains me to say it, because I think that is what you want me to do. However, I can't give you a fairy-tale sort of love."

A wounded look crossed his face, but he shook his head. "I don't need a fairy tale. I want something real. I just want you."

Lord help her, this was even harder than she'd anticipated. But she had to remain strong. She absolutely could not build her entire world around him. Not when he could leave her in an instant. Not when fate could steal him away.

"There are many things I can give you," she said. "Warmth, loyalty, honesty . . . even passion. But I cannot give you my entire heart. It may sound harsh now, but you'll thank me later. When the first blush wears off the rose, your feelings will likely change. Or our careers could take us in different directions. Or our lives might take us down divergent paths. All of that will be easier if we go into this with the understanding that our marriage is based on respect and common goals—not love."

Leo could scarcely believe his ears, and yet Kitty seemed quite serious.

She sat beside him in the little beach shelter, her skin glowing in soft lamplight. Her simple dress, bare feet, and loose hair somehow made her even more beautiful. But her reaction to his declaration wasn't at all what he'd expected. Definitely not what he'd hoped for.

"It sounds like you're proposing that we have a marriage of . . ."—he cleared his throat to dislodge the word— "convenience."

She shrugged, apologetic. "I suppose you could think of it that way. Is that so terrible, though? It's not as if you'd be marrying me for my fortune or I'd be marrying you for a title."

He scratched his head, perplexed. "Obviously. I don't *have* a title. And I don't give a fig about your fortune. If it were gone tomorrow, I'd still want to marry you. Still love you."

"I won't deny that's lovely to hear, but . . ." her voice trailed off.

The truth settled onto his chest like a one-ton cornerstone. "But you don't feel the same way," he said, his voice sounding hollow to his own ears.

"I'm sorry if I seem heartless. I never wanted to hurt you. But I honestly think this would be the best course for both of us."

"How so?" he asked. "What do we have to gain by not giving ourselves completely to each other?"

"You've answered your own question," she said softly. "Love is fickle. Fate is cruel. But if we each hold back a part of ourselves, we never need to fear that our heart will be ripped from our chest. No matter what happens to us or between us, we'll know we can survive it."

A shiver stole over his skin. He'd suspected that Kitty had been scarred by the losses she'd suffered. Anyone would have been. But he hadn't realized how deep the scars ran—and how much they clouded her view of the world.

There weren't many things that frightened Kitty Beckett, but she was absolutely terrified of loving somebody and losing them.

"I'm sorry you've been hurt," he said. "And I understand why you're reluctant to love someone with all your heart."

"Thank you," she said, exhaling. "In spite of that, I do think that we will have a perfectly pleasant future together. We'll pursue our careers and make names for ourselves while we start a little family. And we've already established that we're physically compatible." She shot him a sly smile as a blush stole across her cheeks.

"We *are* good together." He leaned in and brushed his lips across hers in a teasing kiss. "Even when we disagree—which is rather often—we light each other up. Sparks are always flying when you're near."

"Mmm." She pressed her forehead to his and cupped his cheek in her hand. "So you agree this arrangement will work?"

"I'm afraid it won't. Not for me."

She blinked at that, clearly confused, but didn't pull away. "I thought you said we're good together."

"We are." To make his point, he ravished her mouth with a kiss that was hot, hungry, and deep. "I can't help the way I feel about you, Kitty," he murmured.

"Then you're destined for heartbreak," she said, her voice full of regret.

"Maybe I am, but I'm not giving up." He swept her hair back from her face and gazed into her eyes. "I love you, and I want to be your husband. I don't think I've ever wanted anything more. But I won't settle for less than all of you."

Her brow creased and she looked at him curiously. "What does that mean?"

"It means I won't agree to a marriage of convenience."

She slid her hand behind his neck and absently ran her fingers through his hair as she gazed at him, her blue eyes pleading. "Are you certain?"

Hell no, he wasn't certain. Every ounce of him longed to capitulate, to give her anything she wanted. But that wouldn't be fair to either of them. He did not want her to bind herself to him unless she felt the same way he did. He wouldn't lie and say that he'd settle for a marriage of convenience, hoping that over time he could change her mind. He needed her whole heart, and he wouldn't agree to anything less.

"You should have more than 'a perfectly pleasant' marriage. So should I."

"Where does that leave us then?"

"Right where we are," he said smoothly. "In this limbo

where we're more than friends, sometimes rivals, and often lovers."

"We can't go on like this forever," she said, her eyes shining with regret.

"No. But I only need a little more time to make you trust me," he added, sounding a good deal more confident than he felt. "When you're ready to give me your heart, we'll be married. Until then, I shall use any and all means at my disposal to convince you that my love is true."

"Have you forgotten how stubborn I can be?" she asked.

He recalled the image of her when they were teens, wearing a ridiculously lavish ball gown to work and producing a shot glass from the Salty Mermaid. "I haven't forgotten anything where you're concerned."

She pressed her lips together in a thin line and briefly closed her eyes. "I fear you're going to be disappointed, Leo. I don't want to hurt you."

"Do you want to know what I think?" He took her hand and traced circles on her palm with his thumb. "I think that you act as though you don't feel anything, when the truth is that you feel it the most. I think a part of you *wants* me to convince you that what we have is true and lasting. You don't think I'll succeed, but you're hoping I will. I'm here to tell you that I won't let you down."

"Perhaps you're right." She stared down at their joined hands. "Going forward, I shall rely on two old adages."

"What are they? I like to know the rules I'm playing by," he quipped.

"The first is that time will tell."

"I have all the time in the world." He stretched out on the quilt and gently pulled her down beside him. "What is the second?"

Her eyes glowed with anticipation. "Deeds speak louder than words."

"I am very much in favor of deeds." He wrapped an arm around her waist and pulled her close, so her hips were flush against his.

A smile lit her face, and she traced his bottom lip with her finger, tempting him sorely. "I never dreamt my rake lessons would result in such a transformation," she teased. "I fear I have created a monster."

He nuzzled her neck and let his hand glide beneath the hem of her gown, up the inside of her thigh, and between her legs. She opened to him and whimpered softly. "If I am a rake," he murmured, sliding a finger into her, "I'm only a rake for you."

Chapter 22

"It's been almost a fortnight since I've seen you." Leo's mother gave him a peck on the cheek as he went to hang up his hat. "Dinner's almost ready."

"I'm sorry I haven't visited lately. Work and my contest design have taken up most of my waking moments."

He didn't mention that Kitty took up the rest.

In the weeks since their evening in the idyllic beach shelter, they'd been finding opportunities to steal away together. One night, they'd met on a cliff overlooking the sea and counted the stars. On another afternoon, they'd snuck up to his living quarters and he'd made her lunch—which he served to her in bed. And yesterday, he'd visited her at home so that they could put the finishing touches on their designs for the contest.

He could feel her starting to soften toward him. Starting to envision a future where they were a real couple—and blissfully in love.

"Don't apologize," his mother said firmly. "You know I couldn't be prouder. I just worry that you work too hard. You're in the prime of your life, and you're always bent over that desk of yours when you should be enjoying yourself."

"I am enjoying myself," he said, feeling a bit guilty.

He couldn't wait to tell his mother about Kitty, but he had to be sure first. Right now, their relationship felt fragile, and he feared any outside pressure could upend it. Besides, the minute he told his mother, she'd be planning the wedding breakfast and knitting booties for her grandchildren. "You don't need to worry about me. I—"

Leo had been about to sit at the table but drew up short when he saw that only two places were set. "Where's Grandfather? Isn't he joining us?"

His mother dried her hands on her apron and sighed. "I'm afraid he hasn't been feeling well lately. I made him some soup earlier and he's resting."

Leo's stomach sank like a rock. "Sick? What's wrong?"

"The doctor was here yesterday." She sat on the bench next to Leo and squeezed his forearm. "He left a tincture which makes him comfortable enough to sleep."

"You should have told me," Leo said. "I would have come sooner."

"I didn't see any point in alarming you." She tried to console him with a pat on the shoulder, but it somehow made him feel worse.

"I don't understand. He seemed fine last time I saw him."

"Dr. Gladwell says it's probably just a fever, but at your grandfather's age, even common illnesses can take their toll. He hasn't been able to leave his bed in a few days."

"Can I see him now?"

"Certainly." His mother shot him a warning look. "But don't disturb him if he's resting."

Leo strode to his grandfather's room, knocked lightly on the door, and entered. The curtains were drawn and the only light in the room came from a candle on the desk.

His grandfather stirred, opened his eyes, and squinted in the direction of the door. "Leo, is that you?"

"It's me," he confirmed, taking a seat on a stool beside the bed. "I'm sorry you're not feeling well."

"Hand me my spectacles, would you?" Leo found the hint of irritation in his voice somewhat comforting.

"Here you go." He tried to carefully place the glasses on his grandfather's face, but the older man swatted Leo's hands away.

"I can put on my own damned spectacles," he said, wresting them from Leo's grasp. "It's bad enough that your mother won't let me leave my bed."

Leo chuckled. "She's worried about you. If Dr. Gladwell prescribed rest, then that's what you need. I must say, you do look a little pale."

"That's because I haven't seen the sun in three damned days," he grumbled.

"If you follow the doctor's orders, I bet you'll be better before you know it." Leo kept his tone light, but in truth, it was disconcerting to see his wise, usually vibrant grandfather wearing a nightgown while it was still light outside. His face was gaunt, his shoulders slumped, and his arms thin. He bore little resemblance to the virile, energetic man that Leo knew.

"The doc had better cure me before it's time to judge the contest," his grandfather said with a scowl. "If he doesn't, I just might have to march down to the assembly rooms, raging fever, nasty cough, and all."

He'd barely finished uttering the sentence when a violent coughing fit wracked his body, leaving his face red and his breath wheezy. Leo handed him a glass of water and braced his back so that he could take a sip. The fact that he didn't object to Leo's assistance was more worrisome than the cough itself.

Once his grandfather was comfortable again, Leo patted

his shoulder. "The most important thing is that you get well. There's no need to fret over the contest."

"The hell there isn't," he mumbled. "Neither the countess nor the mayor knows the difference between a floor joist and a ceiling rafter. Worse, both of them are easily swayed by outside influences. I need to be there to keep them honest." He paused mid-rant and looked up at Leo. "How's your entry coming along?"

"Pretty well," Leo said. Maybe Kitty's creativity had inspired him. Maybe *she* had. Either way, his plans were some of the best he'd ever done. "Do you want me to tell you what sort of building it is?"

"No." His grandfather held up a wrinkled hand. "I'll find out soon enough. And Kitty's design is almost finished as well?"

"It is." The mere sound of her name brightened the room and made his heart feel lighter. "She's outdone herself."

His grandfather nodded and sank back into his pillow as if their brief conversation had left him exhausted. "That's good. Her entry will need to be twice as good as the rest in order to any chance of winning."

Leo frowned. "What do you mean?"

"Just some idiotic comment the mayor made." He handed Leo his spectacles to return to the bedside table. "He doesn't think females possess the mechanical skills or spatial reasoning necessary to design a building."

"Bloody hell," Leo cursed.

"Precisely."

"Why can't the judging be done blindly?"

"Word of the entries has already gotten out. You know how Bellehaven is. You can't sneeze on one side of town without somebody on the other hearing about it."

"I'm not so sure about that," Leo quipped. "I didn't even know you were ill."

"Good," his grandfather said, punctuating the thought with a satisfied grunt. "I don't need anyone writing my eulogy just yet."

"Don't be ridiculous," Leo scolded. "But if you're not better soon, you might have every unmarried woman above the age of fifty lined up at your doorstep with pies, shamelessly flirting with you as they attempt to nurse you back to health."

"I suppose that wouldn't be an entirely bad thing," he grumbled. "But I'd rather be out of this damned bed."

"All the more reason to follow the doctor's orders."

The old man heaved a resigned sigh. "I haven't a choice. Your mother guards this room like I'm a prisoner of the Tower. I'm hoping I'll be free soon, but you might want to warn Kitty in case I'm not able to judge. Make sure she knows that she has a higher bar than the men in the competition. If the mayor is able to find even a minor flaw in her design, he'll use it as justification for disqualifying her. She mustn't give him any excuse."

Leo's chest filled with admiration and love for his grandfather. "I'll tell her. But I've seen her plans and reviewed them at length. In addition to being creatively brilliant, they're technically sound." He stood and shot him a reassuring smile. "But don't take my word for it. Get better so you can judge her entry for yourself."

"How is it possible that the summer has flown by so quickly?" Kitty mused as a seamstress in Bellehaven's newest shop—Madame Paquet's Boutique—pinned the bodice of the new, shimmering gold ball gown that Clara had designed for Bellehaven's Annual Regatta Ball.

Hazel, who sat on a tufted stool behind Kitty, met her gaze in the full-length mirror in front of her. "Time passes quickly in some respects, and more slowly in others." She placed a palm over her slightly rounded belly. "Your birthday will be here soon, and I confess I have mixed feelings about it."

"Truly?" Kitty looked over her shoulder at her friend and aunt. "Why is that?"

"Well," Hazel began, "in case there's any doubt, I'm ridiculously proud of the young woman you've become. Those of us who are lucky enough to be close to you know that you're even more beautiful on the inside than you are on the outside, which is truly saying something."

Kitty's eyes stung unexpectedly, but she waved a dismissive hand. "I was a brooding, mule-headed, troublemaking girl when you accepted me at Bellehaven Academy. Thanks to you, I am no longer brooding."

Hazel smiled knowingly. "One of the things I adore about you is your ability to lighten up any conversation, but I also know humor can be a shield for you. A way to dodge certain topics."

Kitty waited until the seamstress finished pinning her hem and left the dressing room, then she stepped off the dais and sat on the edge. "I don't wish to avoid difficult conversations—at least not with you. What is it about my impending birthday that gives you pause?"

Hazel absently brushed at the errant curl that always seemed to dangle in front of her forehead. "You'll be coming into your inheritance and will have the means to live as you like, which is a wonderful thing. Financial security is a huge blessing, but your uncle and I wanted more for you."

"You want me to marry," Kitty clarified.

"Yes, but not for the sake of marrying. We want you to be as in love and as happy as we are. And as Poppy and Keane are. You deserve that. I daresay everyone does." She wrung her hands in her lap. "I know you think that a marriage—especially one of convenience—will afford you a degree of freedom, and to a certain extent, you're right. But if you give yourself a little more time, you might find someone who's truly worthy of your love. Someone who loves you."

Hazel was making a case remarkably similar to Leo's, and Kitty's resolve was slipping more and more of late. Every minute she spent with Leo chipped away at her well-laid plans. Made her believe that she could cheat fate this time.

Indeed, she was starting to think that perhaps she *could* give her whole heart to Leo—and that she could count on him to always be there.

"Try not to worry about me," Kitty said to Hazel. "You should be focusing on the babe and your beautiful family."

"*Our* beautiful family," she corrected.

"Yes," Kitty agreed, even though she sometimes felt a bit extraneous as the orphaned niece. Not that Hazel and Blade treated her as such—it was simply the inescapable truth.

In an attempt to change the subject, Kitty asked, "Do you suppose we could stop by Mr. Potter's shop on our way home? I asked him to repair a broken frame from the office." It was the one she'd knocked off Leo's wall when she'd hurled a pillow at his head. He stubbornly insisted that she didn't have to fix it, so the last time she was in his apartment, unbeknownst to him, she'd slipped the broken frame into her large work bag.

"Of course." Hazel shot Kitty a knowing look—the

sort that said she wasn't giving up on the idea of Kitty marrying for love. She was only retreating temporarily and would be advancing her campaign at the next opportunity.

Still, Kitty was grateful for the reprieve, and a short time later, when their carriage rolled to a stop in front of Mr. Potter's shop, she patted Hazel's knee. "Stay here while I run in and retrieve the frame. I shall only be a minute."

Before Hazel could object, Kitty hopped out of the carriage and glided into the shop which was filled to the rafters with odds and ends—the kind that were normally relegated to attics. Mr. Potter repaired everything from shoes to clocks, and he was currently tucked behind the counter, tinkering with a half-disassembled music box.

"Ah, Miss Beckett!" he said, setting down his screwdriver. "I was able to replace the glass for your frame. Allow me to retrieve it from the back and wrap it up for you."

"Thank you," Kitty replied, smiling as the older man swept aside a curtain and shuffled into a room that appeared to be even more cluttered than the front of his shop.

He emerged a few moments later, his spectacles perched precariously on the end of his sloped nose. "Here we are," he said, carefully placing the framed drawing of the stables on the counter for her to see.

"It looks perfect," she said. "Good as new. Thank you, Mr. Potter."

"I suppose it has some sentimental value," he said with a knowing wink.

"Sentimental?" Kitty repeated with a nervous chuckle. "Why ever would you think that?"

The man waved a hand. "Forgive me. I didn't mean to pry. But I couldn't help noticing the inscription on the back of the drawing."

Kitty flipped the frame over but didn't see any writing.

"It's hidden by the frame backing," Mr. Potter explained. No wonder she hadn't seen it before.

"Would you show me?" she asked.

"I'd be happy to." The older man picked up his screwdriver and carefully removed the tacks holding the backing in place, revealing a small, faded pencil drawing in the bottom right corner of the back of the stables sketch.

It was a heart. With the initials K.B. inside it.

Kitty's skin prickled with amazement. Her chest swelled with joy.

Leo really *had* loved her back then—even when she'd been at her spoiled, ornery worst. If his feelings had remained true all these years in spite of their arguments and the distance that separated them, perhaps she *could* trust him with her heart.

If she was honest with herself, she'd already given it to him.

God help her, she loved Leo Lockland.

"Seems like you have an admirer," Mr. Potter said slyly, snapping her back to the conversation.

"Oh, that," Kitty said with a dismissive wave. "I probably doodled it myself ages ago."

"I suppose that's possible." Mr. Potter arched a skeptical brow but smiled warmly. "I'll put this back together and wrap it up for you."

Kitty murmured her thanks and pretended to browse the shop's curiosities while she waited. But all she could think about was Leo's neat lettering and the perfectly symmetrical heart he'd drawn around her initials.

Maybe this discovery was fate intervening. Tapping her on the shoulder. Shaking her free from her past. Proving to her that love *could* last.

When she returned to the carriage with the frame tucked under her arm, she attempted to look breezy and casual. As though she hadn't just realized that she was hopelessly in love.

"Why do you look like that?" Hazel asked.

So much for subterfuge. "I'm just glad Mr. Potter was able to repair the frame."

"Hmm," said Hazel, unconvinced.

Kitty wasn't quite ready to share her feelings for Leo with Hazel. He deserved to know them first. Still, Kitty did want to put her friend's mind at ease.

"As it happens, I may have changed my mind about marrying a rake." She hesitated, then added, "Actually, I suppose the gentleman in question *is* a rake—but he's the sort who I can trust."

Hazel's eyes went wide. "Who?"

"I shall tell you as soon as I'm certain," Kitty promised. "But he's given me every reason to be hopeful, and if it all works out as I believe it will, I think you'll be quite pleased."

"You've been spending so much time on your contest entry of late. I'm surprised that you've had the opportunity to meet someone who—" Hazel stopped midsentence and shot Kitty a knowing grin. "Wait. It's that architect from London, isn't it?"

Kitty's cheeks flamed. "I'd rather not say." Mostly because Hazel's next guess would almost certainly be Leo.

"Well, Mr. Kirkham is very handsome and charming," Hazel reasoned, "and you obviously have a shared passion for design."

Kitty shook her head. "I will be able to talk about it very soon, but I must speak with him first."

Hazel beamed and clasped her hands under her chin.

"This is all so exciting. Perhaps we'll have something special to celebrate at the Regatta Ball."

"Perhaps," Kitty said in a futile attempt to manage her friend's expectations. But the truth was that she couldn't wait to tell her and Poppy how she felt about Leo. She couldn't wait to shout it to the whole world.

Chapter 23

"You're certain I've drawn the stage and proscenium arch to scale?" Kitty asked, frowning at the detailed design that was spread across Leo's grandfather's desk in their office.

"Absolutely," Leo confirmed.

She set aside that scroll, selected another, and smoothed it over the blotter. "What about the dimensions on these elevation plans?"

He chuckled, and the deep, rich sound melted her insides, massaging away some of her anxiousness. "I've checked and double-checked every measurement. Your drawings are perfect. You could submit your contest entry today."

Kitty rolled up all her drawings and whisked them over to her desk. "I think I'll look over everything one more time." She wasn't quite ready to hand her plans over to the judges, especially given what Leo had told her about the mayor's bias against female architects. "One careless error would poison my entire design in the eyes of"—she glanced at Mr. Kirkham, who sat across from her, nonchalantly twirling his pencil, and swallowed her words. "Never mind," she said breezily.

Kirkham grinned. "You're placing an awful lot of faith

in him," he said, inclining his head in Leo's direction. "Don't forget—he's the competition."

She shot Kirkham a sugary smile. "He is, but he is also honorable."

Leo grunted. "Stay out of it, Kirkham. Kitty knows she can trust me."

"We'll see," Kirkham replied vaguely.

"Don't mind him," Kitty said to Leo. "He is simply jealous that my design is done, while he has days of work ahead of him."

"True enough," Kirkham grumbled, reluctantly returning his attention to his plans.

Blast. Kitty had hoped to have some time alone with Leo, but Kirkham seemed to constantly hover about—like he was a chaperone, and she a princess in her first season.

She wanted to tell Leo that despite all her doubts and fears, she was ready to give him her heart. But a declaration like this deserved a special setting. Somewhere private and sweet, idyllic, and memorable. Kitty knew just the spot.

She took a clean sheet of paper and placed it on her desk behind the wall of trinkets so that Kirkham couldn't see it. Then, she set pencil to paper:

I am ready to tell you what is in my heart.

Confessing my feelings is one of the most daring things I shall ever do, and I am terrified. However, I am placing my trust in you. Please, I beg of you, don't let me down.

Meet me at the beach hideaway tomorrow at sunrise. I'll be waiting for you.

She folded the note once, strolled to Leo's desk, and slid the paper in front of him. He looked up at her, his amber eyes curious.

"I made some adjustments to the material estimates," she said, her tone matter-of-fact. "Would you mind having a look?"

He opened the note, arched a brow, and took several seconds to scan the page. When he met her gaze again, his expression was soft. Hopeful. "This looks very good," he said soberly. "I'd only make one modification."

He picked up a pencil, scrawled something across the bottom of the note, folded it, and handed it back to her.

"Thank you," she said, walking briskly to her desk. But she didn't read the note right away. She tucked it into her reticule and took it home with her and didn't pull it out until later that evening after she'd changed into her nightgown and slipped beneath the covers of her bed.

Only then did she gingerly unfold the note and read the line Leo had added at the bottom of the page.

I want every sunrise with you. I'll be there tomorrow. You may depend on me, always.

She read it over and over, savoring every word. In just a few hours, she'd tell Leo that he'd convinced her. He'd made her believe that happy-ever-after wasn't just for other lucky souls. In spite of all the losses she'd suffered, she could have a fairy-tale ending, too.

Unlikely as it seemed, the boy who'd once been her nemesis was now the man she could trust with her heart—and the man who was about to become her fiancé.

Leo gently shut the door to his grandfather's bedroom behind him and joined his mother in the kitchen where she sat at the table, drinking a late-night cup of tea.

"His color looks better today," Leo remarked, relieved.

"Yes," his mother said above the rim of her cup. "He still doesn't have much of an appetite, but—" She held up a finger, retrieved a thick envelope from a basket on the bench near the front door, and handed it to him. "Dear me, I almost forgot this again. This letter came for you over a week ago. I was so worried about your grandfather that I neglected to give it to you."

"I'm sure it's nothing important," Leo said, but the formal script and unfamiliar London return address made him think that this was the letter he'd been waiting for. He stuffed the envelope into his jacket pocket and leaned down to kiss his mother's cheek. "But I should go. I'll be back to check on grandfather tomorrow evening."

Maybe he'd have Kitty with him, and together they'd tell his mother and grandfather the happy news of their engagement.

It was only the start of the beautiful life they'd make together, but each day from here on out was a chance to prove to Kitty that he was steadfast, loyal, and true.

It was also a chance for Leo to prove to himself that he was nothing like his father.

The moment he set foot in his parlor, he lit a lamp, sat down, and read the letter his mother had given him.

Dear Mr. Lockland,

Please accept my condolences on the recent loss of your father.

As his solicitor, I am in possession of his last will and testament. Furthermore, I am fully aware of the unique circumstances of his personal situation. He left instructions that only you and Mrs. Sabrina Lockland should be present for the reading of his

*will. He also stipulated that you would represent the
interests of your mother.*

    *Mrs. Lockland has arranged to travel to my Lon-
don office on the 19ᵗʰ day of August at 11 o'clock
in the morning, and I would request that you make
plans to attend as well so that we may ensure your
father's wishes are honored.*

Sincerely,
Mr. Elmer Abbot, Attorney at Law

Holy hell. Leo sprang from the sofa and paced the length of the room. How dare his father demand that he meet with *her*—the woman he'd consorted with behind Leo's mother's back. He already knew more than enough about her.

She lived in a nearby town called Fayetteville.

She and his father had lived in a cottage together—as husband and wife.

And his father had loved her.

Leo had discovered the sickening truth the day after his twentieth birthday when he'd borrowed his father's jacket and found a note in the pocket.

The note had been signed *your loving wife*—and wasn't written in his mother's handwriting.

And it explained so much. Why his father was away for several days every month, and why, even when he was at home sitting at the kitchen table, he sometimes seemed far away. He always had an excuse, of course. His work as an apothecary required him to travel. He was exhausted from the long days he spent at the shop.

Leo hated how his hand had trembled when he'd confronted his father with the note. He'd hated that he, a grown man, was on the verge of tears.

"I found this," he said, his throat constricting with anger and grief. "A letter from your"—he forced his mouth to speak the words—"other wife."

All the blood drained from his father's face as he ushered Leo outside, away from the house. "I'll explain everything," he said in a hushed voice. "But let's discuss it quietly. I don't want to upset your mother."

Leo snorted in disgust. "You should have thought of that before you went whoring with another woman."

Smack.

Leo lifted a palm to his stinging cheek. It was the first time in his entire life that his father had struck him, but the pain was nothing compared to the shock. The humiliation. The betrayal.

His father stared at his hand as if he couldn't believe what he'd done. "Leo," he'd said shakily, "I'm sorry."

"You're sorry you were caught. How could you?" He was outraged on behalf of his mother, but also for his own sake. It seemed as though the whole world had fallen off its axis. "You don't deserve someone as good and as kind as her."

"You're right," his father said evenly. "I don't deserve your mother, but I love her and you. We are still a family."

"No," Leo spat, adamant. "We're *not* a family. What we are is a farce, and I refuse to be a part of it."

His father dragged a hand through his silvered hair, and the creases on his face looked deeper than ever. "Let's sit on the garden bench and talk."

"I'm already feeling ill," Leo said truthfully. "I don't think I can stomach your excuses or explanations."

"I understand," his father said in a placating tone. "You're hurt and angry. You have every right to be. When you're calmer, I will tell you more. In the meantime, we need to decide how to broach it with your mother."

"No." Leo uttered the word instinctively, reflexively. Because if there was one thing he knew for certain, it was that the truth would kill his mother.

"What do you mean, *no*?"

"I mean you've kept up this charade for God-knows-how-long. Might as well keep it going. I don't want to see her hurt."

His father went very still. "I didn't think you'd . . ." He swallowed as if a knot had lodged in his throat. "I didn't think you'd want to keep the truth from her."

"I hate the thought of lying to her. I can't stay here and pretend we are the perfect little family when you have another wife—and probably a dozen offspring—in another town." Leo cursed under his breath, and in that instant, he knew precisely what he must do. "I'll go to London and find an architect to work with. I'll be out of your life."

"I don't *want* you out of my life," his father protested. "And your mother would miss you horribly." Either he was an impressive actor, or there was genuine anguish in his voice.

But he wasn't deserving of Leo's compassion. "She can visit me in London," he said, resolute. "Or maybe I'll come back to Bellehaven on the days you're in . . . where is it?"

"Fayetteville." His father sighed, defeated.

"Right. I'll be gone by morning. Mother will be sad for a time, but all things considered, I'd say this is the lesser of two evils. I'll leave it to you to console her." Leo took a step toward the house then stopped and added, "When you're not in bed with your other wife."

Those were the last words he'd spoken to his father. He remembered the night like it was yesterday, and the pain was still as raw.

But the letter he'd received from his father's solicitor could not be ignored. If his father had assets that

Leo didn't know about—a distinct possibility given the circumstances—his mother was entitled to her share of them. Hell, as far as Leo was concerned, she was entitled to *all* of them. She had cooked, cleaned, and cared for the man for almost three decades. She deserved to share in any wealth that he'd managed to accumulate despite juggling two households.

Leo would always support her financially and otherwise, but as a matter of principle, she deserved to have some savings of her own—some security and independence as she grew older.

For his mother's sake, Leo absolutely had to attend the meeting, and nothing would keep him away.

Not even his date with Kitty.

The appointment with the attorney was tomorrow morning, and in order to arrive by eleven, he would need to be on the road to London well before daybreak.

It killed him that he'd have to postpone their conversation, and it gave him yet another reason to be angry at his father. But after waiting years and years for Kitty to fall in love with him, he supposed he could wait one more day to hear her say the words.

He just had to make sure she wasn't hurt. He'd write a note explaining why he couldn't meet her as planned, and she would understand. They'd have their whole lives ahead of them. But his mother's entire future could hinge on this one day.

Frantic, he rifled through his desk, found a piece of paper, and dipped the nib of his quill into an inkpot.

Dearest Kitty,
*   I am so sorry that I'm not able to meet you this morning and wish I could have sent word to you at home earlier. It is late in the evening as I write this,*

and I feared that if I left a message at your house it would raise questions with your family. Worse, I was afraid you might leave in the morning before seeing it. I even contemplated scaling the wall below your balcony again to talk to you in person, but that seemed risky, too.

I'm afraid this note was my best option.

There's nowhere I'd rather be than here at the hideaway with you, but I've just received a letter asking me to attend an urgent meeting in London on my mother's behalf. It's imperative that I go, and in order to arrive on time, I must leave Bellehaven before dawn.

I promise to explain the entire situation when I return tonight. I wish that I'd told you the full of it before. If I had, all of this would make more sense.

Please forgive me and know I am counting the minutes until I see you again.

All my love,
Leo

He let the ink dry, folded the paper carefully, and wrote Kitty's name on the outside. Then, he packed a small bag for his trip. Normally, he either took the mail coach to London or rented a coach. This time, however, he decided to call in a favor from somebody who owed him one.

A couple of hours later, while the moon was still high in the black velvet sky, the curricle Leo had borrowed rolled to a stop just off the main road. He grabbed a lantern from the floor beside his feet, hopped to the ground, and followed the narrow path through the grassy reeds to the makeshift shelter on the beach.

The little hut was difficult to see at night. Nestled

between the trees and overgrown with moss, it almost seemed a part a landscape, but the faded blanket at the entrance fluttered softly in the evening breeze, tempting him to go inside and wait for Kitty, the London solicitor be damned.

A true rake would have done just that, but not Leo. He couldn't shirk his duty. All the lessons in the world couldn't change him at his core.

He *had* to go—and there was no time to spare.

He reached into his pocket and hastily withdrew the letter he'd written her along with a straight pin that he'd nicked from one of the fabric sample boards on her desk.

It was difficult to see in the darkness and he pricked himself with the pin twice, but he finally managed to fasten the note to the blue quilt hanging at the entrance. It was in the middle of the entrance where it would be nigh impossible for Kitty to miss.

Now, it was time to focus on his mother and her future.

He scooped up the lantern and dashed back up the path to the curricle, eager to be on his way. As he climbed onto the seat, he thought he felt a cold drop on the back of his neck, so he held out a palm and waited five seconds.

Nothing.

He shrugged, and with a slap of the reins, hurried off to London.

Chapter 24

Kitty had a distinct aversion to mornings. She strongly discouraged conversation before she'd had her first cup of tea and often stifled the unladylike impulse to launch her butter knife at anyone who was intolerably jovial during the breakfast hour.

But on this particular morning, *she* was cheerful. Buoyant. Positively exuberant.

Somehow, although the sun had not yet risen in the sky, she was walking down the path to the beach hut with a spring in her step, making her just the sort of person she normally wished to throttle.

Indeed, given the ungodly hour, there could be only one explanation for her euphoric mood: love.

Heaven help her, she was hopelessly in love with Leo. She loved everything about him. The way he tapped his pencil when he did mental calculations. His tendency to stare at her lips when he thought she wasn't looking. Even his ridiculously meticulous habit of organizing his desk at the end of each workday was oddly charming.

She'd loved him for a while now if she was honest with herself, and it was going to feel so good to let those feelings out. To tell him he'd been right about everything—and that she couldn't wait to spend her whole life with him.

Holding her lantern aloft, she navigated her way through the reeds, surprised to find them slightly wet—as if a storm had swept through during the early morning hours. It already promised to be a warm day, and the balmy ocean breeze rustled the grass as if were gently nudging it awake. It was only a few minutes till dawn.

She'd brought the repaired frame containing the stables drawing with her, thinking it would be a lovely reminder of their first kiss in his apartment—and a symbol of just how far their relationship had progressed. She couldn't wait to see his face when he unwrapped it.

When she arrived at the clearing, she hurried to the rocks, thinking Leo might already be there. He wasn't, but no matter. The sun hadn't peeked over the horizon just yet. He was probably right behind her, on his way down the path.

Giddy with anticipation, she climbed up onto the flat boulders and placed the lantern behind her so that he'd see her immediately when he reached the clearing. She stared out at the ocean, admiring the soft rosy glow that was just beginning to paint the sky. Wishing that Leo was there to see it.

But when the first rays broke through the clouds, she was still alone. She kept turning to look behind her, certain that she'd see him there, smiling like he was as head over heels for her as she was for him.

Doubt started to creep up her spine, but she shook it off.

He was a few minutes late. The old Kitty would have jumped to the worst possible conclusion, stormed away from the beach, and refused to listen to any excuse, but she'd changed. Surely, there was a perfectly good reason that he hadn't arrived before dawn as she'd asked—and as he'd promised.

He was probably on his way right now. She knew him. Believed in him.

So, she waited. The sun rose, the morning mist evaporated, and the air turned humid.

As she stared out at the waves lapping the rocks below, a thought occurred to her. Maybe Leo had arrived before she did. Perhaps he'd gone into the shelter to wait for her and fallen asleep.

She clambered off the rocks, crossed the clearing, and approached the shelter. She skirted a large puddle near the entrance and noted a few twigs littered across the roof, remnants of a summer squall. The blue quilt at the entrance swayed in the breeze and as she swept it aside, something pricked the back of her hand. She paused to examine the quilt and found a straight pin stuck in the fabric. It didn't appear to serve any function and had probably been there for ages. Maybe once upon a time, Poppy had used it to adorn her old hideaway with flowers. Or perhaps she'd used it to pull back an edge of the curtain, allowing a breeze into the shelter.

Alas, when Kitty went inside, there was no sign of Leo. Everything was just as she'd left it the last time they'd visited. The spare quilt was still folded and tucked into a basket on the floor. An old glass bottle still sat on the overturned crate, holding a few wilted wildflowers.

Something was not right. Leo knew how momentous this day was supposed to be for her—and for them. She was ready to banish the demons that kept her from giving him her whole heart, and he'd claimed that was all he'd ever wanted.

But he hadn't shown. What if something awful had happened? Maybe his dear grandfather had taken a bad turn. Perhaps while Leo was riding in the dark, he'd run into a low-hanging branch and fallen off his horse.

She swallowed the awful knot in her throat and hurried back up the path, calling for him just in case he was within earshot. "Leo? Are you here?"

But the only sounds that came back to her were the mocking caws of seabirds and the low roar of the ocean.

Tears burned at the backs of her eyes and slid down her cheeks. Sobs wracked her body.

She had let herself believe in him. Placed all her trust in him.

But here she was, again. Alone.

She should have known better. He'd left her before without a word. Even after returning from London, she'd sensed he was holding back. He'd demanded that she give him everything—her heart and soul—all while refusing to reveal the deep, dark secret about his family.

Life had taught her the harsh lesson over and over again, and still, she'd foolishly dared to believe that she wasn't destined to be alone. But she *was* alone.

The only person she could count on in this world was herself—so she might as well set down that path. She'd go to London. Pursue her career. Live life on her own terms.

In the meantime, however, she needed to be certain that Leo wasn't in trouble. He could be anywhere between the shelter, his mother's house, and his apartment. He had failed her, but she still loved him. If some tragedy had befallen him or his family, he would need her.

She would ensure he was all right, then she'd say goodbye.

She gathered her things, picked up her skirts, and ran.

An assistant in the antechamber of the solicitor's offices greeted Leo and waved him through the door to the small but tidy office occupied by Mr. Abbot. The solicitor was younger than Leo had expected—pale and lanky, as if he rarely ventured outdoors and spent so much time on his work that he occasionally forgot to eat. He had the sort of smile that might have put Leo at ease if he weren't about to meet his late father's second wife. The woman who had constantly pulled his father away from Bellehaven, Leo's mother, and him.

"Please, make yourself comfortable," Mr. Abbot said, gesturing toward the chair opposite his mahogany desk.

Leo unbuttoned his jacket and sat, resisting the urge to nervously tap his foot. At least he'd arrived prior to Sabrina. He couldn't even bring himself to think of her as Mrs. Lockland, the name which should have rightfully been reserved for no one but his mother.

Aware that she could arrive at any moment, Leo came directly to the point. "You indicated that you were aware of my father's situation."

Mr. Abbot shifted in his chair. "I am indeed."

"And is Mrs. Sabrina Lockland aware that my father was married to another woman?"

The solicitor's cheeks flushed. "Actually, he was not."

Leo scratched his head confused. "What do you mean he—" He stopped midsentence, distracted by a sound not unlike a wooden rolling pin with a squeaky handle.

He turned to find an older, slender woman with shrewd eyes, chestnut-brown hair, and a pleasant, freckled face. She sat in a narrow chair with two large wooden wheels attached to either side of it and a smaller wheel centered at the back. A man with sparse silver hair who bore similar features to the woman carefully pushed the wheelchair through the office door and steered it so that she was sitting opposite Mr. Abbot and within arm's length of Leo.

"Thank you. I shall be fine, Marcus," she assured the man, and he retreated to the antechamber, closing the door behind him.

"Mrs. Lockland," the solicitor intoned. "Allow me to introduce Mr. Leo Lockland."

She opened her mouth as if she were about to speak, then inhaled sharply, reached into her reticule, and produced a handkerchief. "Forgive me," she said, dabbing at the corners of her eyes. "I didn't expect you to look so much like him."

Leo swallowed. The hitch in her voice sparked a wave of compassion, something he didn't want to feel. Not for her.

She took a moment to collect herself, then said, "Please, allow me to start over. I realize this must be difficult."

He gave a terse nod, not trusting himself to speak.

"This is all quite unusual," she said evenly. "But I must tell you how very pleased I am to meet you in person. Your father told me so much about you. I feel as though I already know you."

"Then I am at a distinct disadvantage," Leo said curtly. It was yet another punch in the gut—the realization that his father had shared the private details of his life in Bellehaven with her, while Leo and his mother had been completely in the dark about this woman and the life she'd shared with his father.

"Yes, I suppose that is true," she said, thoughtful. "You must have many questions."

Bloody hell. "I have a few," he said dryly. Enough to haunt him day and night. Naturally, he was curious. Had his father had any other children? Had he used a different name? Had he loved his other life more? But mostly what Leo wanted to know was whether any of the best moments of his childhood had been real . . . or whether his entire relationship with his father had been merely a mirage.

"You deserve the truth," she said, her expression earnest. "I will tell you anything I can."

Leo gripped the arms of his chair, determined to control the rage and hurt swirling through him. He wanted to flee the office—and the reality of what his father had done. But he needed to protect his mother from financial uncertainty and, perhaps more importantly, from his father's ultimate betrayal.

"I'd rather limit our conversation to the business at hand," Leo said. He turned to Mr. Abbot and added, "Please, let's proceed with the meeting."

The solicitor blinked, cleared his throat, and shuffled the papers on his desk. "Right. First of all, I'd like to thank you both for coming."

Leo stifled a snort, for it wasn't as though he'd truly had a choice.

"It took some time for me to enumerate all of Mr. Lockland's assets and to address the unique legal circumstances of his situation."

"You are referring to the fact that he had two wives," Leo said bluntly.

The solicitor adjusted his spectacles and met his gaze. "Yes. At least nominally."

"What does that mean?" Sabrina asked, echoing the question in Leo's head.

"Allow me to start at the beginning. Mr. Lockland drafted this will some twenty-odd years ago, when you were still an infant," he said, gesturing toward Leo. "He was not my client at the time, but the document appears to have been witnessed and signed in accordance with the law. His intent seems to have been that Mrs. Sabrina Lockland would inherit the property in Fayetteville and your mother"—he nodded at Leo—"would keep the house in Bellehaven. He specified that all other assets and monies should be split evenly between both women."

Leo released a breath, unaware he'd been holding it.

The terms certainly weren't ideal, but he had to admit they were fair. Indeed, a part of him wondered if perhaps Sabrina might need the money more than his mother. After all, his mother had *him*, and it wasn't clear whether Sabrina had any children or family to look after her.

"But therein lies the issue," Mr. Abbot continued.

Leo's focus snapped back to the solicitor. "I beg your pardon?"

"The will indicates that the monies should be split evenly between his wives, and—well, I'm not quite sure how to say this, but, according to the letter of the law, your mother and father weren't married."

Good God. "That's . . . ridiculous."

"Your father and Mrs. Sabrina Lockland eloped twenty-seven years ago, and their marriage was never annulled. Therefore, his marriage to your mother is not legally recognized."

"No," Leo said, shaking his head. "That can't be true. They lived together as husband and wife for over two decades. Ask anyone in Bellehaven. Surely that constitutes a common-law marriage."

"I'm afraid it doesn't. Not when one of the parties is already lawfully married."

"Perhaps not," Leo ground out. "But you just said that my father's intent was clear."

"It was," the solicitor confirmed. "However, I am afraid that is irrelevant."

"The hell it is," Leo countered, but his stomach churned.
Everything had been an illusion.

His father married Sabrina first.

His parents had never been married.

His mother was entitled to nothing.

"Surely, my mother must have some recourse," he argued, even though he suspected it was futile. "She was unaware of Mrs. Lockland's existence. She is an innocent party in all this."

Sabrina sighed. "Please, Leo—if I may call you that—do not fret over this."

"That is easy for you to say." He dragged his fingers through his hair and took a breath so his voice wouldn't crack. "You didn't watch, year after year, as my mother cooked, cleaned, and cared for us, making our simple cottage feel like a palace. You didn't see her taking care of my father when he was sick or tired. You didn't watch her build her whole life around a man . . . a man who never put her first."

For several moments, the office was unnaturally still and quiet.

At last, Sabrina spoke. "Your father loved you more than life itself. When he talked about you, which was quite often, his whole face lit up with joy, love, and pride. He loved your mother, too."

Leo stared at her, incredulous. "After all he did to us—and to you—how can you honestly say that?"

"I was his first love," she said with a shrug. "I knew him well. We married when we were seventeen, even though our parents urged us to wait, and we were happy. But shortly after, I had a riding accident and my world changed."

"I'm sorry," Leo said sincerely.

Sabrina smiled wanly. "I didn't want him to give up his hopes and dreams to stay home and care for me, so I sent him away. I realize now that my demand was foolish and, in many respects, selfish, but at the time I thought I was doing the right thing. I refused to see him and insisted that he leave Fayetteville. For a whole year he wrote to me and tried desperately to see me. I think I broke his heart."

Leo pressed his fingertips to his forehead. "And that's when he met my mother?"

She nodded. "As far as I know, he never told her about me, but he was very clear that he could not marry her. Which was well and good until . . ." Her voice trailed off.

"She was with child," Leo provided.

"Yes. From that day forward, there was never a doubt in his head as to what he must do."

Leo barked a hollow laugh. "So I am to blame for the whole situation."

"Not at all," she countered swiftly. "*I* am to blame for sending him away. And perhaps he was also to blame, for allowing me to. The point is that from the moment he knew that he would be a father, he never wavered in his love or devotion to you. He begged an audience with me and told me that he intended to marry your mother and give you his name. We tried to get an annulment, but the Church would not grant us one, so he was faced with an impossible choice. Perhaps you can begin to understand why he found himself married to two women."

"I can understand his dilemma," Leo conceded. "But it doesn't explain why he continued to live the lie. Clearly, he still cared for you."

"I won't deny that," she said, lifting her chin. "I cared for him, too. Despite the trials we endured—or maybe because of them—our bond remained strong."

"It didn't bother you that he had another family? Did you not believe that you deserved better?"

"We don't always receive what we deserve, Leo." She sighed. "Maybe I should have turned him away, but his vis-its were the highlight of my month. He told me all about his travels and took me on little trips. He brought me me-mentos from each town he visited and insisted I try new foods and wines. In some ways, he was my window to the world."

Leo grunted. He didn't want to hear about his father's life with her or think about the ways in which she might have needed him too. It was easier when he'd simply—and wrongly—thought of her as the conniving woman who'd stolen his father away. Now he was forced to admit that his father had belonged to her first.

"I told myself that I wasn't hurting anyone," she continued earnestly. "That I only took a small part of him—a part that neither you nor your mother would miss. But I *have* hurt you, and I am sorry for that."

Leo swallowed and looked away. It was far easier to be angry than to be sad, and it seemed that everyone involved had been hurt in some way. Except, perhaps, his mother, who knew nothing of his father's other wife. But even she was grieving.

"There's no point in looking backward, is there?" he mused. "I think our energy is better spent figuring out where to go from here." He turned to the solicitor and said, "I won't stand by while my mother's cottage—her home—is taken from her. So, how do you propose we repair this mess?"

Before Mr. Abbot could reply, Sabrina said, "I think we should do whatever is necessary to honor my late husband's wishes. I will forfeit half of all his assets to the other Mrs. Lockland, and I am willing to sign the Bellehaven deed over to her, if needed."

"That's a very generous impulse," the solicitor said. "However, I strongly suggest that you take some time to mull over your decision. Once done, it cannot be undone."

"I don't need time," Sabrina said, waving a dismissive hand. "I have a spacious home and a modest allowance. Leo's mother deserves that same sort of security."

"You're certain?" Leo asked. Of course he wanted his mother to receive everything she was entitled to, but the victory would feel empty if Sabrina was given short shrift as a result.

"I have everything I need," she confirmed. "This is what your father wanted. More important, it's what's right."

Mr. Abbot initiated a major reshuffling of his papers. "Very well," he said. "I shall review the entire file and prepare the documents to ensure the assets are distributed in accordance with his wishes. I should have them ready in a couple of hours, Mrs. Lockland, if you're able to return and sign them."

"Of course." She turned to Leo, pressed her lips together, then said, "I suppose this is goodbye."

"I cannot tell you how much I was dreading this morning," he confessed. "But I'm glad I met you, and I am grateful for your kindness."

Her eyes welled, and she shot him a tremulous smile.

"May I help you to the antechamber?" he offered.

She nodded, and as he pushed her chair out of the office, she said, "I miss him. I'm sure you feel the loss keenly, too."

Leo mumbled something noncommittal, glad that she couldn't see his face. His feelings for his father were a jumble of anger, hurt, and sadness—a knot he'd likely never untangle.

When they reached the little room outside the office, they found the secretary was gone. The gentleman who resembled Sabrina was slumped in an armchair in one corner, snoring.

"My brother can sleep anywhere," she said with an affectionate cluck of her tongue.

Leo chuckled. "I should go." He was already counting the minutes till he could see Kitty.

"Wait," she implored. "Please, sit for just a moment more."

Reluctantly, he sat in a chair opposite her. He bore her no ill will, but he had little to say to her. Comparing notes of their separate lives with his father was akin to picking at a healing scab. It certainly couldn't help matters, and it could make them markedly worse.

She tilted her head, forcing him to meet her gaze. "Your father hated that he hurt you. He clung to the hope that, in time, you'd eventually forgive him."

Leo grunted, because that was the closest thing to a civil response he could manage.

"I know he was not perfect," she continued, "but he *was* a good man. It makes me happy to know that a part of him lives on in you, and I hope that one day, our paths may cross again."

"No," he said reflexively. "That is, I don't think it would be wise. If my mother ever discovered the truth, she would be devastated."

The night he'd found Sabrina's letter in his father's pocket had been the worst of his life. The mere memory of the confrontation with his father was wrapped up in a pain so fierce that it made his body shake. He couldn't bear to put his mother through that.

"Promise me," Leo continued. "Promise that you won't write to me or try to see me or do anything that might make my mother aware of your relationship with my father."

"Very well," she assured him quickly. "I promise I will refrain from contacting you. But even so, there is a distinct possibility that your mother will one day learn the truth. Our towns are not so very far apart, and we share the last name, after all. Anyone who travels in the area might well question whether we are related."

Leo dragged a hand down his face, muffling a curse.

What Sabrina said was true. Both towns were growing and tended to attract tourists and travelers. "My mother is still grieving. Learning about my father's life with you would increase her suffering tenfold. I need to protect her from that."

Sabrina reached out a hand as if she'd give his arm a comforting pat, but quickly retreated, apparently thinking better of it. Leo couldn't decide if he was relieved or disappointed.

"It's a noble sentiment, Leo—the sort that would make your father proud. But the truth has a way of coming out, and you mustn't blame yourself if you're unable to keep it from your mother."

"You don't know how much it would hurt her," he said. "Or how humiliated she'd be."

Sabrina hesitated a beat. "I think I have some idea of how she'd feel," she said kindly. "And it might surprise you to know that we women—especially those of us not in the first blush of youth—are much stronger than we appear. We've endured physical pain, heartache, and emotional trials . . . and we keep going. Though I've never met your mother, I have no doubt that she's made of sterner stuff."

Leo nodded wearily. Apparently, the lack of sleep was catching up to him. "You've given me plenty to think about on my ride home."

"Some of your questions have been answered," she said sagely. "But now you have new ones. Feel free to contact me any time if I can provide the information you seek. And rest easy knowing that I will not initiate any contact on my part."

"Thank you again," Leo said as he stood and prepared to leave. "I wish you well, Mrs. Lockland."

If anyone had told him that morning that he'd leave the meeting feeling admiration and respect for his father's other wife, he'd have told them they were mad. But the truth was that she was terribly unfit to play the villain. She was far too generous, wise, and kind, which didn't jibe at all with the story he'd written in his head.

Maybe, he thought as he hurried home to Kitty, *maybe stories were meant to be rewritten.*

After all, he and Kitty were once fierce childhood rivals who couldn't agree on something as simple as a stable design, and now they were on the brink of falling in love.

If that was true, perhaps a man who had deceived his wife and son for over two decades wasn't necessarily damned to hell. Maybe, in time, Leo could forgive him.

Chapter 25

"He's not here," Leo's mother informed Kitty, who stood on the doorstep, curious, confused, and hurt.

"We had an appointment this morning," she said vaguely. "I wonder where he could be."

Mrs. Lockland's brow furrowed. "It's certainly not like Leo to miss an appointment, but he has been a bit distracted lately."

"Distracted?" Kitty probed.

"Mmm. It could be the contest, I suppose. Oh, and while he was here last night checking on his grandfather, he picked up a strange letter from London." She shrugged and pasted on a smile. "I'm sure there's nothing to worry about. I suspect Leo's either in his apartment or in the office. Unless you've already checked there?"

"No, I'll head there now," Kitty said. "Please give your father my best. I miss seeing him in the office."

"I know he misses you, too, my dear," she said sincerely. "And he can't wait to see your entry for the architectural design contest."

Kitty thanked her, nodded politely, and set off for town.

By the time she arrived at the office, her feet ached and damp tendrils clung to her neck.

Kirkham looked up as she walked in and blinked. "Are you feeling well? You look a bit feverish."

"I'm fine," Kitty said, too worried to be irritated. "Just winded from my walk. Have you seen Leo today?"

Kirkham twirled his pencil and leaned back on his stool. "No. He's not working today."

"Why not? Did he say something to you?"

"Not exactly, but he borrowed my curricle. He was making a trip to London."

"London?" she repeated as the room tilted. He'd left town instead of meeting her. And to make matters worse, Kirkham knew more about his plans than she did. "Did he mention for how long? Or the nature of the trip?"

"No," Kirkham said with a shrug. "But I assume he'll be back before tomorrow—just in time to turn in his entry for the design contest. If he's not, our odds of winning increase, don't they?"

"Lucky us," she said flatly. She walked to her stool, perched on the seat, and surreptitiously looked around her cluttered desktop in case Leo had left a note. But he hadn't. She placed her elbows on her desk, pressed her fingertips to her temples, and closed her eyes.

"Would you like me to fetch you some water or tea?" Kirkham asked, his voice full of concern.

"No, thank you. I—" She opened her eyes and exhaled. "On second thought, I would welcome a drink. Something of the stronger variety, if you please."

Kirkham arched a brow but slid open a drawer and produced both a flask and glass with impressive alacrity. After pouring a healthy splash of brandy, he reached over her wall of trinkets to hand her the glass.

She gulped it down and set it on the desk with a clunk. Her throat and chest warmed instantly.

"Another?" he asked tentatively.

"No, thank you." As long as she was at the office, she might as well gather up all the pieces of her contest entry and take them to the mayor's house. If she had any more brandy, she'd be staggering through town like she'd stayed for last call at the Salty Mermaid.

She rifled through the stack of papers on her desk, making sure all the necessary pieces of her entry were there: general plans for the theater, detailed drawings of the interior and exterior, framing specifications, and, her favorite, the finishes.

Kirkham cleared his throat. "I sense some friction between you and Leo. Would you care to talk about it?"

"I would not." She swallowed, fearing she'd been too short with him, when he was clearly not to blame for her foul mood. "But I appreciate your concern. I think I shall simply submit my contest entry and return home to rest."

"A capital idea," he said. "In fact, I believe I shall do the same."

Kitty forced a smile as she carefully placed everything in a large brown folder and tucked it under her arm.

Kirkham's forehead creased. "You're going already? Don't you think you should look it over one last time?"

"I've looked at it *ad nauseum*," she replied. "And Leo has checked all my calculations. It's as ready as it can be."

He shifted and scratched his neck. "I'm sure it's brilliant," he said without much conviction. "But one more check couldn't hurt, could it?"

Kitty narrowed her eyes at him. "Are you aware of a particular problem, Mr. Kirkham?"

He heaved a sigh. "I realize I had no business looking at your designs, but I couldn't help noticing the drawing right on the top, which showcases your extraordinary talent for graceful lines and impeccable proportions."

She raised a questioning brow. "But?"

"Upon further examination, I noticed an error."

"That's impossible. Leo reviewed every number."

"He must have missed one," Kirkham said with shrug.

"I'm sure you're mistaken. There's no one more fastidious than Leo." But doubt niggled at her spine. He'd already let her down once today. Maybe he wasn't as perfect as she'd thought.

"Perhaps I'm wrong, but there's no harm in checking. I believe there's a minor discrepancy with the dimensions of the stage." He stood and gestured toward the folder. "May I?"

Kitty inhaled, silently questioning the wisdom of turning down that second drink. "Very well," she said, handing the papers over. "Show me."

He opened the folder and pointed at the number in question. "Here."

She indulged him, scanning the figures and doing a few quick mental calculations—and her stomach dropped through her knees. He was right.

"I cannot believe it." She blinked and took another look, just to be sure her eyes hadn't deceived her, but no. "I forgot to convert these units."

Kirkham nodded in agreement. "I do it all the time. An easy fix."

But that wasn't the point.

She'd missed it. She'd been so intoxicated by her blossoming relationship with Leo that she'd made a careless, silly mistake. One that could have destroyed any chance she had of winning the contest and launching her career.

And he'd missed it, too.

She'd thought he was dependable. That when he gave his word, she could rely on it. That when he'd said he loved her, she could believe it.

Now she wasn't certain of anything. And her head throbbed like the devil.

Kirkham checked her drawing, scribbled some numbers on a scrap of paper, and handed it to her. "I think this is right. You can double-check before you revise the number. I'm happy to look over everything else if you'd like."

"Yes, please," she said wearily. "If you wouldn't mind. I could do the same for your entry, to return the favor."

He waved a dismissive hand. "You look as though you could use a rest. Why don't you go home and lie down for a bit? I'll do a quick review and flag any questions I have."

"I must turn in my entry today," Kitty said, determined to stick to her plan in spite of the fact that the rest of her life seemed to be falling apart.

"Then give me an hour or so with this"—he tapped the folder containing her drawings—"and I'll deliver it to your house myself. I'll bring mine, too, and we can walk to the mayor's residence and turn in our designs together—if that suits you," he added congenially.

Kitty hesitated. She didn't really want to sleep, but it was becoming more and more difficult to keep her emotions in check, and a brief respite in her room, where she wouldn't have to pretend to be fine, was too tempting to resist. "If you're certain you don't mind," she said.

"It would be my honor," Kirkham said sincerely. "Go, and I shall call on you well before the dinner hour."

"Thank you." She started to head toward the door, then paused. She withdrew the wrapped framed stable design from her bag and placed it in the center of Leo's desk. All the heady anticipation she'd felt that morning had fled. Now she was merely fulfilling her obligation to replace something she'd broken. Settling a debt so that she could put the incident behind her and move on. She ignored

Kirkham's curious look and strode out of the office without looking back.

The walk home was only a few blocks. Surely, she could make it there without falling apart. She focused on simply placing one foot in front of the other. Listened to the *click, click* of her slippers on the cobblestones. Tried not to look for Leo in every coach that rolled by or around every corner that she passed.

When the town house came into sight, she picked up her pace. Passersby nodded or smiled, and Kitty kept her head high, ignoring the trembling of her chin and the stinging behind her eyes.

Just a few more yards until she'd arrive at her doorstep, and then two flights of stairs till she reached the solitude of her bedchamber.

She burst through the front door and rushed upstairs to the first landing, when she heard Hazel in the drawing room. "Kitty," she called excitedly, "please come here!"

Oh dear. She had no wish to be rude, but she was currently incapable of smiling and making polite conversation with any guests Hazel might have. "I'll return in a bit," she called back. "There's something I must do," she added vaguely.

"Kitty Beckett," Hazel replied with a combination of playfulness and sternness, "I insist you come see this surprise. At once."

Gads. Well, she'd put on a brave face the whole way home; she supposed she could keep it there for a few more minutes. "Very well," she said as she made her way toward the drawing room doorway, "but I cannot stay very—"

She drew up short and blinked to make sure her eyes weren't deceiving her.

There on the settee, right beside Hazel, was Poppy.

"Look who's returned from London, just in time to attend the Regatta Ball tomorrow!" Hazel teased.

Poppy scrunched her freckled nose and waved a hand. "The ball had nothing to do with it. I thought it was high time the Bellehaven Belles had a meeting." She flashed a wide, sunny smile. "And here we all are."

Kitty stood in the doorway for an interminable second. Then she burst into tears.

Not the delicate sort that one could dab with the corner of a handkerchief. These were hot. Blubbering. Messy.

Before she could even begin to bring herself back under control, Hazel and Poppy encircled her with their arms, patting her back, wiping her cheeks, and telling her that everything would be fine.

But it wasn't and it wouldn't be.

All their well-intentioned coddling only made her sob harder.

Hazel closed and locked the drawing room door while Poppy gently guided Kitty to the settee. Once she was seated, Poppy dashed to the sideboard, poured a glass of brandy, and pressed it into Kitty's hands. "Drink up."

She opened her mouth to say that she'd already had a glass but thought better of it and gulped it down.

"What on earth has happened?" Hazel asked. Worry lines creased her forehead as she handed Kitty a handkerchief.

She blew her nose and took a shuddering breath. "When I woke up this morning, I thought today would be the day I announced my engagement."

"Oh my," Hazel murmured.

"Zounds," said Poppy.

"We were supposed to meet on the beach this morning . . . but he never showed."

Poppy arched an auburn brow. "Who?"

Kitty swallowed. There was no point in hiding the truth. Not from the Belles, at any rate. "Leo Lockland."

"*Leo*?" Hazel repeated, incredulous.

Poppy seemed less surprised. "I thought he was smitten with you."

"So did I," Kitty confessed. "But apparently not."

She proceeded to tell them everything. Or rather, mostly everything. Kitty suspected her friends were capable of reading between the lines.

"I let myself fall in love with him," she said at the end of her recounting, "but today was a splash of cold water. It reminded me of how it feels to love someone and lose them. It reminded me of the vow I made to myself—that I wouldn't marry for love."

"You're overwrought," Hazel said soothingly. "Understandably so. Now is not the time to make big decisions about your future. Wait until you see Leo and hear what he has to say. There could be a perfectly good reason he didn't show this morning."

Kitty realized it was sage advice, but she also heard the unmistakable note of doubt in her friend's voice. She reached for the locket around her neck—the one that had belonged to her mother—and squeezed it in her palm. "Maybe the reason doesn't matter. People leave for all sorts for reasons. In the end, it always hurts. Especially if you love them."

"You're right," Poppy said, surprising Kitty and causing Hazel to frown. "There's no denying it. Loving someone means opening yourself to all sorts of pain. But if you're meant to be with that person, you won't be able to shut them out. They'll keep banging at the door of your heart until you let them in."

"I cannot bear this feeling," Kitty rasped. "This feeling that I'm not in control of my emotions or my future.

For the last couple of weeks I lost sight of what was really important to me. My career. My independence. My peace of mind."

"And you believe those things will be unattainable if you marry Leo?" Poppy asked.

"I think they'd become secondary to love." Kitty stifled a hiccup. "Perhaps his failure to show today was his way of saying that he thinks I'll be better off without him."

For the space of several breaths, her words hung in the air. Neither Hazel nor Poppy contradicted her or tried to make her feel better. Instead, they sat beside her, squeezing her hands as if trying to lend her their strength and ease her pain.

"What are you going to do?" Poppy asked.

Kitty exhaled and straightened her spine. She'd lost her parents when she'd needed them most. She'd fended for herself at strange boarding schools where she knew no one. She'd cried herself to sleep as her friends moved on to pursue their own dreams, their own happy endings.

Somehow, she'd survived all of it. And she'd survive this, too.

Her relationship with Leo had taught her an important lesson. Never again would she make the mistake of giving her heart away.

"I am going to stick to the path I set for myself. After I come into my inheritance, I shall set up house in London and begin my own architectural practice. But first," she said evenly, "I intend to win Bellehaven's design contest." The theater would be her parting gift to the town that had healed her . . . before breaking her heart all over again.

Hazel nodded slowly. "If that is what you truly wish, we will support you. But you should talk to Leo. There may be a reasonable explanation for his absence today."

"There had better be," Poppy remarked in a manner that suggested Leo would do well to steer clear of her.

"It's beside the point," Kitty reasoned. It had been inevitable that Leo would hurt her; it had just happened sooner than expected. "My mind is made up. I'm going to wash my face, take my design to the mayor's residence, and go to bed early so that I'll wake refreshed. I'll spend the day tomorrow packing my things and attend the ball tomorrow night. I shall leave for London the following morning."

Hazel's eyes welled. "Blade and I will miss you terribly."

"I shall miss you, too." Kitty swallowed the awful lump in her throat. "But I'll visit when the baby is born, and you'll come to London, too."

"Of course," she replied with a sniffle. "But it won't be the same as having you under our roof."

Poppy handed Hazel her handkerchief—the only dry one left between the three of them. "Do not fear," she said with a bolstering smile. "Distance cannot keep the Belles apart. We will always find a way to be together when one of us is hurting or in need. Kitty, I know that you have not been able to depend on much in this world, but you may always rely on that."

"Thank you," she said sincerely. "I do feel a little better." Her chest still ached, but at least now she had a plan.

A couple of hours later, as promised, Kirkham arrived on Kitty's doorstep holding one large folder with her entry and another with his. "The one mistake I found in your design at the office was clearly an aberration," he said. "Your drawings are otherwise flawless—and nothing short of spectacular," he added magnanimously.

"Thank you." If she weren't so exhausted and heartbroken, she might have basked in the compliment. Now, she just wanted to officially submit her entry and return to her bedchamber.

Kirkham shot her a sympathetic smile. "Forgive me for saying so, but you look tired. Would you like me to deliver your entry to the mayor's house for you? I'm already going there to take my own."

She debated answering in the affirmative, but after investing so much time, so much effort into her work, she wanted to see it through to the end. "I appreciate the offer, but I will go, too. Perhaps the fresh air will do me some good."

But she didn't feel better after turning in her contest entry, and she took dinner in her room, forcing herself to eat despite her lack of appetite. She picked up a book, thinking it might be just the thing to make her momentarily forget her sorrows. She couldn't seem to get past the first page, but there was something comforting about the weight of the book on her lap, so she kept trying.

A soft knock made her lift her eyes toward the doorway where Hazel stood. She swept the chestnut curl off her forehead and smiled. "Leo is downstairs. He's asked to see you."

Kitty's heart kicked into a gallop. "It's rather late, isn't it?"

Hazel glided into the room and perched on the edge of the bed. "Certainly not usual calling hours, but perhaps this is an unusual situation. Will you see him?"

She wanted to. She wanted to ask him why he'd let her down. Why he didn't love her in the same way she loved him—with every part of her being. She wanted to wrap her arms around him and never let him go. But she knew now that was impossible. Love never lasted.

"I don't think that would be wise," Kitty said firmly.

"Maybe not," Hazel mused, "but he seems rather anxious to see you. Don't you want to at least hear what he has to say?"

"I do. And I will listen, but not tonight." She was feeling too raw, too bruised. "Would you please tell him that I will see him tomorrow night, at the ball?"

Hazel frowned. "Are you certain that's the best venue for your conversation? All of Bellehaven will be there."

"Yes," Kitty said, suppressing the impulse to toss aside her book and run downstairs to him. "I do think that would be best." If they were in the midst of a crowd, there would be little danger of her falling prey to the same heady whirlwind of passion and promises. She'd set her course, and she intended to follow it.

"Very well," Hazel said, her eyes brimming with sympathy. "I will tell him, and perhaps things will seem less dire in the light of morning."

"Thank you." Kitty pulled her knees to her chest as Hazel closed the door behind her.

Two nights and one day. That's all she had to endure before she could flee to London, leaving Bellehaven—and all its poignant memories—behind.

Chapter 26

Kitty didn't want to see him.

Leo didn't blame her for being upset, but he thought that she'd understand why he'd had to go to London on short notice. That she'd give him the chance to explain. And that the truth might even make them closer in the end.

But she'd refused to see him tonight, and he had to respect that.

If he was truly a rake, maybe he'd have thrown pebbles at her window, lured her to the balcony, and tried to sway her with poetry or flowers or flattery. But he *wasn't* a rake, and the reality was that he never would be. Not even for Kitty.

So all Leo could do was wait to talk to her and hope that his explanation was enough.

That *he* was enough.

Though his heart wasn't really in it, he walked to the office. The door had scarcely shut behind him when he saw it—a thin parcel wrapped in plain brown paper lying on his desk. He quickly lit a lamp and sat down, contemplating what the package could be.

Something told him it was from Kitty, and his hands shook as he tore away the paper.

It was his framed stable drawing. With Kitty's decorative accents. And the glass covering was intact. She'd had it repaired, apparently—an undeniably thoughtful gesture.

But he missed the broken glass. He longed for the days of Kitty throwing pillows at his head, causing mayhem in his apartment, and kissing him with unbridled passion.

He hadn't forgotten the heart he'd drawn on the back of his design, and he idly wondered if she'd seen it. But it didn't really matter in the end. If she'd delivered it to him in person, it might have meant something. But she'd left it on his desk as though she were merely fulfilling an obligation. As if she was saying goodbye.

And he couldn't blame her.

With a heavy heart, he gathered up his contest entry, and left it with the mayor's butler, apologizing for coming at the late hour. Then he returned to his apartment, crawled into his bed, and stared at the ceiling for a few hours till exhaustion finally overtook him.

He woke the next morning as confused and miserable as the night before, but took some comfort from the fact that he'd see Kitty that night. He believed in his soul that if they talked, she'd forgive him. More important, she'd remember that in spite of their many differences, there was something very right about them together.

But since the ball was still hours away, he decided to visit his mother, and after a quick stop at the tea shop, he walked into her house and handed her a bag of freshly baked tarts.

"What a lovely surprise!" she said with a teasing smile. "I'm referring to you *and* the tarts, of course."

"I thought Grandfather would welcome something other than soup," Leo said with a chuckle. "How is he faring?"

"Much better." His mother clucked her tongue. "The mayor sent a coach 'round for him this morning, and despite my objections, he insisted on going to the Assembly Rooms to meet with him and Lady Rufflebum in order to judge the contest."

"That's good," Leo said, relieved on two counts. Foremost, that his grandfather was much improved. Second, that he'd provide an objective, unbiased view of all the contest entries—and Kitty's in particular.

Leo sank into the worn armchair in the small parlor, and his mother sat on the settee across from him. "Kitty Beckett came here looking for you yesterday morning," she said casually.

He blinked at that. "Did she?"

"She said you were supposed to meet her but that you never showed. I confess I was a little worried. That's not like you."

The hair on the backs of Leo's arms stood on end, and his mind whirred. No wonder Kitty was upset with him. Perhaps she hadn't seen the note, or something had happened to it, or . . .

Bloody hell. She must have thought that he'd left her. Again.

"You look a bit pale," his mother said, frowning. "Is everything all right?"

"Not entirely," Leo said. "But I hope that it will be." He hesitated, then added, "I went to London yesterday to meet with Father's solicitor."

His mother's eyes widened, and she swallowed. "I see. That must have been difficult for you."

"In some ways," he said truthfully. "But the important thing is that you needn't worry. The house is yours, of course. Once the solicitor finishes his accounting of all of Father's assets, you should receive a nice sum."

She exhaled. "I had wondered. That is, I suppose you now know about Sabrina."

Leo nearly fell out of his chair. "You know about her?" he said, incredulous.

"I've known for several years," she said softly. "Long before you went to work in London. Your father never knew that I knew."

"Why?" Leo dragged a hand down his face. "That is, why did you allow it?"

She shrugged her thin shoulders. "Perhaps the better question is why did Sabrina allow it? He spent the majority of his time with us, after all. I knew that he had another life and I'd hoped you'd never discover the truth. When you and your father had the falling out, I worried that perhaps you'd found out about her, but I couldn't bring myself to talk to you about it. I suppose I should have."

"You were trying to protect me," Leo mused, "at the same time I was trying to protect you."

"I found out about Sabrina when my cousin James traveled through Fayetteville on his way here. He said that while he was visiting a tea shop, he met a woman who was confined to a wheelchair, and she had the surname *Lockland*. Sabrina had assured him that the common surname was merely a coincidence, but I sensed, deep in my bones, that there was more to the story. I did a bit of investigating after that and confirmed my suspicions."

"And you never confronted him?" Leo asked, dumbfounded. "Never called him to account?"

"I was able to put the pieces of the puzzle together myself." She sighed and let her gaze sweep across the cottage as though she was recalling the life they'd made there. "I saw no need to upset the apple cart at that point. We'd been together for so long, and despite all the secrets between us, we were happy."

"Were we?" Leo asked, his voice thick with emotion. "Or was it all a facade?"

"I know it seems inconceivable," she said wistfully. "That I should love a man who was married to another. But I did love him, and we both loved you—very much. He didn't give us all of himself, but he gave us all that he could."

Holy hell. Leo leaned back and scratched his head, flummoxed. He'd learned more about his family in the last twenty-four hours than he had in the last twenty-four years. His mother's words—the part about his father not giving them all of himself—still rang in his ears. Maybe because that's what had hurt the most. Knowing that his father hadn't been one hundred percent committed to them.

And he would not make the same mistake with Kitty. He'd been holding back, trying to show her the parts he thought she wanted to see. But she deserved someone who would give her no less than one hundred percent. He had to be fully himself, and fully invested in her. In *them*.

He only hoped he wasn't too late.

Almost as if she'd read his mind, his mother asked, "You haven't talked to Kitty yet, have you?"

"I tried," he admitted. "She didn't want to see me last night, but I'll have an opportunity to talk with her at the ball."

"Can a mother give her son some unsolicited advice?" she asked with a shy smile.

"Look at me." Leo held up his palms helplessly. "I'm in no position to turn down wisdom, solicited or otherwise."

"When you have the chance to talk to Kitty, don't leave anything unsaid." She paused and blinked rapidly, as if she were fending off tears. "You may think there will be another opportunity to tell her how you feel, but sometimes there isn't."

Leo went to his mother and pressed a kiss to her cheek. "Don't worry. I plan to say everything—and I must hope that is enough."

He gave her hand a reassuring squeeze and was about to retrieve his hat from the hook when a coach rolled up their drive. He hurried out front and helped his grandfather alight from the cab.

"It is good to see you out of bed," Leo remarked, though he couldn't help noticing the dark circles beneath the older man's eyes. "How are you feeling?"

His grandfather responded with an uncharacteristic scowl. "Fine, physically. But I've just come from the Assembly Rooms where the mayor, Lady Rufflebum, and I judged the contest entries, and now . . . I am livid." He punctuated the thought with a coughing fit that folded him in half.

Leo quickly ushered him into the house and helped him settle into the armchair while his mother fetched a glass of water.

"You mustn't let the contest distress you," Leo said.

"I knew it was foolhardy for you to venture out," his mother said more sternly. "You haven't fully recovered yet."

"I had to go," Leo's grandfather rasped, adamant. "The other two judges are making a mockery of the contest. Despite my best efforts to make them see reason, they are hell-bent on using their own criteria to choose the winner."

Leo's shoulder blades prickled with unease. All he could think about were the stunning drawings that he'd seen on Kitty's desk on the night he'd snuck into her bedchamber. She needed to win. She deserved to win. And the world needed her talent.

"I officially withdraw my entry," Leo said. He didn't know if it would make a difference in the outcome, but if the judging wasn't fair, he wanted no part of the contest. "I'll go tell the mayor that I'm no longer in the running."

His grandfather snorted and waved a hand. "It's too late, and it won't make a difference anyway. The winner has already been determined."

"And it's not Kitty?" Leo asked.

He hesitated a beat and shook his head sadly. "I cast my vote for her, but no. It's not Kitty."

Leo raked a hand through his hair and paced the width of the small parlor. "I don't understand. I *saw* her drawings. They're beyond beautiful. They're flawless."

His grandfather grunted.

Leo froze, perplexed. "You disagree?"

"The drawings themselves are exceptional. Everything I dreamed Kitty was capable of."

"But?" Leo probed.

"The numbers, the measurements," his grandfather said ruefully. "There were a handful of errors—too significant to ignore."

"Impossible," Leo said, resolute. "I checked every calculation myself."

"Then she must have adjusted some numbers at the last minute." The older man heaved a weary sigh. "All I know is that the technical shortcomings gave the mayor and countess the opening they needed to support their own pet projects. The mayor likes yours, of course. He wants Bellehaven Bay to be the most fashionable spot for Londoners to spend their summers, and he believes a new inn would allow the town to grow by leaps and bounds."

"I assume the countess cast her vote for Kirkham's entry?" Leo asked.

"Once she realized he intended to name the project the Rufflebum Observatory, there was never any doubt."

"Bloody hell," Leo muttered. To his grandfather, he said, "Kitty can still win. Once I tell the mayor that I'm opting out of the contest, you can convince him to change his vote to Kitty's entry. This contest means everything to her, and a theater as unique as hers would lure as many tourists here as the ocean does."

"The mayor said that it doesn't make sense to build a new attraction like the theater when the Bluffs' Brew Inn is already bursting at the seams. And though I'm loathe to admit it, he has a point. Between the regatta today and the ball tonight, there won't be an empty bed or floor in Bellehaven this weekend."

Leo crossed his arms and exhaled slowly—a futile attempt to relieve the tension coiling inside him. "If each of the judges voted for a different entry, the contest should be a draw, shouldn't it?"

"One judge's vote carries a bit more weight," his grandfather said wryly.

"Lady Rufflebum's?"

He shrugged. "She's funding the building out of her own coffers. I suppose she deserves to have the final say."

Leo shook his head and met his grandfather's gaze. The seed of an idea was sprouting in his head, and though it would require a bit of finesse—the sort that had never come naturally to him—he was determined to give it a try.

If this plan was to have any hope of success, he'd need to draw on every ounce of his rakish charm.

Thank God he'd been taught by the best.

Chapter 27

That night, as Kitty alighted from the coach and walked into the Assembly Rooms with Hazel and Blade, her uncle squeezed her hand and shot her a bolstering smile. "I don't know the source of your sadness, but you should try to enjoy yourself at the ball."

Kitty couldn't see how such a thing was possible, but she supposed she could pretend to do so—at least for his and Hazel's benefit. "You needn't worry about me. I am determined to move on." She strode up the walkway, letting the golden silk skirt of her ball gown swirl about her legs.

"You could always tell me his name," Blade said with feigned nonchalance, "and allow me to teach him a lesson."

"That won't be necessary," Hazel said pointedly. "Kitty can take care of herself."

"Yes," she said, rolling her eyes as if the well-intentioned words hadn't struck a nerve. The truth was she'd always taken care of herself. Not by choice, but by default. Apparently, that was how it was meant to be.

"I have a feeling we shall have something to celebrate by the end of the evening," Blade said in an obvious attempt to change the subject.

"Right," Kitty said flatly. "The contest." She took the arm her uncle offered as they made their way up the staircase to the main ballroom.

"We're so proud of you," Hazel said sincerely. The sapphire ribbon threaded through her chestnut-brown curls complemented her sky-blue gown perfectly. "I agree with your uncle. If this is to be your last night in Bellehaven, you must make it a night to remember."

Blade snorted. "That's not exactly what I said."

Kitty glanced at the slight curve of her friend's belly, which seemed to become more noticeable each day. "Are you certain you feel well enough to be here? If you become tired or sick, you must tell me at once, and we will take you home to bed."

Hazel waved a dismissive hand. "I've been feeling much better for the last fortnight or so. Besides, nothing could keep me from watching them announce the winner of the contest. You've worked so hard for this honor."

"I haven't won yet," Kitty reminded her in a hushed voice, but she hoped beyond hope that she would. She'd poured her heart and soul into her entry, producing the absolute best design she was capable of. If it wasn't enough, then she wouldn't be able to help thinking that perhaps *she* wasn't enough.

"Oh my," Hazel remarked as they approached the ballroom entrance. "What on earth is this?"

Kitty blinked up at the yards and yards of white linen suspended from the ceiling and billowing slightly from the cross breeze. "It looks rather like a sail."

A young man dressed in a naval uniform picked up a bottom corner of the linen sheet and swept it aside so that Hazel, Blade, and Kitty could make their entrance.

It seemed the decorating committee for this year's Regatta Ball had outdone themselves, transforming the usually barren assembly room into a huge ship deck, complete with railings marking the edges of the dance floor, a life-sized mermaid figure suspended from the prow, and silk panels of reds, oranges, and yellows hanging from the walls mimicking the brilliant colors of a sunset. There was even a gangplank leading from the deck to refreshment table, which had been cleverly fashioned from stacks of trunks and luggage. Most of the staff were dressed as the ship's crew, with a few pirates thrown in for good measure. The mayor, of course, wore a captain's uniform.

"How lovely," Hazel murmured. "I feel as though I'm about to embark on a trans-Atlantic voyage—but without the seasickness."

Kitty, however, was feeling decidedly queasy as she gazed around the crowded room, looking for Leo. Saying goodbye to him would be rather like the pain of resetting a broken bone—brutal and excruciating, but necessary in order for the healing to begin.

And she supposed the sooner she was done with it, the better.

But she didn't see his light-brown hair or hazel-flecked eyes among the guests, making her wonder if tonight would be yet another instance where she'd be left waiting for him. Where she was not his priority.

"Ah, there you are!" Poppy glided toward Kitty, her dashing husband, Keane, at her side. As Poppy drew closer, though, she slowed and stared curiously. "My goodness, Kitty. You've always been beautiful, but there's something positively ethereal about you in that dress."

"Thank you. The gown is Clara's design," she said. "And you, I must say, are a vision in peach silk."

"The Belles certainly have come a long way," Poppy

whispered with a saucy smile. She tilted her head, thoughtful. "You were looking for someone just now. Leo?"

Kitty swallowed. "Have you seen him?"

"Not yet. If I do, I shall be sorely tempted to throttle him."

"I appreciate the sentiment," Kitty said, warmed by her friend's loyalty. "But I don't think that will be necessary."

"You're right." Poppy arched an auburn brow. "That gown is all the revenge you need."

Kitty mustered a smile. It was just the sort of thought she might have had herself—if she hadn't felt so hollow and sad.

"Don't look now, but I do believe your first dance partner of the night is on his way," Poppy murmured.

Kitty danced the first set with Mr. Kirkham, the second set with a handsome earl from London, and the third set with Dr. Gladwell's dashing younger brother who was visiting from Somerset. As she whirled across the dance floor, she made witty conversation and executed every step perfectly—so no one would guess that her head and her heart were miles away.

It wasn't until she was going to fetch a glass of lemonade that Leo intercepted her on the gangplank.

His hair was windblown, his jacket wrinkled, and his cravat askew—and the sight of him made her pulse leap, dash it all.

"I apologize for being late," he said breathlessly. "I had something important to—" He stopped midsentence, as if belatedly realizing he was implying that she was *not* as important. "In any event," he said soberly, "I'm here now, and I'm eager to speak with you."

Kitty gazed into his eyes and allowed herself one moment to remember.

Busy days in the office punctuated by hot, stolen glances.

Warm afternoons spent in secluded coves and on wind-swept beaches.

Late nights filled with teasing banter and seductive whispers.

All of it had been lovely . . . but it was over.

"I need to talk to you as well."

"Let's go to the mezzanine," he said, looking up at the small balcony above the dance floor. "It isn't crowded at the moment."

"Very well," she said. "I'll meet you there in a few minutes."

He hesitated, then added, "All I ask is that you give me the chance to explain." There was a note of desperation in his voice. A hint of panic.

"I will listen, Leo. I owe you that much." It wasn't necessary for her to say the next part out loud—that nothing he could say would change her mind.

The fear in his eyes told her that he already knew.

This was Leo's last shot. At happiness, love, and, above all, a future with Kitty.

She stood at the mezzanine railing, peering down at the bustling dance floor, so beautiful that he could scarcely breathe. To any casual observer, she looked calm and composed.

But he could read her better than anyone, and he saw the storm of emotions swirling below the surface. What struck him most, though, was her expression. Both wistful and determined, it made him shiver with apprehension.

He approached and handed her a peach rose that he'd nicked from a huge vase on the refreshments table. "I've missed you, Kitty."

Her mouth quirked into a wry smile, and she twirled the stem between her fingertips. "How very rakish of you—attempting to ply me with a stolen flower and pretty words."

"The flower is stolen. The words are true."

She hesitated a moment and turned serious. "I waited for you," she rasped. "I waited for hours, and you never came."

"I am sorry," he said, resisting the urge to fold her into his arms. "I left you a note. I pinned it to the quilt at the entrance of the shelter. You didn't see it?"

Her gaze snapped to his. "No. It was gone when I arrived. I think it may have stormed overnight."

Leo pressed his palm to his forehead and muffled a curse. "Maybe it blew away, or maybe someone else took it, but that is beside the point. I knew how important that morning was to you, and I should have been there."

"I suppose I would have been less worried if I'd seen your note. If I'd had some inkling why you didn't show." She swallowed and took a moment to compose herself before she continued. "But the truth is that I still would have been hurt. I want to be someone's priority. Not all the time, certainly. But for the big moments. You may think me selfish—and perhaps I am—but I want someone who puts me first."

"That's not selfish, Kitty. It's what you deserve. That's what I've been trying to tell you all along."

"I know," she said softly. "But you didn't put me first yesterday. More important, you didn't put *us* first."

"You're right," he admitted. He could almost see her withdrawing. Slipping away from him. And he was bloody terrified. "I wish I'd done things differently, starting with that night we met at the beach hideaway. You said no more secrets, and I should have told you about my father then. I went to London yesterday to meet with his solicitor."

She tilted her head, curious. "Go on."

He told her everything then. All of it, starting with the day he discovered his father's infidelity, right up to the conversation he had with Sabrina.

Kitty listened, her blue eyes shining with compassion. "You and your father were always so close. You must have been devastated."

"That's why I left Bellehaven four years ago. It's why I didn't say goodbye to you—even though I loved you then." He brushed his thumb across the back of her hand, willing her to open to him, to lace her fingers through his.

But she stiffened and pulled her hand away.

"I couldn't bring myself to explain at the time," he said. "I knew you'd have questions. Questions I couldn't answer without revealing that my father was married to two women."

"I imagine it was terribly lonely," she said. "I would have understood. As much as we argued, we always found a way to compromise in the end. I cared about you."

Leo gazed into her eyes. "I should have trusted you with the truth—both about my family and my feelings for you. God knows, if I could go back and do it over, I would."

"I wish that you could, too." The regret in her voice flooded his veins with panic. "But I believe it was meant to happen like this. To save us from an even greater pain in the end."

"No," he said firmly. "I don't believe that. Think about how ridiculously happy we were over the last couple of weeks we spent together. You were eager to tell me something yesterday morning. I'm here now. You can say it."

His whole world boiled down to that spot on the mezzanine, that moment in time.

Tell me you love me . . . or hate me. Tell me everything in your heart. Just don't say that we're through.

She swallowed. "It's no longer relevant. Happily-ever-afters aren't for everyone. I'm certain you'll find yours someday. For my part, I must content myself with being content."

"Content?" he repeated, incredulous.

"I'm leaving Bellehaven. First thing tomorrow. You'll eventually find someone who can give you her whole heart, and I . . . well, I'll find satisfaction in my work."

No. He couldn't lose her again. "You needn't choose between love and—"

Clink, clink, clink.

A sudden hush fell over the crowd below.

All eyes turned to Mayor Martin, who was tapping a spoon against his champagne glass. Lady Rufflebum stood at his side, the ostrich feather in her hair fluttering as she craned her neck around the room, glaring at a handful of guests who hadn't yet quieted.

"Goodness," Kitty breathed. "They're going to announce the winner."

Holy hell. He'd thought he'd have more time to implement his plan.

"May I have your attention, please?" boomed the mayor.

Kitty gripped the railing as if she were bracing herself for whatever he might say.

If there was one thing Leo hated, it was a spectacle.

But for Kitty, he was about to make one of himself.

And he hoped to hell it worked.

Chapter 28

Kitty silently congratulated herself on making it through the conversation with Leo. She hadn't cried or capitulated, but it had not been easy.

He'd finally poured out his heart—about his family and his feelings.

She'd wanted to take his hand and whisk him away to a secluded spot where they could kiss and hold each other. But she'd stayed true to her decision, reminding herself that she was saving them from greater pain.

In the end, someone was always left alone.

Now, it was well and truly over, and she welcomed the distraction of the contest announcement. She attempted to focus her attention on the mayor and countess, who stood at the helm of the ship deck below.

But out of the side of her eye, she saw Leo tugging at his cravat.

"Are you feeling well?" she asked, frowning.

He pulled the knot of his neckcloth loose and slid it from his neck. "Never better," he said blithely, as he proceeded to wind the cravat around his head and tie it at the back.

"Have you gone mad?"

"Apparently," he quipped.

"Ladies and gentlemen," Mayor Martin intoned, "As your captain"—he paused to tug at the lapels of his gold-trimmed jacket—"I have the distinct privilege and pleasure of introducing Bellehaven Bay's most generous benefactor, the most honorable Lady Rufflebum, who will announce the winner of our architectural design contest."

A smattering of polite applause filled the room as the countess cleared her throat.

Meanwhile, Leo had shed his jacket and was crouching, with one arm stuck inside a large decorative urn beside the railing.

"What are you doing?" Kitty ground out. "Don't you want to hear the contest results?"

"No." He pulled the end of a thick rope from the urn and quickly secured it to one of the railing posts. "I already know what the countess is going to say . . . and I intend to stop her."

"Don't be ridiculous," Kitty said. "She's about to speak."

"We had several impressive entries," Lady Rufflebum crooned. "Three were rather exceptional. But after an abundance of careful thought and consideration, I am pleased to announce that the winner of the contest is none other than—"

"Ahoy! Make way below!" Leo slung a leg over the railing and let the rope drop. The end swung about a foot above the heads of the guests, who gasped, backed away, and looked up.

"You really have gone mad," Kitty murmured.

"Is that . . ."—Lady Rufflebum squinted up at the mezzanine—"Leo Lockland?"

"Good heavens," the mayor cried. "I believe we have a mutiny on our hands."

Leo sat on the railing as if he were oblivious to the

fact that he was perched twenty feet above the ground. His shirt hung open at the collar and with the cloth tied jauntily around his head, he did indeed resemble a rather dashing pirate.

"What's the meaning of this, Lockland?" Kirkham called out, scowling. He stood a few yards in front of the countess, clearly prepared to accept his award. "If I didn't know better, I'd think you were trying to sway the judges."

"Perhaps I'm taking a page out of your book, old friend." Leo winked at Kitty as he gripped the rope and maneuvered his body over the railing. "Wish me luck."

"Don't do this," she pleaded. "You'll break your neck."

But he was already deftly shimmying down the knotted rope, which swung like a pendulum. The muscles in his back and shoulders flexed as he worked his way lower and lower. The crowd looked on, apparently as mesmerized as she was.

When he reached the end of the rope, he used his weight and momentum to swing close to the prow of the ship, then let go and landed lightly on the deck. He jumped onto the edge of the ship, just beside the mermaid, and stood with his feet shoulder-distance apart and his hands planted on his hips.

"On behalf of the fine citizens of Bellehaven Bay," he proclaimed, "I want to welcome those of you visiting our fair town. You should know that we do things a bit differently here, and our quirks are a part of our charm." He turned to the mayor and flashed a wide grin. "Wouldn't you agree, Mayor Martin?"

"Well," he replied, clearly flustered, "it is true we are an exceptional town. I suppose we are a bit unique . . . but also quite fashionable," he added as an afterthought.

"Very fashionable," Lady Rufflebum echoed proudly—
though she, too, was clearly confused.

"We balance respect for tradition with an *avant-garde*
spirit," Leo explained, "and that is why the winner of the
architectural design contest will be decided not solely by
a select committee, but also by all of you."

With that, he strode to the wall covered in sunset-hued
silks, grabbed a fistful of peach fabric, and yanked it
down, pulling it free from its pins.

The guests gasped.

Leo pulled down more silk panels.

Shimmering waves of warm yellows, oranges, and reds
billowed to the floor, revealing a wall papered in scores
of architectural drawings. Elevations, floor plans, and fin-
ishings. Site plans, landscapes, and artist's renditions. All
were neatly tacked to the wall, and above each group of
related drawings, the project name and architect were
written in bold, precise print.

THE BELLEHAVEN BAY INN AND PUB BY MR. L. LOCK-
LAND.

THE RUFFLEBUM MARITIME OBSERVATORY BY MR. V.
KIRKHAM.

And, right in the center, THE ATLANTIS STAGE BY MISS
K. BECKETT.

Her work was plastered across the wall for all to see,
and she didn't feel a whit of fear or trepidation. All she felt
was pride . . . and love. Pride in her work, and love for Leo.

He'd known what this contest meant to her and was determined to make it fair in spite of the suspect judging
process. Leo had found a way to let the townspeople see
her work. He'd made sure she had a chance to shine—even
though it required him to do something uncharacteristically reckless and risky.

"As many of you know," Leo continued, "the winning design will be constructed in the heart of our town, so it seems fitting that all of you should have a say in the judging."

"This is preposterous," Kirkham interjected with disgust. "You're either foxed or mad if you think you can circumvent the rules that were established prior to the contest. The decision rests with the judges."

"It does indeed," Leo replied. "But it's the judges' prerogative to solicit the public's opinion, is it not?"

"The public's opinion?" the countess repeated with obvious distaste. "The public are not funding construction of the project."

Leo flashed her a smile. "You are quite right, as always, Countess. And you are a *most* generous benefactor. I am merely suggesting that the good citizens of Bellehaven should be permitted to see the designs for themselves. Surely, there's no harm in letting them make their voices heard before you and the mayor announce the winner."

She shrugged, mollified by the compliments.

The guests had already crowded to the side of the deck nearest the display of drawings and were craning their necks in order to see the entries.

"The winner is supposed to be announced tonight," Kirkham objected. "We don't have time for these shenanigans, Lockland."

"While I generally give great import to the wishes of citizens," the mayor said with diplomatic flair, "I must agree with Mr. Kirkham. I do not see how we can expeditiously assess public sentiments of these projects."

"As it happens," Leo said casually, "I have given the matter some thought."

"Of course you have," Kirkham muttered.

Leo strode to the refreshments table, opened a large

sack that was apparently meant to look like a ship's cargo, and pulled out a handful of shells. "Everyone here is invited to take one and place it in the vase beneath the design entry of their choice. The voting closes in one hour, and it starts *now*."

The crowd surged toward Leo, who began handing out shells. The guests gathered in front of the drawings, eager to have their say. Some chatted animatedly about the designs; others examined them thoughtfully. And before long, the ballroom was filled with the *clink, clink, clink* of shells being dropped into vases.

Kitty left the mezzanine, descended the stairs, and crossed the dance floor toward Leo. He'd literally transformed himself into a pirate for her. All because he knew what the contest meant to her and understood how it could launch her career. He'd cared enough to descend from the balcony, risking life and limb. He'd created the sort of spectacle that the Bellehaven gossips would recount for years to come. And he'd done it because he loved her.

He was still wearing the cravat on his head, still passing out shells, but when he saw her approach, he froze and met her gaze.

And her insides melted.

It still hurt that he'd left her waiting at their meeting place. But shutting him out hurt more. Maybe that was the problem with true love. It never really left a person. She could say it was over. She could even run away to London. But her love for Leo would always be there, deep inside her, welling up and spilling over at the most inconvenient times.

She swallowed. "Could we talk?"

He smiled, handed the sack to another gentleman, and slid the neckcloth off his head. "Shall we head to the balcony for some fresh air?"

She nodded and glided to the French doors at the rear of the room. The terrace beyond wasn't very big, but if the moon was bright enough, they'd have a view of the bay.

It would be a romantic spot for her to share her heart. And perhaps private enough to steal a kiss.

But just as they were about to leave the ballroom, Kirkham blocked their path, his expression full of disdain. "I could never quite tell whether you two were vexed or smitten with each other, and I doubt you are certain either. But one thing is clear—you conspired to keep me from winning the contest with this"—he waved his hand as he searched for the word—"circus."

"Kitty had nothing to do with this," Leo said. "And you still have a shot at winning. Though your odds have significantly decreased—now that the contest is fair."

"*I* was playing by the rules," Kirkham said, all innocence.

"Then why did you try to sabotage Kitty's entry?"

Her stomach dropped through her knees, and she faced Leo. "What are you talking about?"

"Kirkham changed some of the measurements on your drawings. Almost as if he knew he didn't stand a chance against you otherwise."

She gasped and turned to Kirkham, who was red as a beet. "You altered my entry? You had no right." She'd been so distraught when she left her design with Kirkham that she hadn't even thought to check it again—and she'd never dreamed that another professional would stoop so low.

"You were foolish to trust me—your competition. And you're foolish to trust him, too," he added, gesturing toward Leo.

Kitty curled her fingers into her palms. "He is nothing like you. He is honorable and loyal and good."

She turned to Leo and let her love for him wash away her anger. "It seems that despite my best efforts, I was unable to change who you are at your core. And if you want to know the truth, I'm glad. Though you can be extremely vexing at times . . . I wouldn't want to change a thing about you."

"How very touching," Kirkham said dryly.

Leo ignored him and gazed into Kitty's eyes, his expression hopeful. "Fortunately, I had made a record of all the measurements on your drawings. I hope you don't mind, but I changed them back before I hung up your designs."

Kitty's chest felt like it would burst from happiness. She really could count on Leo. "Thank you."

"Please allow me to offer my congratulations, Miss Kitty." The male voice behind her belonged to Dr. Gladwell.

"Whatever for?" she asked, puzzled.

"Your stunning theater, of course," he said with a chuckle. "It's all people can talk about. They can't wait to see it in the heart of our town." He cast an apologetic glance at Leo and Kirkham. "No offense, gentlemen."

"None taken," Leo said with a polite bow. Kirkham snorted.

"They like it," Kitty murmured, more to herself than anyone else. A part of her worried that her designs were too much. Too whimsical. Too fanciful. Too different.

"You needn't take my word for it," the doctor said, gesturing toward the wall where the designs hung. "Go see for yourself."

Kitty nodded, then she and Leo weaved their way through the crowd toward the drawings. When they reached the front of the line, she could scarcely believe her eyes.

The vase below her entry was overflowing with shells.

They were piled high above the brim and had even spilled onto the ground.

"They love your theater," Leo said softly. "They see your talent. They'd have to be blind not to."

"Your design is impressive, too," Kitty said sincerely. "It may not have quite the same flair or be quite as unique, but it is solid and sound—just like you. Your inn would make Bellehaven a more welcoming place, and your pub would be a place where friends could gather." She paused, then inclined her head toward the wall. "You did this for me, didn't you?"

Before he could reply, Poppy and Hazel hurried toward them, beaming at Kitty. "This is wonderful," Hazel said. "Almost everyone has cast their vote for you. You're all but certain to win."

Poppy wrapped her in a fierce hug. "I couldn't be prouder of you, you know. This is just as exciting as the day we won the regatta together."

"Oh look," Hazel said excitedly. "Lady Rufflebum and the mayor are back on the dais. They must be ready to make their announcement."

Hazel squeezed one of Kitty's hands; Poppy squeezed the other. Leo stood behind her, just as he always had. Somewhat in the shadows, looking out for her. Ready to catch her if she should fall. And she vowed she'd never take him for granted again.

The mayor quieted the crowd, clasped his hands behind his back, and rocked on his feet. "As you have now seen for yourselves, the competition for our contest was extremely fierce. It is gratifying to have so many worthy entries, but one stood out above the rest." Mayor Martin bowed to the countess and said, "Lady Rufflebum, would you like to do the honors?"

"I should be delighted," she drawled. "Without further ado, the winner of the Bellehaven Design Contest is . . ."

Kitty closed her eyes.

"Mr. Kirkham!" the countess exclaimed to a smattering of unenthusiastic applause. "And I couldn't be more pleased to announce that we will soon break ground on the Rufflebum Maritime Observatory!"

Disappointment punched Kitty in the stomach, but she refused to let it defeat her.

"Oh, Kitty," Hazel said, squeezing her shoulder. "I'm so sorry."

"I am surprisingly fine." She turned around to find Leo, but he was already making his way to the stage, pleading her case with the mayor.

"This is a travesty," Poppy grumbled, clearly irate. "The countess wouldn't recognize talent if it slapped her powdered cheeks."

Blade strode toward them, his expression thunderous. "You deserved to win," he said to Kitty. "And I need to leave," he said to no one in particular, "before I say or do something I'll regret."

"Yes," Hazel agreed. "It's probably best if we go."

"There's no need to cut the evening short on my account," Kitty protested. "I'd hoped for a different result, of course, but I shall be fine." And she still needed to talk to Leo.

"Then you are far more gracious than I am," Blade said. "If I cross paths with the mayor, I won't be able to keep a civil tongue in my head. I'll be waiting in the carriage," he added, before storming out of the ballroom.

"Oh dear," Hazel said, watching him leave. "Would you mind if we left now?"

"Of course not. We can go." The last thing Kitty wanted

was for Blade to have a public row with the mayor. She cast one last, longing glance at Leo. He was standing on the dais with the mayor, pointing at the vase beneath her drawings. Still fighting for her. Not giving up.

She wasn't giving up either.

Chapter 29

Later that night, Leo laid in his bed and stared at the ceiling. Despite his best efforts, he'd failed to change the outcome of the contest. Worse, he hadn't been able to change Kitty's heart.

Any stubborn, lingering hope that she might love him was snuffed out when she'd left the ball without even saying goodbye.

In less than eight hours, she'd be in a carriage on her way to London, and God only knew when he'd see her again.

Tap, tap.

He sat up and cocked his ear toward the window, but all he could hear was sound of his own breathing.

Tap, tap, crack.

Holy hell. He jumped out of bed, ran to the window, and found a small, web-like crack in one of the glass panes. Maybe a hapless bird had flown into it, or a young rapscallion was up to some late-night mischief.

But when he raised the sash, Leo found the real culprit.

Kitty.

She stood beneath his sill, her loose hair blowing in the evening breeze, her upturned face limned by the moonlight.

"Don't move," he said, half-afraid she'd disappear if he blinked. "I'll be right down."

He pulled on his trousers, ran down the stairs, and opened the office's back door in less than thirty seconds. Kitty glided toward him, wearing the sort of saucy smile that never failed to make his heart pound.

"You broke my window," he said.

She walked past him, her silken hair brushing the bare skin of his chest. "You didn't respond to pebbles. I had no choice but to resort to something bigger."

"So you reached for the nearest boulder?" he countered, following her back up the stairs to his apartment.

She glanced over her shoulder at him and arched a brow. "Perhaps I shall find a way to make it up to you."

Leo blinked and said a silent, fervent prayer that he was not dreaming.

Kitty walked into his sitting room, reached into the bodice of her gown, and produced a folded paper, which she handed to him.

"What's this?" The paper was warm from being pressed to her skin, and he barely resisted the urge to sniff it.

"Something I'd been saving—for quite a while now. Have a look."

He lit a lamp, opened the paper, and recognized the drawing immediately. "The gargoyle-fairy house. I remember it well. I teased you because I was intimidated by your talent."

She inclined her head. "To be fair, I deserved a bit of teasing. I tossed out most of my old drawings, but I saved this one."

Leo scratched his head. "You wanted a souvenir of our argument?"

"I suppose I did," she said thoughtfully. "I'd thought

it would make a fitting wedding gift—when you finally found your fairy bride."

He folded the paper and handed it back to her. "Keep it. If I can't marry you, I'm not going to marry anyone. Not even a fairy."

She moved closer—close enough that he could see the brilliant blue-green flecks in her eyes—and pressed the paper into his palm. "As it happens, I want to marry you, Leo Lockland. Not just because it is practical and convenient. Not because I know we'd have a perfectly pleasant life together. I want to marry you because I love you with my body, mind, and soul."

"Thank God," he rasped, cupping her cheeks in his palms. "What changed your mind?"

She circled her arms around his neck, pulled him closer, and pressed her forehead to his. "I know love is a gamble, and I might end up hurt. But I'm willing to bet on you. On us. I'll gratefully accept the happiness that Fate is bestowing on us—whether it's for five days, five years, or five decades. Loving you is worth the risk. It's worth any price."

She brushed her lips across his. Teased his mouth open with her tongue. Ran her palms down his chest.

With a growl, he scooped her into his arms, carried her into his bedroom, and laid her across the mattress. "I will never leave you, Kitty. Not if there's breath left in my body, not if I can help it. You're everything to me."

Tears welled in her eyes. "That's lovely—even if a true rake would never say such a thing," she added with a wobbly smile.

"No? Would a true rake do this?" He loosened the laces on the side of her gown and, with one firm tug, pulled down the bodice.

"He might," she said, her breath shaky. "Among other things."

Leo shot her a wicked grin, then dipped his head between the swells of her breasts. Using his teeth, he lowered the top of her corset, exposing taut buds to his hungry gaze. "Better?"

"I have noticed a marked improvement." She speared her fingers through his hair and arched her back as he suckled one tight peak, then the other. "Of course, one should never settle for a satisfactory rating . . . when there is unlimited potential."

"I couldn't agree more." He ran a hand beneath her gown and up the inside of her thigh, teasing the folds at her entrance and finding the spot that made her thrust her hips and fist the sheets. He kissed his way up the column of her neck and ran his tongue around the shell of her ear.

"I want you, Leo," she murmured. "Now and always. I need you."

He stripped off his trousers and what remained of her clothes, then laid on his side, pulling her back against his chest. He held her close as he eased inside her, savoring the weight of her breast in his hand and the sigh that escaped her throat when he kissed the skin at her nape.

He thrust faster. Harder. Deeper. Rocked against her round bottom as he slid a hand over her hip and caressed her in all the places she liked. Bringing her to the brink. Daring her to come.

"Don't," he whispered. "Not yet."

She moaned in protest and clenched her muscles around him, almost making *him* come.

"I think we both should," she said raggedly, "because I'm not certain I can wait . . ."

Her voice trailed off and she cried out as her body pulsed around him. Whimpered as waves of bliss vibrated through her. Clung to him as the last echoes lingered in her core.

Then he climaxed, too. Finally surrendering to his own pleasure—and bringing her with him again. He murmured her name over and over, like a prayer. And though they'd lain together before, this was different.

This time, he knew that Kitty was his, always. He pulled the sheet over her body and held her as she drifted off to sleep, loving the feel of forever.

A few hours later, he caressed her shoulder, gently nudging her awake.

"I thought you loved me," she grumbled without opening her eyes.

He chuckled and kissed the back of her neck. "I do. More than anything."

"Lies. If you truly did, you'd let me sleep." She pulled the blanket tight around her and nestled her head into his pillow.

"I know you're not particularly fond of mornings." He slipped out of bed and began dressing. "But I thought you might like to return to your own bedchamber before anyone realizes you're gone."

She moaned and sat up, looking delectably disheveled.

After kissing her thoroughly, he reluctantly helped her back into her gown, and they skulked through the dark, empty streets of Bellehaven, hand in hand.

"I'm sorry about the contest," he said sincerely. "I honestly thought Lady Rufflebum would change her mind when she realized how popular your theater would be. I suppose that in the end she couldn't resist the allure of having a landmark named after her."

"I am disappointed," Kitty admitted. "I wanted the theater to exist not just on paper, but in the real world. I wanted to be able to walk through the doors, dance across the stage, and sit in a balcony seat."

"I wanted that, too. Not only for you, but for Belle-haven." He brushed his thumb across the back of her hand. "Perhaps someone in London will recognize the brilliance of your design and build the theater there."

"No," she said firmly. "It wouldn't be the same any-where else. But, thanks to you, at least I have the satisfac-tion of knowing people loved the idea. I thought winning was the only thing that mattered, but maybe what I really needed was validation. To know that there are people who respect my work."

"This is only the beginning," he said soberly. "We can live and work wherever you like, but I am certain people all over England are going to fall in love with your designs as surely as I've fallen in love with you."

Her smile made his heart take flight. "It would be nice to spend time in London and visit other places around the countryside," she said, "but your mother and grandfather are here. My uncle and friends are here. It's where home will always be."

Warmth blossomed in his chest. "If we're blessed with children, we'll teach them to build sandcastles before they can walk—so they can win the Sandcastle Festival every summer."

"And we'll have them swimming and rowing a boat by the age of three so that they can bring home the regatta silver cup."

"I'm glad we have that sorted," Leo said as they ap-proached Kitty's house. "Now I just have to hope that your uncle gives us his blessing when I ask for your hand."

"He will," Kitty said with a devilish grin. "And not just because he wouldn't want me to run off to Gretna Green. I think he likes you. He respects any man who stands up for what he believes in, and now he knows you believe in"—she paused to kiss his cheek—"me."

They stood on the pavement outside her front door, their fingers laced together, reluctant to say goodbye.

"I'll never be a real rake, you know," he said. "I tried to be one for you, but I can't give up my straightedge ruler. And I'll probably always be inordinately fond of numbers."

"You're a rake when it counts," she said with a sly smile. "But more important, you're the man I love."

"They've been in there an awfully long time," Kitty said. She tapped the toe of her slipper against the Aubusson carpet in a staccato beat and kept one eye on the closed door of her uncle's study where Leo had an audience with both Uncle Beck and Poppy's husband, Keane.

"I would not worry." Hazel sipped her tea as if it were a perfectly ordinary afternoon. As if Kitty's whole future wasn't being decided on the other side of that door. "The gentlemen are probably having a celebratory glass of brandy."

Poppy shrugged nonchalantly. "Either that, or a challenge has been issued and they're naming their seconds."

Kitty narrowed her eyes at her friend.

Poppy scrunched her freckled nose in return. "Someone needed to lighten the mood."

"I know Uncle Beck will be pleased about Leo," Kitty reasoned. "Maybe even ecstatic. But for some reason my heart is racing and my fingertips are numb."

Hazel batted her eyes innocently as she reached for a scone. "I wonder if your symptoms might have something to do with a lack of sleep last night."

Poppy's eyes went wide, and she turned to Kitty, silently demanding an explanation.

Good heavens. Heat crept up Kitty's neck, but she was

saved from having to respond because the study door finally opened. The men emerged, and the wide smile on Leo's face told her all she needed to know.

"I hope everyone is satisfied," she said with mock irritation. "All of you insisted I should marry for love, and it seems you shall have your wish."

"We couldn't be more pleased." Hazel set down her cup and gave Leo a kiss on the cheek. "Welcome to the family."

"Thank you," he said sincerely. "I shall do my best to make her happy."

Poppy gave him a warm hug as well. "You don't make a very good pirate," she teased, "but I've a feeling you'll make an exceptionally good husband. Congratulations. Our Kitty is special, indeed."

Blade wrapped her in a hug and kissed her forehead. "I'll ring for champagne," he said.

Kitty clasped her hands beneath her chin and beamed at Leo. Her fiancé. Her very handsome, kind, devoted fiancé. "Engagements and champagne are two of my favorite things," she said with a blissful sigh. She couldn't imagine feeling any happier than she did in that moment.

But then, the spry butler, Simpson, appeared in the doorway and cleared his throat. "Pardon the interruption. There's a gentleman, Mr. Holland, here to see Miss Kitty."

"To see me?" Kitty repeated. "I don't know anyone by that name."

"Nor do I," Blade said. "Shall I have a word with him? Send him on his way?"

"Wait," Poppy said, frowning slightly. "Keane and I met him at the ball last night. He was there with his wife. A charming couple—from Newcastle if I recall."

"Then we must make him feel welcome," Kitty said.

"He can join us for a glass of champagne. Please show him in, Simpson."

A few minutes later, an older gentleman with a kindly face, an expertly tailored jacket, and a northern accent joined them in the drawing room. He greeted Poppy, who introduced him to Hazel, Blade, Leo, and Kitty.

"I am delighted to meet all of you," he said politely, "and I hope you'll forgive the intrusion. I felt compelled to pay you a visit, Miss Beckett, because my wife and I are utterly enamored of your theater design. She was once an actress—and quite accomplished. She's worked in dozens of theaters, but she said performing on that stage would be a dream."

Kitty's eyes stung, and she blinked back tears. "That means the world to me. Thank you."

"We recently purchased thirty acres of property here in Bellehaven, just a couple of blocks from Main Street," Mr. Holland continued. "We believe your theater belongs there, overlooking the water. Indeed, now that we've seen the designs, we can't imagine constructing anything else."

Kitty swallowed and set down her champagne glass with a trembling hand. "What are you saying, Mr. Holland?"

He smiled widely. "We want to build your theater, and we'd like to hire you as the lead architect."

The words echoed in her head, and her shock turned to unbridled joy.

The room erupted in cheers and congratulations—all for her. Leo was grinning from ear to ear, mirroring the happiness she felt inside. Poppy and Hazel held hands and danced right there on the carpet, as if they could scarcely contain themselves. Blade and Keane nodded, both of them beaming like proud papas.

Kitty reached for her locket, rubbing the silver casing

between her thumb and forefinger. She would have given anything to have her parents there at that moment. But she was far from alone. She had a whole room full of people who believed in her, loved her, and would always stand beside her.

She'd thought she'd have to move to London to chase down her dream.

But, as it turned out, the dream had found *her*. Right there in Bellehaven.

She cleared her throat and addressed Mr. Holland. "I've never undertaken a project as big as this one," she said. "But together, I think we could make something beautiful for this town."

The kindly man smiled widely. "That's a yes, then?"

Kitty extended her hand and shook his. "That's a yes."

Epilogue

Bellehaven Bay, two years later

Kitty, Hazel, and Poppy strolled down South Street, arm in arm, while the lovely ocean breeze rustled their skirts, and the sunshine warmed their faces.

Kitty felt as though her heart could burst. "I'm so glad you both could be here today."

"Are you jesting?" Poppy asked, her tone incredulous. "We wouldn't miss it for the world."

"Well, I'd understand if you weren't able to make the trip." Hazel had recently opened a new school for orphaned girls in London and was busy hiring teachers and enrolling new students. Poppy and Keane had been at their country estate, overseeing major improvements to their tenants' cottages and building a bridge connecting some of the more remote houses to town. "You have so much on your plates—and small, adorable children to boot."

"That is true," Hazel said. "But the Belles always come together for the important moments—and this is one of the biggest. We're so proud of you."

"You haven't seen it yet," Kitty pointed out. "For all you know, it could be a monstrosity. A ghastly eyesore."

"And I could sprout a mermaid's tail tomorrow," Poppy said with a chuckle. "Possible, but extremely unlikely."

Kitty shot her friend a grateful smile. "The construction

was completed in record time, thanks to Leo. He visited the site daily, checking that every element was built precisely according to the specifications. But I can't help feeling apprehensive. The townspeople have such high hopes for this theater, and I should hate for them to be disappointed."

"They will adore it," Hazel said, confident. "I'm not nearly as certain that the first stage performance will be a resounding success," she added with a chuckle.

"Nonsense," Kitty said. "Jane has done a brilliant job of preparing the students for the play. Lucy clearly has a talent for directing, and Clara's costumes are breathtaking. I couldn't be happier that the first production to grace the stage will be presented by Bellehaven Academy."

"The girls have raised an impressive sum," Hazel said proudly. "They're donating every farthing to the foundling home."

Poppy sighed happily. "Lucy and Clara are kind, courageous young women. You know, I think they could be Belles in the ma—" She drew up short as they rounded the corner and gaped at the view of the theater. "Zounds," she breathed.

Hazel covered her mouth and gazed in disbelief. At last, she said, "Kitty. It's giving me gooseflesh—in the best possible way." She took a few more steps so that she could see the entire front of the building. The towering statues of Poseidon and Aphrodite at the entrance, the grand marble terrace, the shimmering domed roof. "It's a work of art."

Kitty had to admit that the cerulean-blue ocean, the pale-pink sky, and the wispy white clouds provided the perfect backdrop. "Stop it, both of you, or you shall give me a big head. Even worse, you might make me cry, and you know how much I detest showing weakness."

Poppy clucked her tongue. "It's always the ones with the toughest exteriors who feel things most deeply."

Kitty rolled her eyes and turned to face Leo, Blade, and Keane—the trio of dashing men who were bringing up the rear. "Come on then," she said matter-of-factly. "If you lot insist on dallying, we shall miss the opening act."

After the show, Kitty stood on the huge terrace outside the lobby, overlooking the sea. "It's everything I'd hoped for," she admitted to Poppy and Hazel. "Not the building *per se*, but the way people are moving in it. The way the girls performed on the stage. The way the audience sat on the edges of their seats. Before it was a shell, but now it feels . . . complete."

"No one is in a hurry to leave," Hazel noted. "They're all lingering, enjoying the company and the view."

"And we have a few additions to the crowd as well," Poppy said with a grin. "Look who's here." She hurried across the terrace to her redheaded, freckle-faced daughter, Alexa, who was toddling toward her and Keane, her harried nurse in tow.

Blade proudly rolled a pram toward their group, and they all gathered round, marveling that his and Hazel's cherub-faced boy, William, could sleep so soundly in the midst of all the commotion.

Leo pressed a warm hand to the small of Kitty's back and handed her a glass of fizzy champagne. "You are an unqualified, smashing success," he whispered in her ear. "Congratulations."

"Back when we were both apprentices, I wouldn't have believed this was possible," she mused.

"Which part?" he probed. "Seeing one of your beautiful designs come to life or being blissfully married to your childhood nemesis?"

"I wouldn't have believed either. But I am delighted to have been proven wrong on both counts." She gestured toward another building site, half a block away. "At the rate construction is going, your inn will be open before winter, and we'll be celebrating that, too." Mr. Holland had wisely decided that the inn would be an excellent business proposition, given the influx of tourists the new theater was bound to bring. Indeed, Bellehaven was growing so fast that Kitty and Leo had more projects than they could handle on their own.

Interestingly, however, construction had not yet begun on the Rufflebum Observatory, although the countess had repeatedly assured the townspeople that they were set to break ground any day now. Apparently, the delay stemmed from a few design flaws that Mr. Kirkham needed to address, but since the gentleman had been sacked from his uncle's architectural practice, it seemed unlikely that he was capable of salvaging the observatory project.

No one in Bellehaven seemed to mind.

"I have a surprise for you tonight," Leo said, snapping Kitty's attention back to the present.

Kitty arched a brow. "What sort of surprise?"

"No hints." His rakish grin made her knees wobble, but she merely sipped her drink . . . and let her imagination run wild.

"We're not going home?" Kitty asked. Home was the spacious suite of rooms they'd been renting in town. With Kitty's inheritance, they could have bought a mansion to rival Lady Rufflebum's, but she and Leo liked being close to his mother and grandfather. As an added bonus, if they opened their windows, they could often smell the delicious aromas coming from the bakery.

"We need to stop by the office first," Leo replied vaguely. The sun had begun to set, and the buildings along Main Street seemed to glow in the twilight.

"Is this part of the surprise?" she asked.

"You'll see," he said. "We only have one block to go."

"I'm not fond of surprises." She tossed a bouncy lock of hair over her shoulder—a dead giveaway that she actually *adored* surprises. God, he loved her hair flip. Hoped she'd still be doing it after her golden curls faded to gray.

"Is that so?" He squeezed her hand, and she shot him a reluctant smile.

"Perhaps I like them a little," she conceded.

They walked faster as the office front came into view. They'd recently had the new name of their company, *Feline Building Design*, painted on the large picture window. *Feline* was a nod to their first names, and if someone had told Leo eight years ago that he'd name his practice after a cat, he'd have told them they were certifiably mad.

Now, the sign made him smile, because it was a symbol of the life he and Kitty were building together.

The bell above the door trilled as they walked inside. Not much had changed in the last two years. Leo's grandfather's desk remained positioned at the front; his and Kitty's were at the back.

His was neat as a pin.

Hers was a study in chaos.

They strolled to their respective desks, sat down, and faced each other over the eighth wonder of the world—her great wall of trinkets.

Kitty propped her chin on her laced fingers, her blue eyes sparkling with anticipation. "So, Leo Lockland, what do you have for me?"

The sound of his full name rolling off her lips still made his heart skip a beat.

"Remember this?" He pulled out a framed drawing. "You gave it to me on the day we became engaged."

She smiled as she studied the faded, creased depiction of the gargoyle house. "Some of my finest work," she said with a chuckle. "Of course I remember. I wasn't sure you'd saved it," she added, clearly touched.

"That's not the surprise." Leo reached into the basket beside his desk, pulled out a large scroll, and unrolled it on his desk. "This is."

Kitty hopped off her stool, came to stand beside him, and let her gaze flick across the design. She frowned, opened her mouth as if she'd say something, then closed it again.

At last she said, "These look like actual plans . . . of the gargoyle house."

"That's exactly what they are."

"Do we have a new client? Someone with the eccentric tastes of, oh, Satan?"

He laughed. "It's more charming than eccentric, I think. Definitely more whimsical than demonic. I thought that perhaps *we* could live here."

She blinked at him, dumbfounded. "But you detest this house."

He shook his head. "I only pretended to."

"You said it wouldn't fit in the character of this town—and you were right."

"You said you'd never be content to blend in—and I'd never want you to." He cupped her cheek in his palm and brushed his lips across hers. "My home is wherever you are," he said. "But I *like* the gargoyle house, and if you like it, too, I think we should build it."

She erupted in laughter, the hearty, genuine sort that never failed to make his body thrum.

"I think we must build it." Her finger drifted across the plans and stopped at a room just outside the main bedchamber. "Especially since this nook will make a fine nursery . . . for our first gargoyle-fairy child."

He froze and met her gaze. "Kitty?"

"Do you think we could complete construction in about seven months' time?"

He pulled her into his arms, picked her up, and spun her around the office, certain his heart would burst. "How shall we celebrate?"

She tilted her head, pretending to ponder the question. "I have a few ideas."

"As do I," he growled.

She ran her palms down the moss-green waistcoat he'd purchased during his rake lessons. "We could go home to bed."

"Or we could slip upstairs to my old apartment," he countered.

"Or . . ." Her eyes lit up the way they always did when she had an inspired idea. She knelt on the stool, perched on the edge of his desk, and tugged on his cravat, pulling his hips between her knees. "We could stay right here. Unless you're worried your desk will become untidy."

"Are you jesting?" He swept the scroll to the floor, leaned her back across the warm wooden surface, and ran a hand up her side. When she lifted her arm, she bumped her teacup, causing it to clink against the saucer.

He paused, steadied the wobbling cup, and brushed a tendril from her face. "Are you worried about your trinkets?"

"No," she said, her expression serious. "They were

important when life seemed fickle. When I desperately needed something to hold onto. But now I have you, and our families, and the family we're making together. I have love."

"Now and forever," he promised.

She pulled him on top of her, held his face in her palms, and kissed him with all the emotion and passion whirling inside her. "I love the sound of forever."